The Turkish Trap

Jack Dylan

ISBN: 9798694321259

CONTENTS

Chapter 1

Turkish Coast 13th October 2006

The trap in Kapi Creek

22:00 hours. Location: 36°42.05'N 28°55.65'E, six miles south of Gocek, southbound in Skopea Limani.

The slightest crescent moon lightened the dark surface of the water with a pale metallic gleam. In the distance the lighthouse on Kizil Island cut its regular sweep through the warm night air. The faint background glow in the eastern sky from the lights of Fethiye dimmed the brilliance of the lighthouse, and made the darkness seem even more complete. To the north the Taurus Mountains bulked mistily behind the wooded coast. Ahead to the south, but only visible in silhouette, were the islands of Tersane and Domuz, leading to the hooked peninsula of Kapu Dag with its sheltered anchorages and hidden coves.

The boat scythed through the water at high speed. It

was capable of speeds that nothing else on the coast could match. The twin V12 Mercedes marine diesels emitted a deep throbbing bass tone. Unlike the showy millionaire motor yachts that passed by day, the noise was deliberately muted through the underwater exhausts. The twin stainless steel propellers produced an irresistible thrust as the powerful craft scored a white foaming trail through the dark water.

The skipper's hands gripped the wheel more tightly than usual. His eyes peered into the darkness, watching intently for a dark shape in the faint silvery reflection that might be a small boat invisible to their radar. His face was marked by the tense muscles in his cheeks. One more minute was all they needed. He planned to cut the engines well before they were visible from the sheltered anchorage. The journey was crazy he thought. Why had they left it so late to let them go? Why risk everything with this high-speed dash in the darkness? He knew the answer and had to accept it. He wiped the thoughts from his mind and kept sweeping the darkness with his eyes, using the more light-sensitive part of the retina away from its centre by looking to the side or below where he really wanted to see. If there was an obstruction in the water he would swerve the boat before he had time to form the thought. His thinking didn't become conscious until after he reacted. Lives depended simply on reflexes.

The navigator's eyes did not leave the glowing screen for a second. He could see the outline of the coast with the islands that would soon be left to port, and the shape of the bays dead ahead. The crew wore their dark combat gear with no sign of the usual reflective markings. No-one spoke.

"Minus One skipper," at last the voice of the navigator came crisply through the headphones. He immediately started the slow-down and the unspoken tension began to rise in the red-lit closeness of the bridge. As the speed dropped so did the pointed bow of the sleek craft, until they were cutting through the water with minimal wake and strangely sinister lack of noise. Had there been anyone to see, they would have been puzzled by the silent gliding speed of the shadowy craft.

As preparation for the next stage began, the surge of controlled excitement remained masked on the darkened faces of the crew. Hatches opened on their hydraulic rams, and the black-clad figures hauled their carefully prepared equipment onto the rear deck. They went about their tasks speedily and with practised confidence. The quiet efficiency of their preparations made talking superfluous.

*   *   *

Alexander Fox poured the traditional celebratory tot of ship's rum into each of the six waiting glasses on his yacht's cockpit table. The bottle rattled slightly against the rims of the glasses, and he noticed Maggie's questioning and worried look as he returned the bottle to its place near the binnacle. He sat on the pristine royal blue cushions in the open cockpit of his yacht. They were moored in what had once been his favourite anchorage on the coast. It had been spoiled for him, or perhaps he had spoiled it himself, but his paying guests were oblivious to the darker shadows in his mind. They were simply enjoying the final night of their week cruising the Turquoise Coast of ancient Turkish Lycia, relaxed by the generous quantities of wine with their dinner, and warmed by the feeling of achievement.

"God you're a lucky man Alex," said the London accountant wistfully. "You have the perfect job and the perfect location. I'd give anything to be able to do this."

"Ah sure somebody has to do it," grinned Alex using his well-practised formula. Privately he thought that if Bruce had the slightest inkling of what lay below the peaceful-looking surface he would be scurrying back to his safe job in London as fast as he could. But he knew he had to play along with the mood.

"I think on behalf of all of us," started the doctor with unusual formality, nodding to include Bruce and their two wives, "I would like to take this opportunity to propose a toast to our skipper Alex, and his irresistible mate.."

"Steady on there Jack," laughed Maggie.

"No I use the term advisedly. I know what I mean, and I don't apologise for it. Obviously Alex will agree with me anyway. But as I was …."

"Oh get on with it Jack," urged Bruce a little testily.

"I'm trying to but everyone keeps interrupting," stammered Jack, "What I'm trying to say is how much we have all enjoyed the week, and how much Alex and Maggie have done to make it the perfect cruise. So let's raise a glass to toast our superb skipper and mate – and many happy sailing days together."

The six people in the cockpit raised their glasses and the four paying guests seriously intended that this was an experience they would repeat. Alex and Maggie relaxed in the warmth of the genuine appreciation, which seemed to be the norm when people first experienced a week of sunny Mediterranean sailing.

"Well I have to say that you have all done really well," started Alex in response. "We have enjoyed having crew who actually wanted to learn and who were able to do so much of the sailing themselves."

"Hear, hear," agreed Maggie, enjoying the ritual bonhomie.

Alex felt rather than saw a slight movement in the boat. As if a wave had passed, the bow seemed to dip ever so slightly and the stern to rise – just a subtle shift that none of the others had noticed. He automatically looked forward and was stunned to see a black-clad figure haul itself over the bow of the boat and land crouching on the foredeck without a sound. Something about the silence and the strength with which it was done conveyed instantly that this wasn't just another teenager climbing the mooring rope after a swim. There was such menace and power in the action that the possibility of resistance didn't occur to him.

Alex started to rise to his feet. He looked round as he rose, for he sensed another movement at the stern. His heart sank as he watched an identical black-clad figure step lightly from the jetty onto the stern of their boat behind Maggie. Without looking, he knew as he felt the movement of the boat that another was stepping aboard behind him.

Unseen by the celebrating yacht, hidden by the western hillside, the sleek speeding craft had performed a final turn and slowed to a gentle halt. Two rubber dinghies had instantly separated from the white craft, followed by a third just seconds later.

Surprise was as important to them as speed for this

part of the operation, so they had motored with muffled engines gently into the anchorage. Had Alex been watching, he would have seen the dark shapes make unhesitatingly for their target. The jetty to which Alex was moored ran east to west across the inner southern end of the bay. The bow of his yacht was pointing out of the bay to the north, the stern closely moored less than a metre from the jetty. There were about ten other yachts similarly moored, with Alex third from the outer, western end.

One of the dinghies had come ahead of the other two and with night-vision binoculars identified Alex's yacht. A black figure had attached a signal light low on the bow, invisible to those in the yacht's cockpit, but clear to the other intruders.

A second dinghy made for the outer end of the jetty, and a black figure swung effortlessly onto the walkway. Simultaneously an identical figure from the third dinghy climbed silently onto the inner end of the rough, wood-planked construction.

There was no hesitation or uncertainty about the way they moved along the wooden surface. The suddenness, silence, and the black unmarked combat-wear allowed them to reach Alex's stern before anyone registered their presence.

A split second after Alex became aware of the black figures, Maggie and then the four guests started in alarm as they became conscious of the intrusion that had fractured the warm mood of the evening.

The figure that Alex sensed behind him spoke,

"Mr Fox." It was issued as a statement more than a question. Alex was already half-way to his feet, and it was as if this was sufficient answer to the implicit question.

"Mr Fox, you are under arrest from the Turkish Sahil Guvenlik, the Coastguard. We have a warrant to search your boat, and you will be taken to Headquarters for questioning. All of you are required to remain below in your cabins."

"You can't do this," started Alex with an uncharacteristic hoarseness in his voice. His shakiness conveyed his shock, but also an element of embarrassment. He hadn't seen the crewman who even as they spoke was readying the boat for departure. The engine started, lines were cast off, and the yacht moved under the command of the black clad figures. There were now five of them on board, Alex later guessed the final two had stepped from the yachts on either side of him, but at the moment he was in a state of shock, not able to think.

Maggie and the four drunk, frightened and tentatively outraged guests were directed down the companionway to their cabins inside the yacht. Alex was under no misapprehension about the irresistible nature of the invasion. The speed, assurance, and professionalism of the operation left no doubt about its authenticity, and he knew that it was already too late to try any form of resistance. In fact there had never been a moment when it would have been possible.

"Just do as they say," he said flatly to the others, his voice a dull fraction of his earlier confident self. "We'll get this sorted out later but for now there's no point in arguing. Just do as they say and we'll be all right."

He knew that the searchers would very quickly find what they were looking for. The operation had been so suddenly successful that there had been no warning – not even the 15 seconds he needed to jettison the package overboard. Why had no-one seen them coming? How could they have appeared without The Greek's men getting the warning to him? Watchers in Gocek and Fethiye, as well as on the water, were supposed to be ready to warn them of any unusual movements. He knew that the other boat waiting for tomorrow's rendezvous must have been the subject of a similar operation. It was over.

Chapter 2

Mugla regional jail: Saturday 14th Oct 2006

Alex in jail

Alex sat on the edge of the bed. It was a rough metal construction, hinged to the wall on its inner edge, and supported by two metal legs on the outer corners. The mattress was thin, stained and smelled distinctly of stale urine. The blanket was similarly uninviting. Alex was still dressed in his sailing clothes, but his deck shoes had been removed when he was delivered to the cell.

He was anxious about Maggie. When he was bundled from the coastguard launch into the waiting jeep, he had seen his yacht alongside the coastguard jetty, but he could pick out only the coastguard crew as they secured the mooring ropes. He had no idea if Maggie had been transported to this regional jail or kept in Gocek. He hoped the latter.

The jeep had arrived at the jail at about 4:00 a.m., and they were obviously expected. He was marched briskly into a bare, harshly lit guard-post, where he was searched and processed by the admitting guards. Paperwork from the delivery guards had to be stamped, signed, exchanged, and filed. The Ottoman Empire's administrative legacy lingered on. Once inside the clanging gates, two sleepy-eyed guards took him to a cell on the first floor, down a disinfectant-smelling corridor lined with metal doors. They indicated that he should remove his shoes, which they took away, and without any exchange of words pointed him to the bed and locked the heavy metal door. He heard their retreating footsteps and wondered what they were finding to laugh at as they disappeared from his hearing.

He didn't even try to sleep. He listened for sounds that would let him know if Maggie was brought to the same place. He couldn't work out why she would have been brought separately. Perhaps she was safely in the relative comfort of the coastguard station in Gocek. About thirty minutes after his arrival, he heard the same process repeated three times. He thought he could hear three sets of footsteps make their way down the corridor each time. He could distinguish the solid confident steps of the guards in their regulation boots, and the softer shuffling sound of a reluctant prisoner wearing everyday shoes. There was no conversation to be heard, but as the last of the three doors was slammed closed, he heard a shouted exclamation which could have been in English. He wondered if the other prisoners were connected to the operation that had captured him. Without being able to consciously analyse why, he was sure that none of the shuffling footsteps had been Maggie's.

His thoughts went back to the long and complex

path that had led him from peacefully humdrum married routine, to a bare, stinking cell in a Turkish jail. But strangely his spirits were not deflated. He was numbly resigned to his own incarceration but he was worried about Maggie, what she was thinking; what she was experiencing. He went back to piecing together the combination of stories that had drawn together Dublin, London, Edinburgh and Turkey. Making sense of the sequence of the unfolding histories kept his mind active and was sufficiently absorbing to at least reduce his consciousness of the cell.

Chapter 3

Dublin: December 2005

James Findlater:

James Findlater was 45 today. To boost his morale he put an extra shine on the classic brown brogues, and chose his second best remaining Magee tweed jacket. He looked at himself in the mirror and approved the well-pressed grey slacks, the discreet check in his jacket, the knitted tie and the slightly country-style Jaeger wool shirt.

James needed to boost his morale. His minor public school, his moderate academic performance, and his well-bred accent had led to a career founded more on his family connections than on his own brilliance.

'Redundant at 44' seemed like a death sentence. It certainly explained why he lived in a down-market flat in what the estate agent had euphemistically called an "area with potential". He checked his tie again and marched in a vaguely military style down the stairs to make his way to the golf club he could no longer afford.

James was burdened with a disturbing level of insight into his situation. He suffered no illusions about his qualifications or his ability. His father had seen to that. He knew exactly how unappealing he was to potential employers. He wouldn't even employ himself, and that didn't make the situation any more bearable. He knew that he couldn't survive long in his current state. His money would soon run out. He felt that his sanity was hanging by a thread. He imagined what it would be like to be in the identical situation, but blessed with impregnable self-confidence. Some of his ex-colleagues in the bank had exuded such confidence, and despite being a similar age to James, had picked up jobs right away. James didn't think he would. Perhaps this lack of confidence was so pervasive that it escaped as soon as a potential employer opened the envelope with his application. Like some pernicious vapour, the air of pessimistic desperation leaked out and damned the process.

So far he had been invited to two interviews, neither one of which he could bear to remember in detail. Lack of confidence bred lack of coherence. He had stumbled and stuttered through answers so badly that he was glad to escape, and didn't even bother to wonder if he might have been successful.

He caught the bus in the general direction of the golf club. It simply wasn't done to arrive by public transport, so he skulked off the bus half-a-mile away from the entrance, and tried to give the impression of someone enjoying his Sunday walk.

At 3:00 o'clock James escaped from the golf club. He

cursed himself for making the double mistake of going there in the first place and then letting "Cunningham hyphen Browne with an e" know that it was his birthday. He had taken no pleasure whatsoever in the birthday drinks since he had to buy them, nor in the otherwise adequate Sunday lunch. By economising all week he could just about afford the price of the lunch for one. The cost of the drinks was going to provoke a premature crisis in his cash flow. In the foulest of moods James contemplated avoiding the little reading-group that he had agreed to attend. If he hadn't promised Lavinia so absolutely he would have taken the bus straight home. As it was, his well-ingrained sense of duty saw him trudging rather than striding down the winter-grey tree-lined road, to the fine block of Georgian apartments where Lavinia's group was waiting.

Chapter 4

Lavinia: Dublin December 2005

The party

      Lavinia, in her early thirties, had found herself the beneficiary of a modest but comfortable inheritance, and was energetically turning her life into the sort of existence she wanted, rather than the pampered and constraining cocoon that life with her mother had been. Too much money, too many romantic novels, and a streak of perfectionism in her personality, had left Lavinia as the perpetual bridesmaid. However part of the grieving process for her mother had been the liberating decision to start organising life for her own enjoyment, and not to hold on to the incapacitating dream of the perfect relationship that just didn't come her way. She now was fit, healthy, and was enjoying taking initiatives in organising her life. The reading group had been going for about eighteen months and was working so well that she wanted to recruit some new members to the original group of herself, William, Steve and Sinead. Hence the introductions of the studious and serious Simon, and poor James, whose circumstances she vaguely appreciated, but whose poverty she hadn't fully grasped.

Steve was the least likely but increasingly the most active member of the group. About 35 years old, he seemed to scrape a living through a mixture of basic temping jobs in Dublin offices, along with his vague status as occasional artistic agent for a small number of long-standing friends who were singers or actors. He habitually wore jeans, sometimes with a t-shirt, sometimes with a casual sweater that looked expensive but was probably on its second owner. Lavinia had never been able to tempt him to give all the details of his artistic agent role and she had stopped prying. Steve had emerged as an insightful and humorous group member, and better still, was working on his own novel. The glimpses they were allowed of his personal life added to the mystery. There were hints of a prosperous past ended by the untimely death of his father. His frequent illnesses and sometimes gaunt face had been explained after the first few months by his revelation of what it was like to live with his regime of anti-retroviral drugs. His domestic arrangements seemed to involve moving back to live with his widowed mother, but his social life did not appear to be curbed by any maternal disapproval. Lavinia found him strangely inspiring, and she promised herself that she would learn from his honest ability to be himself, whatever the complexity and problems that lurked in the background.

Sinead was a more obvious group member. She was a mature student in her late twenties. She had studied Anglo-Irish literature at Trinity, so brought greater knowledge of classic literature than the others could offer. Her new studies could hardly be more different. She had decided to reinvent her career, and had enrolled for an accountancy course as a way of getting out of the badly paid office job in the university and into the blossoming industrial opportunities in the newly-successful European Ireland. Short, chubby, and with the features that people unkindly labelled as "homely", she was a practical, able and energetic member. The book group afforded her a welcome contrast to her dry accountancy studies. She usually dressed in a three-quarter length black wool coat that owed nothing to fashion, but this afternoon was wearing an uncharacteristically stylish black linen trouser suit – with a long jacket that disguised her dumpiness. Lavinia had been amused and touched to discover that the fashion advisor who had taken her shopping was none other than Steve.

"Has everyone grabbed something to drink?" Lavinia raised her voice to try to make sure that she was heard by all the members of her strange little group of friends.

"Of course I always say that Turkey is the new Greece," continued William, content with the tall thin glass of gin that matched his own physical characteristics – tall, thin, and positively bubbling. His angular frame was, he thought, stylishly clad in jeans, but they had an incongruously formal-looking sharp crease down the long legs. They sat neatly over the surprisingly small and highly-polished black Barker loafers that he thought right for this semi-formal party. He wore a fine woollen sweater in bright yellow over a check shirt and tie, and looked as if he felt quite pleased with himself. William enjoyed his status as a slightly mysterious businessman and auctioneer, who had brought an apparently successful business from Edinburgh to Dublin. His thinning hair was still a definite brown, and he had convinced himself that people would not guess that he tinted it. The worry lines on his face and a slightly hunted look in his eyes appeared when his guard slipped and he momentarily stopped projecting his chosen buoyant image. He continued, "and quite honestly I can't understand why anyone would buy property anywhere else these days. In fact, just yesterday…"

"Simon," Lavinia interrupted again, "what can I get you?"

"Nothing at all at present thank you," responded the ever-correct Simon.

Lavinia as hostess had earlier almost chosen her conventional little black dress, but at the last minute had decided to be more daring, and wore a multicoloured extravaganza of embroidered flowers on a light flowing fabric. It was cut to hang sensually, and moved with a swing as she walked. She was enjoying showing off her new liberated style. Simon meanwhile was dressed as conservatively as he spoke. Lavinia wondered if she should encourage him to break out from the cheap chain-store shirt, tie, slacks and blazer that he had worn every time they had met. Perhaps his scholarship from Pretoria University was not very generous. She decided to be tactful.

"As I was saying," continued William with a slight increase in volume, "the property market in Turkey is going to be the hottest investment opportunity this year. We have three new developments…"

"Excuse me sir, but is there not a risk that failure to gain entry to the EC…" Simon was cut short.

"Don't you worry about that! Whatever happens, people are going to want sunshine, sand, and cheap food. Can't lose I'm telling you. Take our Bodrum apartments, last year they sold at £75k, this year…."

"But surely the threat of terrorism is becoming greater every…."

"Don't you believe it sonny," countered William a little brusquely, his accent just beginning to slip.

"James, how lovely to see you!" Lavinia raised her volume, partly because of her anxiety to make James welcome, and partly out of frustration at William's continuing dominance.

"Do come in. What can I get you? G & T all right? William would you mind awfully getting James a drink? Simon come and meet James, I don't think you met him last week."

As William obediently made his way into the kitchen to find the gin, tonic, ice and lime, Lavinia quickly drew the two out of earshot.

"You've got to help me. This is going to be a disaster. James, you know my sister Hermione?" James nodded, but was puzzled. He was out of touch with the backstabbing character assassination and rumour mongering that passed for the social whirl round Dublin, but he was sure that Hermione had not been part of Lavinia's world for years.

"O God, I can't believe this is true. You won't believe it. You couldn't invent it – It is too awful to be happening."

"Lavinia, will you please tell us what you are talking about. Simon and I will help if we can, but you really need to explain."

"Where the hell do you keep the lime Lavinia?" came a voice from the kitchen.

"In the fruit bowl in the corner – there should be one started."

"Got it. Sliced and ready! Won't be a second."

"Oh no! Look I can't explain now. Just please you two be ready to rescue me. Don't run away, and please, please help keep things going."

"There you are James," burbled William amicably. "And what mischief are you three cooking up? You look like three school-kids caught smoking in the toilets. Come on, spill the beans."

At that moment the door opened again. Two figures appeared, one of them recognisably Lavinia's sister – the same svelte good looks, the same dark hair, and the same twinkle of mischief in her eye. Hermione was wearing a tunic-style grey and pink top over tight black leggings, and looked every inch the successful and confident journalist. However it was the other who caused the affable smile to leave the previously bubbling William's face. In contrast to the suavely chic Hermione, she looked distinctly masculine. She wore a severe trouser suit in a dark pin-stripe, and sported an Oscar Wildean green buttonhole, matching the pale green silk tie tucked neatly into the suit-top. Like a punctured clown, William gasped for air. His mouth worked at forming words, but nothing emerged. His tall gin hit the tiles with an explosive crack.

"Don't worry William, I'll get you another. Everybody I'd like you to meet Hermione, my long lost but never-forgotten dear sister. And this is Pat, Hermione's new partner. William I'm awfully sorry I should have said something, but I didn't expect Hermione till later. I was going to tell you. Honestly."

"Pat!" William exclaimed a little hoarsely. "I had no idea……"

"Oh honestly William. You are a scream. You'd think that I was a ghost. When I heard that you were going to be here I just couldn't think of a better way of announcing the news. But really darling, I thought you were just a little more blasé than this. Don't think I can ever remember a grown man dropping his drink when I walked into the room!"

Chapter 5

William: Dublin December 2005

Philosophising

It was Monday afternoon, the day after the end of the world in Lavinia's, and William was walking up Grafton Street, avoiding the temptation of a sticky bun and coffee in Bewley's. The embarrassment of the previous afternoon had forced him to think long and painfully about his shortcomings; his long catalogue of mistakes; and where he was going with his life.

His preoccupied wanderings led him through force of habit into the old market near the corner of St Stephen's Green. He walked through the multi-coloured alleyways, his eyes roving aimlessly over the curious mixture of third world handicrafts and discarded first world junk. He was cursing himself for the laughable sequence of ill-considered decisions that had punctuated his life so far. His self-flagellation was interrupted when his eyes stopped their unseeing roving and came sharply into focus. In one of those strange mental connections that seem to work unconsciously, he suddenly saw it. A bit like the odd sensation when, without conscious analysis of the piece or the space, he unexpectedly found he knew exactly where a piece of a jigsaw fitted. It was just suddenly there.

He had read an article in one of the auction journals about the price that the Pears Soap Company was prepared to pay for a lost piece of their history. It was a rather crude little china advertising gimmick, showing a mother washing the hair of her mud-stained child, with the scolding words "You Grubby Boy" wrapped round the base of the ornament. All that Pears could find were pictures of the item, and it was the one gap in their collection of advertising memorabilia. Even so, he had been astounded to read of the enthusiasm with which they were searching for an undamaged example. And there it was – looking at him from between a scrappy old lampshade and an obsolete portable tape player.

It cost him one Euro. His ever-optimistic assessment convinced him that he was going to sell it for hundreds. That meant that he could pay enough of his bills to give him some peace of mind for the rest of the month.

William had ended up in the auction and antiques business by accident. He had intended to be something totally different, but that was typical of the quality of his planning and his life. He still hated to think of the sequence of ill-advised decisions, or sometimes the absence of decision, that had led him to the precarious career he had carved out – teetering from one successful sale to the next three disasters. He didn't just act as auctioneer. Like most of his colleagues he couldn't resist a little buying and selling himself – not just the odd antique, but worse still the odd bit of land, the not-to-be-missed overseas investment opportunity. He was having a bad spell.

He reflected on his decision making. In restaurants he always put off ordering what to eat until the waiter was looking expectantly at him, and everyone else had chosen. At that moment, when there was no more room for thinking, the decision usually came easily. Earlier, when there was time for exploration, analysis, and imagining alternatives, he appeared paralysed. However his brain was far from inactive. He could see the options from so many points of view. He could usually see possibilities so many steps ahead that apparently simple analysis became a major undertaking.

So he had been very pleased with himself, he remembered. For once he had been spontaneously decisive. The waiter wasn't hovering, the deadline didn't loom. His first career choice had been initially briskly decisive.

He had finished university in Dublin and was back in Edinburgh itching for something different. VSO floated into view. Voluntary Service Overseas. It sounded romantic, exciting, and a little scary. He researched it; wrote his application; and in due course impressed at interview. He knew he had it.

His mother didn't see it that way. He could still remember the letter she sent him when she heard the news.

"Now first of all you are not to worry about me. I will be fine. Dorothy will look after the shopping I think (she's awfully good – but you know she isn't well at all) and Tom will fix that lock on the back door. You mustn't worry about it. It is great that you can get away – you must be so organised to have everything ready to leave for such a long time. I've been a bit tired but mustn't complain. The important thing is that you have a good time and don't worry about me. Mum"

In other words, "How can you possibly do this to me, I'll probably die while you are away enjoying yourself!"

Then a chance encounter with his old supervisor in Dublin raised the chance of a research post for a year, possibly two. It would be a superb career opportunity to work with this respected name. The research was not just interesting; it was sexy, current, and potentially big news.

He accepted. It was another briskly decisive move. The apology to VSO was difficult, but he was full of self-righteous satisfaction at the responsible decision made without agonising. He would start in Dublin in October.

The letter arrived in Edinburgh on a Saturday. A Dublin postmark. Trinity Psychology Department. "Dear William, I am very sorry to have to tell you that as the research funding has been withdrawn, I will not be able to…." Shit.

A friend brought him to an auction near Haddington the following week. Davy's father was a minor auctioneer and dealer, so he knew his way about. They pooled their money to buy an old desk – he'd now call it an escritoire – and made what seemed like a fortune when they sold it the same day to a city centre dealer. He was hooked. The rest, as they say, was history. "More like tragedy really," thought William.

.

Chapter 6

James: Dublin December 2005

The day after the party

James lowered himself onto the cold park bench. He had not ended up there deliberately. The only deliberate thing about him this afternoon was the way he had to concentrate on placing one foot after the other without tripping or staggering.

James's world was a harsh mix of simple economic constraint and vividly expansive imagination. He no longer had a car; that had gone with the job. He still found it embarrassing to admit that he didn't have one. He hated the bus – the unpunctuality; the corners of the floor that were never properly cleaned; the smell.

He had spent the morning in the library, using the free internet access to explore and to dream. He had researched GPS receivers – the sort you can hold in your hand while they pick up the satellite signals, process them, and tell you to within 3 metres where you are on the face of the earth. They even showed the direction of travel and the precise speed. He was fascinated by the technology and longed for one. He fussed loudly in the library over securing a printout of his list of GPS units, and carefully folded it into the inner pocket of his jacket before at last allowing himself to take refuge in O'Neill's bar, possibly for lunch.

Lunch didn't seem necessary after his second pint, and he relaxed into the fuzzily carefree state of the early afternoon drunk. He maintained a reasonable show of respectability with his good-quality jacket, and his shirt and tie, but by 3:00 o'clock he was a mess. He stumbled up Grafton Street to St Stephen's Green, and sat on the bleak wintry bench as the false euphoria of O'Neill's evaporated and guilt seeped in.

Yesterday in Lavinia's had been awful. For once he had been more embarrassed for others than for himself. In fact the awfulness of the situation had provided a welcome relief from feeling that he was the subject of the whispered conversations. Poor William. He must be looking for a stone big and heavy enough to crawl under even now. He had never met William's ex-wife Pat before. He hoped he would never meet her again. What on earth could they say after that debacle?

He suddenly saw William striding into the park through the corner gate some hundred metres away. James's instant reaction was to avoid him. It was an unthought, instinctive drive to avoid an embarrassing and complicated encounter. He made for the little bridge over the duck-pond, surprised at his unsteadiness, and didn't look back. He might have noticed William's wave had he risked a glance.

Luckily William was more mentally alert than James. He was fired with positive emotions and optimism. The find of the little piece of china had banished the negative, self-denigrating and regretful analysis of his mistakes. Like the flick of a switch he was back in the grip of the pleasure of victory. It wasn't much perhaps, and had he stopped to think about it, William would have been surprised at the irrationality of his mood-swing. The potential profit from his find was trifling compared with the financial ups and downs he had suffered in the past. It was infinitesimal compared with the money he nearly made in Edinburgh. But moods aren't logical. It took him soaring from the dark depths of his perception of utter failure in life to the sunny pleasure of the better days, the times when he clinched the deal, spotted the valuable item among the rubbish, and walked home with more money in his pocket than all the grey-suited administrators, civil servants and accountants that he disdained.

William spotted James lurching towards the little footbridge over the duck-pond. He could recognise even at a distance that James was unsteady in that determinedly focused style of the unpractised drunk. Chuckling momentarily at the dissolute sight, William strode benignly after James.

"I think you need a steady arm to get you back home," he said warmly as he easily drew level with his quarry.

"Oh, William. Yes. Thanks. Sorry."

"Look, let's wander round the park a bit while you tell me what you're up to."

"Afraid I had a bit too much at lunchtime. Not

feeling great this morning. Awful day yesterday. Look here….."

"I'm the one should be suffering after that – but for some reason I'm OK about it now. So don't worry. Unless you'd really like an excuse for a little more escape from harsh realities into a warm snug bar?"

"No more to drink. I shouldn't drink you know. I'm no good at it. I feel awful the next day. I really shouldn't drink."

"Funnily enough you aren't the first person I've ever heard say that. I don't think you'll be the last either." The two of them walked slowly along the curving paths that led around the bandstand, under the trees and gently towards the far corner of the Green, where William planned to get James onto a bus for home and some food. They suddenly felt a reciprocal warmth that stemmed from the glimmerings of recognition of their own failings in the other. Fellow-sufferers in the lonely and dispiriting underworld inhabited by middle-aged men facing their conspicuous failures, and their uncertain futures. .

Chapter 7

Alex: London 2002

For years Alex had entertained a vague ambition to own a classic car, and an idle past-time was to scan the small ads in the Sunday papers, or to browse some of the enticing web-sites that specialised in classic motor cars. Not just cars of course, but 'motor cars'.

He noticed gradually over the months the existence of a small specialist dealer in Putney. They dealt exclusively with classic Mercedes 'motor-cars' and sounded as if they were a cut above the dubious second-hand car dealers who were dabbling in the market. Most of the cars they advertised were far too expensive for him, but he had noticed once or twice they listed cars that were perhaps twenty or thirty years old and were described as "future classics".

One particularly quiet Friday morning in the office he picked up the phone and dialled the Putney number. A cultivated voice chatted in a friendly way about his interests, and fairly quickly established that he was firmly at the "modest" end of the market.

"Look, I don't usually deal in 107s, but they will soon be real classics. You know the models? They were the SLs and SLCs in the 1970s and 80s."

Alex confessed that although he recognised the model he didn't really know much about them. In retrospect that may have been a mistake.

"I have a 500SLC here that is an absolute cracker. It's so good that I keep on using it myself but I really must sell it. Totally practical as an everyday car but stunning performance and absolutely classic looks. Rare as hens' teeth as they were never officially imported to the UK. Too fast and too expensive they thought. We only got the 450SLC. This one had the new light alloy V8, the new gearbox, and this particular example has the light alloy body panels that make it really special."

How could he resist at least going to see it? No harm in that. It would provide a bit of entertainment on this dull and depressing Friday. So he took the tube to Earl's Court and changed to the Wimbledon line to Putney Bridge. He followed the directions over the bridge, down the steps and soon found the dealer. There were four or five older classics – one covered by a dust sheet – and the gleaming bronze SLC.

Alex remembered being thoroughly seduced by the whole operation. The dust-sheet was ceremonially whisked off the 1930 limousine, ("asking a hundred grand for that"), and the pristine 1960s SLs ("starting at about twenty-five grand before restoration"), before being allowed to sit in the ("priceless, actually") racing SL that was too original to think of restoring. He was suitably primed with the magic of the marque, and its association with his distant boyhood heroes of Moss and Jenkinson, and before them Fangio and Carraciola. They took him for a drive in the SLC and he was hooked.

Pitiful really – but he could later actually remember the exchange of comments back at Putney when he played at being the street-wise buyer but really was putty in their hands.

"That rear window doesn't seem to wind down?"

"Don't worry that's just stiff from lack of use, WD40 will sort it."

"You didn't say it was left-hand-drive!"

"But all of these were. Not imported to the UK you see. This one was a special order from the factory and collected there by the one owner."

"The carpet looks a little worn."

"You are better with matching mats over that anyway. I'll be getting a pair made that match the carpet and it will all look like new."

"The petrol consumption must be awful."

"If you only do eight or ten thousand miles a year you are probably spending only about £1,000 on petrol. Let's say this drinks it 30% faster – that's only £300 a year - to drive this!"

He was seduced and ready to be comforted by the pat answers. When they went into the office to inspect the bulging "history" file, he was irretrievably lost. Pathetic he knew – but it really was impressive. It seemed a wealthy Greek restaurant owner in London ordered the car, collected it himself from the factory, and used it solely for the annual drive across the continent to visit his family, a routine that had long since ceased. Hence the relatively low mileage, or kilometerage as it was. There were receipts covering 20 years with every detail of its life and maintenance,

Before the Friday afternoon was over, they had shaken hands on the deal and Alex was back on the tube rehearsing his speech to Liz – who was still hanging on firmly to the marital bonds, but with occasional flurries of such exasperation and rage that he should have known they were on the downhill path, with an impossible climb back to their version of peaceful harmony.

However he was still approaching his marriage with the same blind unreasoning faith that he later realised he had exhibited in his business. Like a pathetically slow-learning laboratory rat, he persisted unreasonably with behaviour patterns long after he should have realised that they no longer resulted in positive outcomes. He displayed an almost heroic ability to soak up the set-backs and disappointments. What in the short-term might be an admirable quality, in the longer term was painful and destructive.

The news of the SLC didn't totally derail Liz. She was slightly flummoxed, as this was something she hadn't seen coming. She had probably run through the scripts in her head for a bankruptcy plea; probably a malpractice claim from a client, spiced up with the absence of professional indemnity insurance; certainly for the uncovering of an affair with a younger woman; without doubt for the drama of discovering that a business trip had involved no visible business but a double room receipt. She was primed and ready to blow on any of those scenarios, but the SLC took her by surprise. She even laughed. Alex thought that secretly she might have liked the picture of them doing their romantic "grand tour" in a classic Mercedes sports car. Most of all he just took her off-guard as she hadn't rehearsed it. So he had his car, and the extension to the mortgage to pay for it seemed like a minor detail in the great scheme of things.

They really did love that car, even though it cost a fortune to keep it running properly. That sticking window turned out to be a burned out motor. The air-conditioning system which hadn't even featured on his list of queries set him back an unbelievable £3,000. However they did love it, and it become both a shared feature of their planning and one of the few things that gave them a joint focus in a positive plan for a grand continental tour. They thought that they would take a month the following spring – probably May – to drive through France, Germany, Switzerland, the north of Italy, and down the Adriatic coast to Greece. Vague plans, but at least a shared excitement.

As part of the planning Alex decided to look up the SLC's previous owner. Perhaps they would retrace his steps. Perhaps he would have some good advice. Certainly Alex expected he would be an old man, delighted to see his previous pride and joy restored to mechanical splendour, and about to re-enact the sort of journey it was built for.

So one autumn evening he found himself driving in the leafy avenues of Hampstead, looking for Iannis Katharos. It was later he discovered that the name could be loosely translated as Johnny Clean, or perhaps even as

Honest John. The irony was, in time, a cruel taunt.

Chapter 8

Alex: London November 2002

Alex visits Katharos

When he found the SLC's owner Alex had the most bizarre greeting. He had telephoned Katharos, and the old man had reacted in a way that at first Alex thought rather suspicious and cautious. He put it down to cultural and linguistic differences, for Iannis, despite his years in London, still spoke English with an accent and inflection that was almost stage Greek waiter.

Alex pulled up in the driveway of the red-brick extravaganza – it was Hampstead but with the Greek excess of decoration at every opportunity. The lace curtains tied back in fancy patterns; the flowers around the doorway; and the Greek tiles in the porch were all indicative of clinging to national identity rather than of a desire to integrate in his adopted city.

Iannis spoke in Greek to the readily-identifiable son who emerged from the house with him. They couldn't miss

Alex's arrival as it had triggered movement detectors that brought on a battery of halogen floodlights.

He exhibited a muted interest in the SLC, having a grunting amble around it as he heaved his overweight frame ahead of the trail of expensive cigar smoke. He ushered Alex into the house with that insistent Mediterranean arm around the shoulder, but said his son, also Iannis, would like to look around the car – so Alex left the keys.

Iannis senior took him to a back room in the house where in the midst of an over-upholstered, and over-heated plushness, he insisted that Alex accept a generous glass of Metaxa 7 star.

He asked where Alex had bought the car and how much he had paid. Alex wasn't ready for such a blunt question so told him. Katharos grunted. He asked about the trip planned for the spring, and Alex waxed lyrical about the splendours of his plan. Katharos dismissed with a wave of the fat cigar the details of the route to Greece, allowing only that he used to take the fastest route which in those days was through Yugoslavia but avoiding Albania. He advised against Albania in the route. "All crooks on that border," he said rubbing thumb and fingers together expressively.

He was more interested in Alex's Greek destinations, which of course included Athens, but were vague otherwise.

"You must go to Thessaloniki," was his advice.

"Don't go to the Peloponnesus. Too much tourists."

So they talked about Salonika, the route from Athens and the places to stay.

Young Iannis came into the room and there seemed to be an almost imperceptible nod to the father before he handed the keys to Alex.

"Good car. I hope you have pleasure in owning and driving it. It was important to us and we thought it was gone. Thank you for coming and good luck."

Iannis Junior had almost accent-less English, and Alex realised that he was being dismissed.

"What's your hurry, here's your hat," was Alex's old family expression for the feeling.

They both stood and ushered him back to the car, exchanging some muttered words of Greek on the way. Whatever they were, Iannis senior seemed content and nodded between puffs on the everlasting cigar. Alex left them his business card for no good reason other than habit, and drove back home not entirely rewarded by the experience. At least, he thought, it did give us a firm recommendation about where to go in Greece. He even thought that closer to the date he might ring old Katharos again to see if there were any contacts he would like him to make, or messages he could deliver in Greece.

Sometimes his own naivety amazed Alex when he looked back on it all.

.

Chapter 9

Alex

London 2003 – the Grand Tour

Winter turned to spring as Alex's researches and plans for the journey filled the dark months with positive possibilities. At last it was time for Liz to pack her bag and join Alex on their magic carpet ride to the long list of foreign cities. The maps and city-guides had been bought and organised, and they had revelled in the evenings debating the merits of one route over another, each pointing to their proposed solution on the big Europe map spread on the floor.

Not long before they left Alex had a phone call from old Katharos.

"Are you still planning you journey Mr Fox?"

Alex was very tempted to reply that their "chourney" was just about organised, but resisted. He was slightly surprised to hear from him, as he had seemed, Alex thought, a bit gruff and off-hand when they met.

This time he was being the affable old friend, and Alex could almost see the fat cigar being waved as he spoke.

"Mr Fox, my cousin in Salonika is so happy to hear my old car is alive. He wants you to be his guest as a favour to me. You must stay one night, two nights, as long as you like. They have nice taverna. Near the beach. You like it. I send you address and little present for my cousin's wife. What date I tell him you coming?"

Alex was actually quite glad to have the prospect of a fixed point and a potentially helpful local contact, so he responded enthusiastically to the idea. He promised to let him know the exact date later, but said he knew it would be in the third week of the trip which would make it the second week of May. That was good enough for Katharos, and sure enough, next day a package was hand-delivered to Alex's office with a map, some very specific instructions for finding the taverna, and a fat envelope for Katharos' cousin's wife. It was very firmly sealed with tape all round, which Alex took as a slight insult. As if he'd want to pry into the family exchanges of greetings!

At the end of the second week of April, Liz and Alex 'motored', as one does, to Folkestone, and gingerly negotiated the SLC over the ramps and humps of the Eurotunnel train. The feeling of excitement started properly when they left the Tunnel in Calais and looked forward to the drive down through France, Switzerland, Italy, Slovenia, Croatia, and Macedonia. Liz anticipated excitedly the sights of Paris, Milan, Verona, Venice, Trieste, and even Zagreb and Belgrade. It really was going to be a drive through European history.

The Grand Tour of 2003 was memorable. It was

superb. It exceeded their expectations in every way, including the extent to which Liz and Alex enjoyed one another's company, and found themselves agreeing on where to go and how long to spend there. It was like being transported back twenty years to happier and less complicated times. They argued only a little over the map-reading, which was always a problem. Liz struggled hard to meet Alex's demanding standards for a navigator, but it just wasn't compatible with her natural urge to enjoy the scenery and wonder at the history.

The drive down through France, Switzerland and Italy was the stage of tentative relaxing and testing of one another. They couldn't believe that they were able to agree and enjoy the process of touring. By the time they were motoring across from Milan to Verona and Venice, they were really relaxing. They seemed to have accepted by then that they actually were going to make a success of the trip. They weren't waiting for the angry words or the sharp retort. The slight tension and wary anticipation during the first five days seemed to dissipate as they completed another landmark and another journey without a fight.

They decided that once in Greece they would go to Thessaloniki as the final stop on the trip, before taking the fastest route back home, so they had a few days in Athens in perfect spring weather. It was another memorable time. The new Acropolis museum still wasn't open, but the benefits from the preparations for the Olympics were obvious all round. The traffic was just as daunting as they remembered it, so they stayed in one of the new hotels to the east of the city, now connected by the Olympic transport system to the city centre and only taking about 15 minutes to travel. They sat in little squares in the Plaka; wandered the streets round the old market at Hephestou St; even made it to the Acropolis early in the morning to beat the queues. It brought back mostly warm and good memories of the backpacking trips that they made as penniless students twenty years earlier. As Alex remembered, they were always good at travelling and exploring together. It was just the other bits of married life that they made a mess of.

Athens was probably the highlight, because by then they were thoroughly relaxed. They each could sense the other's relaxation, so even the shadow of the potential for quarrels seemed to have been burned away by the bright Greek sunshine. The associations with ancient times – and so far as they were concerned their ancient times were twenty years previously – probably helped. They tried to remember the little hotel in the Plaka they had stayed in. The fact that they couldn't find it didn't matter at all. The atmosphere was still there even though most of the businesses had changed hands. The kafeneions in tree-shaded squares were busier than they remembered but essentially the same. The foreign exchange students were dramatically more numerous; the grey or greying couples also more numerous; but thankfully the local business-people and shoppers were still confidently in their seats at their favourite establishments. Still they were putting the world to rights, still bemoaning the price of everything, and more than ever complaining about the state of the traffic in Athens. The Olympic construction projects had given them a whole new impetus. It was great fun to use the little Greek that Alex had learned to overhear the complaints which could almost be sufficiently understood through the facial expressions and the gestures. They just had to hear about the "Provlemma Olimpiakos" and see the face to get the general idea.

Eventually they made the drive north to Thessaloniki, and followed Katharos' instructions to find his cousin's taverna. Alex did take the precaution of ringing from Athens to warn them they were coming, and had a businesslike conversation with the cousin.

They arrived early evening in Nea Agathoupolis on the coast just southwest of the main town. It was still early season so there were only four or five other groups in the taverna – which turned out to be much bigger and more tourist oriented than they had anticipated.

The hugs, kisses, and formal welcoming process gave the other diners a great floor-show. They must have thought Alex and Liz were visiting royalty, or maybe just cousins. The same interior designer who had worked on the Katharos house in Hampstead had been at work in the taverna, but hadn't been so restrained. Their bedroom was a frilly extravaganza, every possible surface coated in lacy doilies and mats. It really was quite charming and Liz thought they had probably been given the best room in the house. The package for the cousin's wife was unceremoniously whisked away to be opened privately. Alex decided not to feel it a slight.

Katharos' cousin Adonis took command of the evening. While the women kept well in the background, Adonis and cousin Toni joined Alex and Liz at a table where wine just kept coming, and plates of mezedes were constantly refreshed. They had just about reached the point of exchanging enough eye-contact messages to say to each other 'time to go' when the main course arrived. It was a kleftiko – a rich slow-cooked stew that was so good they were able to eat and drink more than they imagined possible. By the last little coffee and inevitable Metaxa, they had been told the history of the taverna, how wonderful Thessaloniki was compared with Athens, and had found themselves agreeing to being taken by the cousin on a tour of the city.

Liz and Alex crawled off to bed exhausted by the concentration required to converse with well-meaning strangers and to cope with the excessive bonhomie and hospitality.

They were meek as lambs when Adonis announced they would take his car, and were told to give the keys of the SLC to Toni 'in case it has to be moved'.

They later agreed they didn't really enjoy Thessaloniki. The combination of Adonis' bombastic style as a tour guide, the endless monuments and ruins they 'must see', and the loss of control of their time became wearing. By the time they returned to the taverna they needed to sleep, and by the time they woke late in the evening, only the women seemed to be around. They thankfully were allowed to eat quietly in a corner, just the two of them, content to let the conversations from the other tables wash over them, and carefully avoiding eye-contact with any of the other diners who might use it as an opportunity to draw them into their discussions.

They escaped relatively early to bed so didn't see Adonis until they met at breakfast the next morning when he returned the keys of the SLC and wished the pair a safe journey. Since Alex hadn't told him yet that he and Liz had agreed in their room that they had to escape, had to get back to taking the world on their own terms and in their own time, he was slightly miffed but also relieved. It seemed to be a family trait to convey with minimum subtlety when one's visit was complete. He handed Alex a similar little package to the one they had brought, similarly securely taped for Iannis' wife.

So they drove back to the north, concentrating on covering ground rather than stopping for the sights. It was a relief to be back on their own again, and Alex more than Liz relished the effortless cruising across the face of Europe. The old SLC was still drawing admiring looks most places they stopped, and probably some looks of awe and sympathy at the petrol pumps. They drove more directly up through Macedonia, Austria and Germany, before reaching France and the Tunnel again for the return home. It was still a drive of about 2,500 kilometres, although that was some 500 shorter that the scenic route out.

Alex phoned Iannis Katharos a couple of days after their return to London, and he seemed keen to meet soon for a drink at his house. Alex offered to send him the package by courier as he wasn't ready for more verbal battering but Katharos was politely insistent and Alex agreed that he should visit the following evening.

Once again the floodlights announced his arrival and the two generations of Katharos were there at the car door before he had time to think. Effusive greetings and more Mediterranean hugs had him ushered away from the car before he had time to extract the keys or lock the door. When he gesticulated his need to lock the car the arm round my shoulder continued to draw him into the house amid reassurances that young Iannis would see to the car.

"Trust us Mr Fox, your car will be safe."

Alex remembered reading somewhere that only someone who is lying ever says, "Trust me." He felt uneasy, but politeness meant it would seem foolish to resist the hospitable arm that propelled him again into the recesses of the house.

This time he was surprised to find a table spread with little dishes of mezes. There were olives, little cubes of feta, dolmades, and even delicious little bits of fried kalamari. Again he was mildly surprised that the packaged greetings from Salonika were slipped immediately into a drawer of the desk, but the pressing hospitality took over and it was an hour before he could demonstrate that he had consumed enough ouzo and mezes to be allowed to escape. This time Iannis Junior appeared just as he was gathering himself to launch into the expected profuse thanks for the delicious hospitality.

Again Alex noticed the barely perceptible nod from one to the other, the pursed lips, and the sudden switch from never-ending offers of yet another meze or just a small ouzo, to the farewell handshakes.

"What's your hurry, here's your hat," once again.

.

Chapter 10

Lavinia: Dublin December 2005

The day after the party

Lavinia opened her eyes and saw nothing. Nothing other than the strange sparks of light left over in her eyes from the daylight outside. She waited, looking around as they subsided, and the total utter blackness took over. After a minute, she noticed a faint glow which oriented her and restored her sense of balance. A faint straight line of light was coming from under the door. She promised herself she would fix the seal.

She was now able to work out where the switch must be, and explored the wall tentatively with her fingers. A click, then a red glow illuminated the room. Beside her, glowing in the red light, was a stainless steel shelf and sink. There were black plastic bottles of chemicals on the shelf, which despite tight seals seemed to exude their sharp smell. On the draining board of the sink were three large plastic trays, upended and draining – one white, one red and one green, and smaller grey one. Opposite, Lavinia could make out the shape of the enlarger on its solid wooden table, looming against the black wall behind. On the floor she could feel the coarse weave of the ancient coir matting, and see the white cable of the power lead.

After the social catastrophe of the previous afternoon, Lavinia had decided that a day of solitude and creativity would help restore her spirits. She always found that the satisfaction of creating beautiful images on glossy black-and-white paper left her feeling rested and more philosophical about life. Today was going to be a test of that theory. Lavinia was dressed for the dark-room. She was wearing an old pair of jeans, an old work-shirt, and a blue apron that was no longer respectable enough for the kitchen. Her long dark hair was drawn back and held by a coloured elastic band, and her old trainers betrayed the occasional splash of chemical from past endeavours. She had decided that the best thing to drive out the bad memories would be to focus on something totally different, so she had chosen a roll of black and white Ilford FP4 film that she had used last October in Turkey. Even thinking about the task ahead helped her relax. The images of the little sun-drenched anchorages and the unspoiled landscape soothed her mind. She sighed for the remembered pleasure of sailing and swimming in warm blue seas in an idyllic corner of the ancient world.

She had answered a small advertisement in the Sunday Times. "Perfect Sailing on the Turquoise Coast", the heading had suggested, and for what seemed not a lot more money than a package holiday, promised an opportunity to sail with four others on a skippered yacht.

Some long-unrealised urge and an idealised mental image of the possibilities had combined to give Lavinia the courage to answer the advertisement. She had discovered a small-scale operation run by an individual living in London and using his Turkish based yacht for some commercial chartering. The yacht looked just beautiful in the photographs, and even to her inexpert eye and vivid imagination promised safe but exciting voyages. Part of her new-found sense of adventure persuaded her to risk her individual booking, and she kept at bay her natural worry about the other passengers never mind the unknown skipper. In the event it was one of those experiences that had rewarded her bravery, and increased her inclination to take new risks and find fresh experiences.

They had turned out to be a guest party of only 3, the others a couple who took the bow cabin on the yacht. Lavinia had enjoyed the space of her own double-cabin in the stern, and had discovered a new world of technical terms, at first worrying sensations, but ultimately the exhilaration of being propelled by the wind across idyllic seascapes. She had loved almost every minute of it, and had learned rapidly enough to be genuinely useful to Alex the skipper and his sailing partner Maggie. While the her fellow guests wanted to enjoy their own company and be transported passively, Lavinia had found herself becoming unofficial crew, and had learned how to operate the anchor windlass, coil the warps, and tie a clove-hitch on the fender ropes.

She had brought along her newly purchased Canon camera. It was an expensive SLR, deliberately not digital, and she had decided to use black and white film to try to capture images that she could process herself back in Dublin. She was fired with the imagined pleasure of creating evocative images that were in a different class from the everyday colour snaps her friends routinely showed her. Every day, as she and Alex brought the yacht into one delightful cove after another, or on one occasion into a bustling port, she saw endless images that she wanted to capture on film. Once she had carried out her self-imposed yachting duties, she took her camera and wandered the jetties and the shorelines. She took hazy early morning seascapes, looking across the great Gulf of Fethiye towards the distant high mountains. She captured bright sunny images of the yacht at anchor, or moored to one of the impossibly rickety-looking jetties. She even risked taking the expensive camera in the dingy, with Alex on the oars, to take photographs from almost sea level of yachts, anchorages, bays, hillsides and jetties.

So today as she prepared herself for the careful process of producing prints, she felt the calming influence of the distant perspective suffuse her agitated mind, and she slowed into the meticulous routine of the darkroom. As she had been reliving the warm memories of the original scenes, and even experiencing a slight pang of missing Alex's company, she had been carefully placing the four trays side by side, and filling the first with developer, the second with stopping chemical, the third with fixer, and the last with clean running water. Without having to focus her thoughts on the mechanical tasks she had checked the temperatures and adjusted the thermostat on the tray heater. After about 10 minutes of peaceful preparation and reminiscing, all was ready. She chose a set of negatives from their first evening on the yacht.

They had sailed from Gocek to a beautiful little inlet called Kapi Creek. She could still remember her sense of overwhelming awe at the peace and beauty of the place. They had enjoyed invigorating sailing winds during the day, and the sheltered bay was suddenly quiet and welcoming after the excitement. They had arrived mid afternoon, and only a couple of other yachts were already there, so Alex had time to show her how he organised the yacht with the right ropes and fenders for their mooring to the jetty. She wasn't much help that first day, but was already fascinated and enthused by the process. She watched Alex expertly reverse the boat to the jetty, shouting greetings to his friends who were waiting to help. The ropes were thrown with no drama and Alex had brought the boat to a standstill about a metre from the jetty before going to the bow to secure what he later explained to her was called a lazy line. The details were a bit of a blur to her that first time, but she drank it all in and had been quick to grab her Canon and step ashore to try to capture the images she wanted of this idyllic location.

She remembered walking back and forwards along the beautifully rickety jetty as she captured frame after frame of hillside, reflective water, yachts, and local children. The jetty was her photogenic ideal, with old weathered wooden slats nailed to a rustic underwater framework of unfinished pine trunks. It had been a totally intoxicating and captivating experience. When Alex called her back to the yacht for a swim and later for the ritual pre-dinner raki, she still was not satiated with capturing her images of the creek. So when evening came she had the camera by her side, and brought it to the taverna table on the shore as the five of them shared the bread and wine in what felt like a sacramental celebration of the ancient coast. Alex, she remembered, had been restless and had almost spoiled the atmosphere of the waterside dinner, but once he left them to do something back on the boat, they settled down as a foursome and found the conversation came easily and philosophically. She had used the firm wooden table as a base for the camera as she continued to experiment with wide aperture shots in the gathering gloom. And she had even tried some time-exposures looking out over the bay in the moonlight, with two little boats posing perfectly in the moon's reflected beam; two timeless silhouettes in the ripple-interrupted path of light across the water.

Lavinia back in the darkroom switched on her anglepoise lamp, carefully gripped the first set of six negatives by its edges and slid it out from the protective sleeve. She held the negatives up to the light and tried to visualise the finished prints. A couple of the negatives looked under-exposed, and she feared that at least one might have been blurred by some movement during the long exposure, but the late-night shot of the two boats in the moonlight looked crisp and clear. She checked the negative for dust, and gave it a light squeegee between her fingers before slotting it into the holder from the enlarger. She put it in apparently upside down, so that the projected image looked the right way up on the enlarger table. Once she was satisfied that all was well, she clicked off the anglepoise, returning the room to a dim red glow, slipped the negative holder into the enlarger, and switched on the enlarger light.

The projected image was still in negative but was now much larger and easy to examine. The dark parts were where most of the emulsion had been affected by light and had therefore not washed away in the developing chemicals. This retained emulsion would resist the enlarger light passing through to the sensitive paper on the enlarger table, and would turn out light or even pure white in the finished print. The lighter parts of the negative represented the areas where the original image had been dark, the emulsion had not reacted and was washed away in the chemical processing so would allow lots of enlarger light through and turn out black or grey in the print. She adjusted the size and focus of the image until the ripples of the moonbeam and the two little boats were larger, clearer images than she had been able to see on the night in Turkey. She still couldn't work out what the boats were doing - probably some sort of fishing - but liked the composition and contrasts of the image. When she was happy that everything was well-focused, and the important aspects of the image were eye-catchingly placed, she made her test strips to work out the ideal exposure time. When she was satisfied with the settings she at last slipped a glossy sheet of 10 x 8 paper into its place, and made the exposure. Once the exposure was complete, she slipped the sensitive paper into the tray of developer, pressed the timer start button, and gently rocked the tray as the seconds ticked by. The trick she had learned was to keep things moving, just gently, but never allowing the chemicals to sit still on the print. The gentle rocking of the tray kept the chemicals washing back and forth over the active surface. After only about 15 seconds the image was emerging, and after 20 it looked clear, but she knew to keep processing it until the specified minute had elapsed. She knew that consistency was crucial in achieving good results.

After the minute she lifted it with tongs into the red tray holding the chemical that stopped the process, and then into the final green tray containing the fixer. One more minute and she was able to turn the anglepoise on again to examine the still glistening wet print. It looked promising in the dim light. She knew from experience that what looked marginally too dark in the darkroom would look well in daylight. This print was a satisfyingly contrasty study. There was an enormous amount of firm unblemished black – no dust particles had interfered. Across the black was the jagged bright white rippling reflection of the moon's light, interrupted by her two mysterious boats in silhouette. She allowed herself a flutter of self-congratulation at the production of a really striking image before slipping it into the fourth tray with the clean running water.

Lavinia continued to examine negatives, and produce prints for the rest of the afternoon. As she had hoped, the combination of soothingly meticulous routine, and her absorption in a technical yet artistic process, had driven everything else from her mind. She had produced nine prints she hoped would still look good in daylight and was wondering about what to tackle next when she noticed the time. She had been alerted and wakened from her concentration by the ringing of the telephone in the distance. It was 5:45 already, and she hadn't realised the afternoon had gone. Having forgotten to bring the cordless phone into the darkroom, she decided to let the caller leave a message and set about clearing up the darkroom. Each of the trays of chemical had to be carefully funnelled back into its own labelled bottle. The trays, tongs, and the whole sink area had to be washed thoroughly to prevent the corrosive attack of the chemicals. She tidied the enlarger, put the dust-cover in place, and at last opened the door, pulled back the lightproof curtain and emerged into the evening gloom with her wet tray of finished prints.

Chapter 11

Alex after the tour

Alex's diary after the tour 2003

When he thought about it afterwards, the visit to Thessaloniki had been a bit of a puzzle. While they had been glad to see the area and tour the city, the atmosphere had jarred a little. After weeks of being totally in control of their own time and decisions they both found it hard to give in to being organised by Adonis and his family. Also, the oddness of the contrast between the fulsome welcome and the dismissive departure niggled Alex from time to time. For the first night and the following day they were the honoured guests and were treated like royalty. The final day it was almost as if they had been finished with – time to go. It had probably been because it fitted so well with their own inclination that they hadn't spent a lot of time thinking about it, but as the weeks passed and the holiday achieved a different overall perspective, he became more conscious of how the time in Thessaloniki had been the watershed. Up to that point they had all the time in the world, were relaxed and happy. They were their own masters. From that point everything was different, and an urgency about getting away had dominated. In fact as soon as they left Thessaloniki, the focus changed to getting back home quickly and safely. Alex wasn't sure to what extent the interaction with Katharos' cousins caused the change in mental orientation, or if it was simply inevitable because of the passing of the most distant point of the journey and the start of the return home. The more he thought about it the more certain he was that the interactions in Thessaloniki were to blame. The bloody Katharos people had broken the spell, invaded their self governing and exclusive democracy in their own Grand Tour. Things weren't the same from that point on.

They arrived back in London in the first week in May, and London was warming up as usual for a late spring. Liz and Alex were also warming up for their final bout, with an annoying series of little squabbles throughout the summer.

Alex had returned to a London that was depressing and difficult after the unexpected pleasures of what he and Liz still referred to as their Grand Tour. The escapism that had made the trip so enjoyable gradually showed itself to be just that. It had been an escape from the realities of the rest of life.

He walked listlessly from Tottenham Court Road tube station to his office and pushed through the heavy outer security door with more of a feeling of dread than of enthusiasm. Alex's office was small. It was also dark. However it was relatively inexpensive for the area because of the size and basement location. He flicked on the light, and the same old annoying buzz from the fluorescent light hammered home the message that he was back to an imperfect reality.

Poland St didn't sound too impressive but the postcode was central. Alex was conscious that not too many doors along from his entrance, further away from Oxford Street and closer to Soho, the seediness of the area became more obvious and more oppressive. The occasional new coffee bar and even an oxygen bar didn't really counterbalance the number of handwritten signs that appeared in doorways. "Blonde busty model" was the basic message, with occasional references to Page 3, or to the model's familiarity with English. It was sufficiently central to make it easy for him to reach other central offices easily, but it had never proved to be an office where he felt comfortable entertaining clients.

When business had been good, five years earlier, Alex had rented two bright offices on the first floor. He had employed a secretary and from time to time rented the top floor conference room for meetings and seminars. He reflected on the financial and literal decline of his business that had seen him progressively give up the full-time secretary; then one of his two offices; before finally moving to the cheapest office in the building – the dark 10 sq metre basement cubby-hole that depressed him more each month.

Alex had been a bright student back in the 70s, but his Business Studies degree hadn't really enthused him. It had been the recommended passport to a well-paid job in what his father always referred to as a blue-chip employer. It probably could have been, but Alex didn't respond well to the corporate culture he found himself in. A job with a major confectionery manufacturer had been a mixture of pleasure at the steady income and the unusual bonus of a company car – a Vauxhall Cavalier it had been – mixed with horror and boredom at the realities of the Graduate management scheme.

In the 1970s it had been the norm for big companies to organise a series of placements in all the different aspects of the business so that their bright new managers knew everything "from the shop floor up". Unfortunately the responsibility for organising such schemes usually rested with an elderly manager who had to be found gainful employment until his retirement date finally arrived. "How times change," thought Alex, who knew just how brutal companies had become, and how little room there was for sentiment in allocating jobs or avoiding redundancies. The result was that he was imposed on one unprepared and unwilling host department after another, with a series of less-well-qualified managers whose chief concern in relation to Alex was to "teach him a thing or two," or perhaps "take him down a peg or two."

Alex had found himself with a seemingly endless list of small shops in the no-mans-land of peripheral Birmingham. He had to visit the shops to take orders, which could have been done by telephone, and to "merchandise". This seemed to him to consist largely of tidying the display of his employer's unhealthy produce, moving the display of competing products if he could do so without annoying the shopkeeper, and assembling the never-ending series of cardboard display aids that proclaimed the latest offer. "10% Extra Free." "New

Nuttier Recipe." He hated the repetitive meaningless futility of it all.

He lasted for two years before finding a less well paid but infinitely more interesting job as Business Development Manager in a small packaging manufacturing company. He flexed his mental muscles and even utilised his old degree course notes as he helped the owner to draw up strategic plans, present business plans to the bank, develop marketing strategies, activity plans, and even management by objectives for the bemused production supervisors and workers.

He thought he had probably done a good job for the company, even though he knew the older workers sniggered sceptically at his business-school ideas and terminology. It was when he found that the owner's feckless son was to be appointed over his head that he decided he had no answer to nepotism.

As a reaction against two unhappy experiences he decided to emulate his old lecturers and get into the apparently much more agreeable academic world. While he had thoroughly hated a lot of the seemingly pointless activities of the past five years, he found they could be described in ways that made his experience sound very impressive. The combination of two years with a major household name and three years virtually running a small company sounded good to the academic selection panel, who were privately a little worried about the thin-ness of their own claims to experience in the world of business.

Alex at first took to the academic environment with exemplary enthusiasm and energy. Students reacted well to his lively style and his ability to tell genuine stories from recent commercial experience. He became a popular teacher with positive appraisals, and year by year moved up the salary scale. However ten years later he emerged grumbling from yet another long boring departmental meeting and realised he was no longer happy. The teaching that he had loved was now a lesser part of his job. Departmental administration and haggling over budgets was more of his life, and the future looked as if it was going to be yet more of the administration and less enjoyment.

Alex took the plunge into self-employment in 1990, when he could see that he could pick up work that the University was losing. He set himself up to deliver management courses to the medium sized companies that wouldn't pay the top rates demanded by the international business schools and better universities. He found himself back doing what he enjoyed most – sharing his know-how with people who wanted to learn. He was a good performer, and generally went down well with the clients who used him. So for some heady years, Alex was making money. In fact he was making much more than his old academic salary, and avoiding all the parts of the job he hated. His marketing had been very simple. He contacted all the companies that had used the university in the past, and offered them deals that saved them money. His old networking skills paid off, and he settled into a life where his calendar was full, even though it meant that he was living most of his life in a series of not-very-inspiring conference hotels round the south of England.

Nobody needed him during the long summer months – in fact July and August were a total waste of time for the business, so he and Liz had started taking themselves off for long holidays to France and then to the Mediterranean. It was during those well funded years that he started to indulge his dream of sailing – at first with tuition and then more confidently on his own. By the end of 1996 he was ready to buy himself a yacht. A very excited Alex visited the Boat Show in January '97 and, trying to look relaxed and experienced, examined the mid-sized yachts on offer. He finally picked a roomy, stylish French Jeanneau that would be ready by the spring. He paid his deposit, and went home bubbling with excitement. A yacht! In the Med! Him!

He saw the downturn coming. A deadly combination of negatives seemed to take his feet from under him at the end of the 90s and start of the 2000s. At first he found his clients spending all their money on IT in preparation for the "year 2000" problem. There was less money for the sort of management courses that he could deliver. When that problem was past, and business should have been picking up for him, he found there was an inescapable trend towards the sort of formalised procurement that made it impossible for old friends to pass work his way. He had to bid in competition with all the slick large companies, and however much his friends wanted to give the work to him, he just couldn't compete. So by 2002 Alex was clear that the last couple of lean years were not just a temporary problem. He knew he had a long term and fundamental problem.

The escape to the Grand Tour had probably been irresponsible, but he didn't really care. He was facing the end of his business career and he might as well enjoy himself. That was how he felt on the better mornings. The other mornings were times of despair and regret.

He settled himself to look at his diary and to think about his options. He could see at a glance that most of the appointments in his diary were for meetings with people who had used him in the past, and were really just old friends agreeing to see him from time to time. In terms of bookings for work that would pay a fee, he had nothing in July or August, and just a couple of days in June and September. He knew it wasn't looking good.

Alex telephoned his accountant.

"Hi Sam. Can we get together for a serious chat?"

"Oh dear, Alex. That usually means something unpleasant. How bad are things?"

Sam knew from the last couple of years' accounts that Alex was making less money than he needed. He had advised him to get out of the business while he could still pay all his bills and go back to a university job. Sam didn't know that it was no longer so easy to do that, so Alex put off the evil day.

"Pretty bloody terminal so far as I can see. It really isn't worth my while keeping an office with all the expenses that go with it."

"How's next Friday afternoon for you – say 2:30?"

"What do you need me to bring?"

"All the usual stuff that you always do – accounts for the year so far, work plans and projections. By the way we haven't even started on last year's tax return. You'll probably have some losses on that so we can talk about that too."

"Thanks Sam. See you next week. I'll dig out all we'll need. Shouldn't take too long unfortunately."

"See you Alex. Let's hope it isn't as bad as you think. You've still that house haven't you? And the boat? Not to mention a working wife?"

"Yeah, all of those thank goodness."

"Could be worse then"

"Yeah, see you next week."

"Bye. Love to Liz."

Alex put the phone down. Yes the house in Chiswick was undoubtedly his greatest asset. His yacht and his car were depreciating but still worth something. But what about his 'working wife'?

Liz had gone back to work after the tour with a lot more enthusiasm than Alex. She worked for Shipham's estate agency and seemed to virtually run their Marylebone office. She obviously enjoyed it, and was making a successful and well paid career in it. But he knew they were going to have to face some harsh realities about their future – together or apart.

In the years that Alex had been busy, they had fun planning their holidays and making the house as attractive as it was well-located. The 90s were successful and rewarding for them both, and they had focused on building their respective businesses and making money rather than on raising a family. But Alex had been a less than perfect husband, and Liz had suspected that his time away from home wasn't as celibate as he maintained. When Alex's money became less plentiful, there were fewer treats to create the feeling of positive activity. The more they found themselves together in the evening with no excitement planned, the more they annoyed each other and allowed little arguments to become serious rows. Liz had threatened to leave him in the heat of many rows, but only twice had come really close to actually doing something. Alex had the ominous feeling that the next big row would be the last.

He was right. He came home from his session with Sam with a greater depression and gloom than he could ever remember. He hadn't been able to give positive answers to Sam's probing questions about the evidence for optimism in the business. All the signs were that it was in terminal decline. Sam's advice had been to give up right away.

"Leave the office empty and try to negotiate a transfer of the lease. Cease the telephone lines, stop paying for the web-site that had been a total waste of money anyway. Start applying for jobs and sign on for whatever benefit you can qualify for. Put time and energy into applying for a good salaried job and do it from home," had been the stern advice from his old friend and one-time supporter.

So Alex was in a fatalistic mood when Liz decided it was time to give him the benefit of her wisdom and insight.

"I've been telling you for years you needed to do things differently. Look at John Shipham. He saw the way things were changing and moved with the times. You wouldn't listen. You thought you could keep going with your old pals giving you crumbs of work when it suited them. Well you were wrong. And I don't know what you're going to do now."

It wasn't, in retrospect, the approach designed to soothe his battered ego.

Next morning they both were reflecting on the night before. Alex was reflecting in the unusual spaciousness of his sole occupation of the double bed, while Liz was experiencing the slightly dusty and unused atmosphere of the spare room. It was odd to be experiencing the house from a different angle – the light; the sounds; the physical shape of the room were all slightly disorienting. Liz felt good. She felt empowered – as if she had done something positive. At last – she had done something positive about getting out of this relationship that was as stale and dusty as the spare room she lay in. She was planning and wondering. She wasn't going to make up. She wasn't retreating. One of them had to move out as she wasn't going through the excruciating nonsense of sharing a house but not a bed.

Alex was bruised. He was resentful. He had come home expecting support and sympathy and instead had been kicked when he was down. He looked forward to the apology from Liz. At least this morning he would get a bit of pampering to make up for the unjustified battering from last night. He expected that he would soon hear Liz making some breakfast – but then was uncertain. It was Saturday and he always was the first up. He usually went to buy the papers before the long lazy breakfast that took them half-way to lunch-time, and sometimes ended up back in bed. Perhaps he should stick to that familiar routine – it had the advantage of getting him out of the house while Liz emerged from the spare room. He imagined it would be painful meeting on the landing as they emerged from their separate rooms.

He strolled down to Chiswick High Street, gradually imagining more positive outcomes to the day. Perhaps it was a good thing really – a chance for them to create a new, fresh basis for getting along together. Liz would help him get himself sorted out. He would take Sam's advice - give up the office and set himself up a workspace in the spare room at home where he could start his new project of applying for jobs. "Treat it as a job in itself" had always been the trite advice he had read about job-hunting. He started to plan a different pattern to his days. He even started to feel a little lightness in his spirit at the relief from admitting that he should give up the office and escape the negativity of his collapsing self-employment. He bought the papers and popped into the boulangerie to buy a couple of croissants and a large pain au raisin to share. It was a celebration breakfast in a way.

Alex and Liz both approached breakfast with a positive and determined air. They both had the hint of a smile not quite formed, but twitchingly ready to appear. As soon as Alex saw Liz he recognised the incipient smile and knew that she had been thinking the same sorts of things that he had. He was preparing the reconciliatory response he would graciously utter. Perhaps he should get in first and reassure Liz that all was forgiven and things were going to be better.

As soon as Liz saw Alex she recognised the slightly cocky swagger in his step, and the twitching hint of a grin that he was hopeless at controlling when he had some good news to break. He was a hopeless poker player. But she was relieved. He had obviously been building up to this break-up just as much as she had. He probably had already phoned whoever it was he currently had as a secret soul-mate to say he would soon be free. They both tried to speak at once.

"Don't worry about last night – you were really

justified in having a go," was Alex's start.

"Well this is it at last," was the simultaneous contribution from Liz.

She was standing in the kitchen with a mug of the freshly made coffee clutched in her right hand, her fingers wrapped around the warmth and poking through the unused handle. It was a typical pose and Alex's heart was ready to melt. They each processed the words from the other and smiles disappeared as they wondered if they had heard what they thought they had heard. Both had been so focused on what they were going to say that it took them time to register, analyse and comprehend what was happening. At one level it seemed to take seconds. At another level they both saw instantly what was going on. The croissants and pain au raisin were wasted that morning.

Chapter 12

Alex London:

Summer/Autumn 2003

Alex found living on his own an odd mixture of tentative pleasure at being in control of things and occasional depressing emptiness. He was well organised and his new flat was still satisfyingly clean and fresh. He had the first floor of a redeveloped terrace house close enough to Clapham Common to be accessible. Once they had agreed that this really was the time to separate, Liz had taken control. Her estate agency know-how meant that Alex found himself being told what was going to happen rather than planning it himself. Liz was going to buy out his share of the Chiswick house. He argued that he had paid more of the mortgage than she had, but his lawyer persuaded him that such an argument would get him nowhere. So the property-savvy Liz ended up with a big house in Chiswick to split into modern apartments, while Alex was found an attractively converted apartment in Clapham – but crucially with no debt. Liz had happily taken on a loan to buy him out, and it was enough to buy outright the new apartment. Although he resented Liz being able to stay in Chiswick, he knew that he was in no position to take on another mortgage. Another year or two and he might start again, but with his business winding up, and arguments with his office landlord about continuing payments for the now empty office, he was well and truly cornered. Liz, with her steady salary, had been able to turn the whole situation to her advantage. He was sure that in a couple of years the value of the two, or was it four, apartments she would then own would dwarf the loan she had needed to sign up for. She was building her own property business on the wreckage of their marriage but there was nothing he could do about it.

"Irreconcilable Breakdown" was the official terminology which apparently would eventually lead to an uncontested divorce. More legal fees, more depressing realisation that his place in the world had shifted. He started to realise how many parts of his old life had been based on the marriage. The simple availability of someone to talk to in the evening had never struck him as something he would miss. But like someone bereaved, he often found himself in the strange metachronistic thought pattern where he realised he had been looking forward to telling Liz about the amusing incident during the day, or the idiocy of the bank clerk. Almost daily he found his brain going through the anticipation and the almost instantaneous correction. At times he could laugh at it, and bizarrely even found he had anticipated telling Liz about the crazy process. But it chipped away at his inner self. It chiselled out an empty space inside him, which sometimes felt physically painful and empty – but he couldn't find any way of filling it.

He created routines for himself. Differentiating between work days and weekends became an obsession. On weekdays he had his strict rule about being at his desk by 9:30 in the morning. He still received professional journals redirected from the office, and still logged on to the websites where he trawled through the notifications of contracts that he could bid for. He had quickly found that just applying for jobs wasn't going to work. He was too old for most of them – even though employers were trumpeting their equality policies. He could absorb himself in one form of activity after another, and found that the emptiness could be ignored for hours at a time. On good days, when he had found something that interested him and needed some reading and research, he could even carry the feeling of positive purposefulness through his solitary lunch and into the afternoon. It was as if the positive momentum could be kept moving right through the freewheeling parts of the day. If he achieved something purposeful in the part of the day he labelled work-time, he could go to the kitchen in the evening with an air of success. He moved positively. He was decisive about what he was going to cook, and prepared it efficiently and with enjoyment. His movements were brisk and competent. He cooked well, and enjoyed the process. He could sit and eat while listening to Radio 3 or sometimes Radio 4 before settling down with a book and some background music from his collection. He had at least been able to hang on to his Linn hi-fi and most of the CD collection that he had built up over the years. A warm glow of positive achievement could leave him feeling energised and motivated, which later translated into proper relaxation and rest. Sometimes these good spells lasted for several days, and he woke in the morning looking forward to getting to the desk, looking forward to the feeling of progress, and eyeing himself in the mirror to see someone building a new way of living and a new sense of himself.

The fragility of the good days frightened him. The simplest failure could sabotage his mood and leave him unable to function. One Thursday he had started well enough, but when he opened the morning's post he was notified of an outstanding account for the old office telephone. It wasn't a large amount, but if he paid it, he wouldn't have enough in his account to buy wine for the weekend. His mood spiralled down. The derailing of his plan for the day deprived him of the activity that kept his mind off the negatives always lurking there to depress him. He couldn't create his feeling of achieving something, and the absence of that feeling meant that the vacuum inside could take him over. The pain returned, the feeling of worthlessness felled his fragile confidence, and his personal vicious circle of being disabled from doing the very things that rescued him from this state, left him hurt, limp and pointless.

He shambled into the kitchen confused by the emptiness. Sometimes it felt as if it was his empty stomach, but it didn't translate into appetite. Quite the reverse, and he had to remind himself that if he didn't eat he would feel even worse. He opened the fridge and moved the jars of pickle to the side to see what else was there. He rejected the eggs, and thought the pate looked old. He closed the fridge and opened a cupboard. After closing the cupboard he stood leaning with two hands on the edge of the worktop, shoulders stooped, and physically inches shorter than he had looked and felt the previous evening. He couldn't decide what to eat. Nothing appealed. He could make a sandwich but didn't feel like it. An omelette would be easy and quick. He could take something out of the freezer, but he couldn't be bothered to hunt through it or to defrost anything. He walked heavily out of the kitchen and into his living room. The papers from yesterday were still lying around and he spiralled further down as he hated the messiness but couldn't be bothered to tidy it up. He kicked the papers out of the way and sat on the edge of the settee. He hunched forward, hugging his stomach like someone with a pain. He cursed and rocked back and forwards for a minute. Then with a burst of energy he stood up and went to the hall cupboard where he pulled on some outdoor shoes and a jacket. He hauled angrily at the front door and went down the stairs to the outside world knowing that he had to walk, to keep moving, to make his limbs work or he was lost in the wallowing emptiness and grief for something vague that was no more.

He walked with his head angled down, not looking at other people other than to avoid bumping into them. Making his way to the Common he walked along to the Underground Station but didn't go in. He thought of going somewhere but nowhere seemed worthwhile. He crossed the road because the pedestrian crossing beeped and beckoned him rather than because he wanted to. He walked along the High Street and purposelessly walked into Sainsbury's, picking up a basket as he went. Walking along the aisles he thought he should buy something to eat. Some bread? Some ready-made soup? A salad? He was paralysed by an inability to decide and hated himself for it. The impatient mothers with their push-chairs sighed pointedly as they manoeuvred past him. At last he decided he would buy a sandwich and take it back to the flat. He lifted one of the wedge-shaped plastic boxes and put it in the basket. As he walked to the tills he imagined the lonely flat and put the unappealing box on the nearest shelf. He walked back out of the shop and wondered how many degrees of difference there were now between him and the homeless tramp in the dirty red sleeping bag in the next doorway. The way he felt today there wasn't much further to fall.

Alex wandered along Clapham High Street getting in the way of the busy pedestrians and reacting huffily to the impatient exclamations as people had to slow or turn to avoid him. It was lunchtime, and there was a pub across the road. With a burst of decisiveness he went more briskly back to the pedestrian crossing. Walking more uprightly and purposefully he crossed the road and made his way into the newsagent to buy a paper to read with his lunch. He reached for his usual copy of the Independent, changed his mind and went for the Guardian in case there were public sector jobs he should check, and went to the counter. Shamefacedly he stammered his apologies and put the paper back when he realised he had no money in his pockets. He cursed himself again and strode angrily back towards the flat. At least he was moving faster and looking as if he had somewhere to go. He looked back across the road to the red sleeping bagged figure and shuddered slightly as he turned away.

He opened the door of the flat to hear the last ring of the telephone. Just missed it. He threw his jacket into the cupboard and dialled 1471. It was a number he vaguely remembered with a Bristol code, so he scrambled back to the old filofax to scan through the people and companies that he knew there. Eventually the number matched – of course – one of his old contacts who had used him to run training sessions for the management team from time to time. He dialled the number and asked for Ron.

"Hi Ron, sorry I missed the call – just working on something else. Good to hear from you."

"Alex – you are a hard man to track down. I tried that office number of yours and couldn't get any sense out of them. They said you had left but didn't know where. I actually remembered about Liz working in the estate agency so I tried her. Hope I haven't put my foot in it!"

"Don't worry. All water under the bridge now. Liz and I separated in June and I'm working from my new place here," he lied.

"So how's business? Any chance of doing another little job for us?"

Alex tried to control his breathing but failed. Rather breathlessly and hoarsely he said,

"Sure. What would you like and when. I'll come down and chat unless you want to trek all the way to London to talk."

He was still in business.

Chapter 13

Alex London: September 2003

Alex and Jack in the wine bar

Alex finished the phone call, put away his filofax and threw himself on the settee. He uncharacteristically punched the air like a reality show winner, and leaned back on the settee.

"Yes," was all he could say, "Yes, yes, yes!"

The flat suddenly seemed too small, too confining for his expansive mood. Remembering to lift his money and credit cards from the bedside table, he once again grabbed the jacket and closed the door behind him. He exuded energy and positive intent as he strode back towards the Common. A date in his diary for a meeting next week, a 3-day event a few weeks hence, and "the usual" allowance of preparation and writing up time had changed his world. The pubs in Clapham seemed too depressing for his good mood, so pausing only to phone his old friend Jack who worked at the top of Regent Street, he set off by tube to

Oxford Circus, from where it was a short walk down Regent Street and behind Liberty's renovated shop-frontage, to the welcoming intimacy of Kingly Street and his favourite old wine bar.

"'Bout ye!" shouted Jack from the dim rear narrowness of the bar. He was from Northern Ireland and, especially when having a drink, tended to use deliberately exaggerated colloquial phrases like the abbreviated "what about you?"

Jack had already bought a bottle of New Zealand Sauvignon Blanc, and a chilled glassful was waiting for Alex on the mellow wooden elbow-shelf.

"Bloody wonderful," sighed Alex as his shoulders relaxed and his face beamed with a strength of emotion fuelled by the earlier depression. The soaring rise of his mood was better than could be appreciated by anyone who hadn't shared the depths of the empty, lonely wasteland earlier in the day.

They settled in to a warm, philosophical late afternoon and evening of reminiscence, swapping stories of their mutual friends from years gone by. Jack maintained a coruscating disdain for any sign of soft romanticism, so was a good resolve-stiffening partner for Alex. He quizzed Alex about the state of his business and just as dispassionately about the relationship with Liz.

"Just as well out of it," was his verdict.

"Out of what, the business or the marriage?"

"Bloody both of them. Reckon Liz really screwed you over the house because she knew you couldn't do a thing about it. And so far as the business is concerned you might scrape by with the odd bit of work but only if you have absolutely zero overheads. I really don't know why you held on to that office so long, and I reckon you should change the sort of work you target. This guy Ron is a good example. Like everybody else he probably has a spending threshold below which he doesn't have to go to tender. So if you try to sell all your work in small chunks, each of which is below the limit, you'll do far better than you were doing competing for the big jobs."

"But I don't know what that limit is. It's bound to vary from one firm to another, and to be lower in the public sector where I got lots of work."

"You haven't thought of ringing each of your old friends and asking them have you?"

"Shit."

And so the evening went on. It seemed at the time to be reasonably sober and to be a good mixture of serious thinking and analysis, interspersed with enjoyable and light hearted story-telling. The Viognier made a good follow-up to the Sauvignon Blanc, and slipped down far too easily. The Australian Brut sparkling was a mistake.

Next morning Alex suffered as he always did after excessive alcohol. He had slept badly, felt tired, and the depressive effect of the alcohol left his mood shaky and self-accusatory. The euphoria of the previous afternoon and evening seemed a false and foolish mistake. His optimism had disappeared and he shuffled round the flat with the pointless air of the moodily disaffected.

The phone rang.

"Hello," rasped Alex, realising as he croaked that it was the first word he had uttered that day, and his throat wasn't really awake yet.

"You sound rough! Thought I'd give you a bell to remind you that the world hasn't come to an end, you have some work to do, and you are actually a lucky bastard." It was Jack, who knew him better than most, and was familiar with Alex's self flagellation following a night on the town.

"God almighty! How do you do it? You must have had at least as much as I had last night and you sound fine this morning."

"Ah it's the constant supply of youthful maidens that keep me young and healthy. Either that or the constant practice. Anyway, how are you and what are you doing?"

"I'm sick, sore and depressed. What do you think? But thanks Jack, I'm actually feeling a bit better since you rang. The head still hurts but the world isn't ending I don't think."

"Silly bugger. You have the world at your feet – well bits of it. When are you off to Turkey again by the way? Don't forget I'm still waiting for my call to crew for you on that tub of yours."

"Yeah, I know, and I'll organise something, but this year I've just been ignoring it. The big tour in the spring and then the disaster with Liz have all left me rather out of it, not in the mood for spending the money on an air-fare."

"Probably too late to go this year anyway. It's October next week, and you have work to do. What happens to the yacht while you're in London?"

"Mostly it sits in the marina, but my old friend Momer uses it a bit for short charters so that it makes enough money to cover expenses."

"So it actually makes money for you? I always was surprised that you could bear the cost of maintaining it out there, and hadn't realised it was quite the opposite."

"But it isn't much. Momer hasn't time to do a lot of organising, and I don't want him to lose control of who uses the yacht, so I'm happy if there is just enough income to pay the marina and the annual haul-out and maintenance. Pretty stupid really when I'm not using it. What do you think?"

"You've said it. If you aren't doing much work in the UK, why on earth aren't you out there enjoying yourself and organising a bit more income?"

"I suppose I've been drifting a bit – feeling badly done by and reckoning if I'm doing no business in the UK I shouldn't be away spending money."

"Well if I were you, which I'm not, and I know it's easy for me to say, but I think you could sell more charter time on the yacht for half of the year, and work on jobs like Ron's the rest of the year. Sounds like a tempting lifestyle to me."

"A bit idealistic if you ask me. But I'll think about it. Might need to think about advertising skippered charters - you see them sometimes in the Sunday papers – always fancied doing a bit of that."

"Well there you are then. That'll be a standard fee for one of my consultations."

By January 2004 Alex was making ends meet with his small chunks of consultancy work. Jack had been absolutely right about ringing round his better contacts to find how he could avoid their strict spending limits – and had been delighted to find that they were as keen as he was to think about small jobs that were simple to administer and avoided the paperwork of endless formal procurement procedures.

Through October and November he actually felt as if he was making some money again. December was a non-event, but by January he was starting to see a reasonable amount of work for the spring. The income was just about matching his spending, but it meant he had no surplus for buying himself new clothes or treating himself to a really good dinner.

He decided to take Jack's advice about the yacht also, and with his help cooked up a small ad for the Sunday Times. It was horrendously expensive for such a small insertion, but he decided it was potentially worthwhile. So he ploughed on with it.

It was more productive than he expected and by the end of January he had dealt with a dozen queries about taking a week on the yacht. Just a few firm bookings, but it looked as if he was in business.

Life had been looking up in other ways too. Maggie was her name and she quickly transformed Alex's life from the depressive solitude that threatened to make him a prematurely grumpy old man into an almost adolescently excited "lover". Alex thought that at last things might be working out the way he had dreamed they could. He might be scraping by financially, but he had a girlfriend 12 years his junior, the sex-life of a twenty-year-old, and the prospect of a summer in Turkey with Maggie on the yacht – he was counting the weeks.

.

Chapter 14

London: April 2004

Katharos calls Alex

"Mr Fox."

The unmistakable tones of Katharos greeted Alex.

"You are a hard man to find Mr Fox. But here we are at last."

"Sorry about that but things have been a bit complicated since last year."

"I think you might be interested, Mr Fox, in a little proposition I have for you. Come to my house tonight at 8:00 o'clock and I will explain."

"Look, I'm in a different position now – I'm separated from Liz, and I'm selling the car. I won't be doing any more trips like the last one."

"I know about your situation Mr Fox. I'll see you tonight." And with that the line went dead.

Alex held the receiver in his hand and looked at it accusingly. As if he could extract from the inanimate object some apology or some explanation for the extraordinary summons from Katharos.

"Well bugger him," was his first reaction. "I'm not going to be summoned at the drop of a hat to his bloody Greek presence. Who does he think he is? What makes him think I'll drop everything and attend to his whims?"

So at 7:55 he was driving towards the Katharos home in Hampstead, still fuming a bit, but curious to know what the old man had up his sleeve. He was driving his sensible car, a 1995 Golf, which could hardly have been a greater contrast to the magnificent Mercedes SLC that had brought him into contact with Katharos in the first place.

He drove into the driveway, braced for the explosion of light from the array of security lights. As before, the door opened before he was out of the car, and the familiar cigar-puffing figure lumbered out of the house to meet him.

"Good efening Mr Fox," he rumbled, with the voice that had tasted the smoke of countless cigars and enjoyed hundreds of litres of fiery spirits. "What have you done with the Mercedes Mr Fox?"

"I'm afraid it had to go. It's back with the dealer I bought it from. I needed to have a sensible car for London so it was time to let it go." He wasn't going to tell Katharos that he no longer had a garage or driveway, and no longer had the money to keep the expensive old car on the road. Nor did he confess that he hadn't been able to sell the car – it was sitting waiting for a buyer in the dealer's garage, and continuing to cost him money. Circumstances were very different from just a year earlier.

"Come inside Mr Fox."

He followed Katharos into the house and again they

went into the claustrophobically plush room at the rear. Iannis Junior was already waiting, standing unsmilingly by the desk. No mezes had been laid out, but the bottle and two glasses were waiting on the small leather-trimmed table between the two armchairs.

The old man groaned down into his chair, then leaned across and poured Metaxa brandy into the two glasses. Alex accepted cautiously, wondering why Iannis Junior wasn't joining in.

"Eis eiyeiya sas" murmured his host before sipping the brandy from the heavy straight glass. Alex raised his glass and followed suit.

"Now Mr Fox, you will require some explanation. Thank you for coming tonight, but you will understand that the situation has changed for you since last year."

"I don't see what…"

"I have a job that I would like you to complete for me. It involves your yacht in Turkey, and a simple task of collecting a small package and bringing it to London for me."

"Look here…."

"But this time I am prepared to pay you for your trouble. I will pay you £5,000 for the safe delivery of the package, and I happen to know that this would be very useful to you."

"Look, I don't like the sound of this at all. Why would you pay me for something that could be posted? I really don't want to get involved in anything illegal – as I assume this is?"

"Mr Fox, I have taken considerable trouble to check up on you and your business. I know everything there is to know about your debts, your old office, your failure to find work, and the trick that your wife has played on you."

"Now hang on there, that's none……"

"Mr Fox I think you should listen. You need the money I can give you, and what I am asking will be of no trouble to you at all. Everything will be arranged and it is just a discreet way of bringing some merchandise to me that is of a very personal nature."

"Look – it is obviously smuggling of some sort that you are asking me to be involved in. I'm in enough of a mess as it is without getting into worse trouble."

Alex stood up defiantly and was slightly disconcerted by the lack of reaction from Katharos or his son. Neither moved to restrain him. They looked faintly bored with his predictable response. There was something else to come.

"Iannis, show Mr Fox the photographs."

Alex felt a brief moment of giddiness as he tried to keep up with what was happening. Iannis Junior lifted a brown envelope from the desk behind him, and slipped from it a set of black and white photographs. They were 10 by 8 inches, and glossy, but as they were spread out on the desk for Alex to see, he at first couldn't make sense of them. There were dated close-ups of what he realised was the back of his old Mercedes. A shot of the interior of the boot made no sense at first, but the next shot suddenly opened the flood-gates of realisation. It showed a compartment in the boot that was not normally visible or accessible. Behind the left rear wheel arch, there was a generous space which ran from the wheel arch to the rear of the car. On the right hand side of the car it provided space for the heavy duty battery. It hadn't really struck Alex that there wasn't a matching volume on the left. The photograph showed how the floor of the boot had been skilfully remodelled to leave a slight recess to match the battery tray, but sealed with inconspicuous silicone gel was a panel that could be removed to reveal a space large enough to hold three or four wine bottles – not that it would be used for something so innocuous.

The next photographs gave Alex the most sinking feeling of being trapped that he had ever experienced. There was what amounted to a picture story starting with the empty compartment in London the previous spring; the car in Greece; an unidentifiable hand placing a package in the compartment; and next, dated after Alex and Liz's return to London, another unidentifiable hand removing the package. The final photograph showed the package opened out on what looked like a garage floor, revealing six smaller plastic-wrapped bundles, familiar from all those television stories of successful interceptions of drug smugglers.

"You're blackmailing me," Alex croaked. It came out more as a hoarse whisper than the firm accusation he intended. "You set me up and now you're blackmailing me."

"Mr Fox I didn't ask you to contact me. I didn't ask you to present me with an opportunity to re-start a route that I thought was history. You presented yourself to me, and the offer you made to take packages to my relatives was your idea not mine. You presented yourself to me and I could not refuse the opportunity. Don't tell me you were so naïve not to think there was something a little out of the ordinary going on? No matter. We are where we are today. I would prefer not to use these photographs. There is no suspicion of any sort relating to your last trip, so you are totally safe unless you force me to send this evidence to the authorities. Look at it as my insurance policy to ensure that you provide me with one more little service, which will be of no inconvenience to you, and for which I am prepared to pay you generously."

Alex's brain was gradually piecing together the new information that was assailing him. It wasn't just data, but it was an emotionally charged revelation that made it harder to process.

"How did you know about the yacht?" He challenged Katharos, who laughed without a smile and said,

"Mr Fox, I see that you really have no idea how much information I have about you. Would it surprise you to know that you have £125.75 in your bank account, and that you have no further money due to arrive until after you have invoiced your friend in Bristol?"

"I demand to know how you get this information. I am going to walk out of here and go to the police with this scam."

Alex made to go for the door, but hesitated with his hand on the door handle feeling un-nerved once again by the lack of movement from either Katharos to restrain him.

"I see you are thinking Mr Fox," rumbled the old man in a sickeningly self-satisfied way. "You know that I will have ensured there is nothing to be found in this house and no record of any wrong-doing on my account. The police will investigate your car, which I know is still sitting in Putney, and will find traces of smuggled and highly illegal substances. All I need to do is maintain I know nothing about it, or perhaps to say that you approached me to try to sell your smuggled drugs. I can apologise for not letting the authorities know but I didn't take you seriously at the time – I obviously should have. They will find no way of involving me, but even if they fail to convict you, you will find that your new girlfriend is not willing to remain with a drug smuggler; your clients will not wish to use you; and your ex-wife will not thank you for ending her career also. So you see the only person you can damage is yourself Mr Fox."

"I don't believe a word of this. You're bluffing. You'd be in serious trouble if I went to the police. I'm leaving right now, and I don't advise you to try to stop me."

"By all means Mr Fox. I wish you good night. I anticipated that you would need time to think about all this. I will telephone you tomorrow with your instructions. Good night Mr Fox."

With that Iannis Junior swept the photographs into their neat pile once more, slipped them into the envelope and closed them in the desk drawer. He then reached behind Alex to open the door for him, and with a display of politeness that had only the merest hint of threat ushered Alex down the hallway and out to his car. Alex found himself meekly going along with the process, and let himself into the driver's seat of the Golf. Rather than close the door Iannis Junior leant forward so that his head was inside the car beside Alex's.

"You will realise I think that my father is a very careful and well-organised man. If you discuss any of this with your friend Jack, or with anyone else, we will know. All you will achieve is to involve them in the case as accessories after the fact. If they don't go to the police they are guilty. If they do go to the police the consequences for you are unpleasant and inevitable. Good night."

The door closed with a firm, solid, confident thud. Alex felt like the small child who has blundered into an adult world where the rules and the stakes are very different from anything he had experienced before.

He drove slowly back to Clapham, looked around carefully as he locked the car, and let himself into the flat with the air of a man expecting to find a nasty surprise behind the door. He looked up and down the street one last time, eyeing carefully the mini-cab that drove past, before pouring himself an unusually large malt whisky and sitting lost in thought.

Chapter 15

William in Dublin

William's story

One significant side-effect of his involvement in the reading group was to give William the inclination to try to write himself. Lavinia encouraged him, and promised to give him honest feedback when he produced something. He decided to try to write a practice-piece about his life to date. Not as a testament, but as something that he needed to stand back and have a think about, and something that he surely could write about if he could write about nothing else. So shortly after the chance encounter with James in St Stephen's Green, William sat himself down and started to type. He imagined Lavinia reading it at first, but once past the first few paragraphs the writing and recollection took on an independent life of its own and no longer needed an audience in mind. He didn't title it, but just started:

My start in the auctioneering business was as accidental as it was fun. Back in Edinburgh after the complete cock I'd made of my career plans I was still really in student mode. Pints of Deuchars in the Canny Man were an easy substitute for my pints of Guinness in Toners, Mulligans, and all those other welcoming refuges round central Dublin. Having turned down the offer from VSO I couldn't, I thought, go back to them. Perhaps I should have. The offer of research then the failure of funding really was a good explanation for my behaviour, but in my youthful mindset I didn't find it easy to retrace my steps.

"The path of least resistance", was what my mother used to accuse me of taking. That really annoyed me at the time because it was absolutely accurate. I was so easily led I now feel a flush of shame, but best not to dwell on it. Davy, my entrepreneurial auctioneering friend, provided the perfect path of least resistance. I didn't have to fill out applications or go for interviews.

We were at first useful "runners" for Davy's father, who would send us in his Volvo estate car to the seemingly endless sequence of auctions in the countryside around the city. We didn't even have to do the research, he just told us where to go and what to look for.

Davy had learned the business without consciously realising he was doing it. Years of watching his father meant that he knew the basics, could recognise quality, and knew what would sell quickly in the city. Within weeks we were supplementing our earnings from his father by picking up items on our own behalf, and passing them on through the big auction houses. No wonder my mother disapproved. We made enough money to finance our social life by working a couple of days most weeks. It was irregular, and some weeks were lean, but others were unexpectedly profitable. If you have ever felt that roll of notes in your pocket from an unexpectedly good deal, or a lucky win on the horses, you will know just how addictive it is. You instantly forget the bad weeks and enjoy a sufficient "high" to see you through to the next one.

A strange convention in Edinburgh is the combination of legal practice and estate agent. It is normal there for a firm to be equally active on both fronts. Some add the auctioneering business and it becomes a virtuous circle. The estate agency feeds the legal business with conveyancing. Both create opportunities for the auctioneering business either clearing houses that are sold or furnishing those that are bought. It is the ultimate "well as it happens we could help you out there" business. Many clients become customers for all three businesses.

To cut a long story short, the path of least resistance led to Davy's father suggesting to us that we take the lease on a shop next door to his friend Sandy's legal and estate agency business. It was actually a sublet of part of Sandy's building and was part of the same façade. We could share facilities, have a ready stream of business, and be a little more respectable and established than the wandering dealers that we were becoming.

So naturally we did that. And naturally enough business flourished.

I still had lots of friends in Dublin, and some of my old year-mates now worked in London, so my social life became a three-ring circus between the three capitals. International rugby weekends provided some of the annual structure, but so did all the other conventional excuses for supposedly civilised debauchery and drunkenness that were the staple diet of the well-educated professional class in Dublin and Edinburgh.

I didn't miss a chance for those weekends where hazy memories and mind-numbing hangovers were the norm. It was on one of those International rugby trips to Dublin that I woke up one Sunday morning in Jury's Hotel in Ballsbridge with someone snoring gently beside me. I had no recollection of meeting her but assumed I had lured her back to my room. It was part of a pattern that is probably recognisable as an indicator of serious personality disorder and certainly of alcohol abuse, but it goes something like this:-

Thumping headache and urgent need for a pee wakens you in the morning. "Where am I" is a high priority question. Home can be quickly ruled out as a location, so some remaining brain function hazily feeds in "Dublin, hotel, everything OK". You try to move to get to the bathroom but any movement shifts the throbbing pain in your head so you stop. Having started your body moving, the need for a pee becomes more pressing.

It is generally around this phase of the low-level brain function that the presence of someone else in the bed creeps into the approximation of consciousness that you are left with. A strange mixture of pride, apprehension and panic usually follows, depending on how much recall of the night before has survived. Being a gentleman, you check the memory for any sign of a name that might be associated with the companion. That is a risky moment. It is all too easy to grasp at a name that floats into your apology for a mind. It often turns out to be wrong. Experience leads to caution at this point.

So there you are, lying in bed, wrestling with puzzles that would test Einstein, and your brain seems to have packed up. The headache demands attention, but perhaps if you ease your neck and shoulders it will help. You have to pee but you can't risk moving. If you let her wake first she'll start the conversation so you might not need to remember the name. The packet of Resolve in the bathroom is becoming irresistible. (How do you know there is Resolve in the bathroom? – Well of course you do. There has to be. There always is.)

Thirst. That's the other thing. Like a lost soul in the desert you'd give anything for liquid. Funny how Coke can be so right at a time like this. Surprising they don't market it on that basis. If you're feeling queasy – as you usually are – flat lemonade is medicinally advised.

So there you are, torn by conflicting demands to be asleep and be awake; to lie still and to get up for a pee; to avoid disturbing the throbbing head and to get to the bathroom for some magic powder; to avoid being sick – but you don't know if getting up or lying still will work best. And you're trying to wrestle with all this stuff on the basis of about three functioning brain-cells!

The good old body usually sorts things out. Large quantities of beer of any sort lead to quite remarkable disturbances of the digestive system. In general the darker the beer the more serious the consequences – but that rule isn't hard and fast. In any case, large quantities of internal gas seem to be produced at times like these, and in a totally fair world you'd just be able to let rip.

However there are two problems. First, you have company and the little remaining bit of brain function does seem to be disproportionately concerned with avoiding further embarrassment. So being a gentleman you resist. Secondly, the magic little mechanism in your anus or your sphincter or wherever it lurks that enables you to determine if the pressure is purely gaseous or if it is solid(ish), is not a reliable performer on mornings like this. What you think to be a potentially decorous little fart may have quite another outcome planned.

So when the pressure builds up to demand release, the only safe place to be is sitting on the toilet. That's just something you learn. All those plans to let your mystery companion waken first come to nothing when your body conspires to let you down and force you to move – now – quickly – but gently.

So that's how I met my wife Pat. Not exactly the introduction my mother would have intended, but functional nonetheless.

Pat really took control from that first hazy moment. She was in no position to be judgemental about my behaviour the night before, as she was obviously just about as vague as I was. She even took the initiative over the names issue by unashamedly admitting she had seemed to have misplaced mine. There is something bizarrely intimate yet distant about making introductions in a hotel bedroom the morning after some part-remembered excesses. However we survived the first strange moments and then shared the gradually returning recall of the night before.

"Oh shit, I've just remembered about that nightclub! Do you remember threatening to punch that English bloke?"

"That was just because he kept pawing me and asking to dance. By that stage I fancied you."

"Where did we go after that?"

"We left just after that and tried to get a taxi."

"I remember that. We got one didn't we?"

"In the end yes. Had to walk to the Green for it – half-way back here."

"Where did we lose the rest of the crowd?"

"They were still in that nightclub when we left. Your friend with the tweed cap was asleep in the corner."

"That's Davy. It's his safety mechanism. Once he passes a certain point he just quietly falls asleep in a corner, while the rest of us drink more than we need and get into trouble. The only problem is we sometimes forget him, and he wakes up later with no sign of us and no clue where he is or where to go. Good initiative test. Should be part of the SAS training I think."

"Do you fancy Bewley's for some decent coffee?"

"Almost as much as I fancy a Bloody Mary in Davy Byrnes."

"That's a plan then. First one then the other."

Who could resist a woman like that! I certainly couldn't. Path of least resistance again. She was passably attractive in a slightly masculine way, had a good figure, but most importantly she slipped seamlessly into my way of life. She enjoyed the rugby weekends, loved the social noisiness of the crowd, and was not at all prissy or *disapproving.*

Chapter 16

William and Pat

Edinburgh in the 90s

William was getting used to the idea of writing his account of life so far and found it easier than he had expected to carry on with the story of how his relationship with Pat had developed.

Pat liked the idea of me and my "business", which I probably painted in a more favourable light than I should. But over a six-month period, she became part of the travelling social group, part of my life, and we both, without really discussing it or thinking deeply about it, allowed ourselves to be swept along with the natural flow.

The "natural flow" was determined in good part by other people's expectations. Pat achieved peer approval from my friends easily. She fitted in with our plans and our self-indulgent habits. I found that friends, especially Davy, took it for granted that she and I were an item, and assumed she would join us in Edinburgh, Dublin, London, Cardiff and even Paris. Pat was working in Dublin selling advertising space in one of the glossy society magazines, and dabbling a little in fashion journalism. It was an easy-going life with no problems about taking long weekends, so we settled into a routine of Pat coming to Edinburgh every other weekend – if we weren't off elsewhere for a rugby weekend.

By spring of the next year I was being asked increasingly frequently if and when we were going to give everyone an excuse for a big day out. Was the wedding going to be in Dublin or Edinburgh? Being a fairly unsubtle lot, these questions were asked in front of Pat, and I suppose we assumed that it was the natural thing to do. I was making enough money from the business for us to be relaxed about Pat finding a job in Edinburgh later. So by late summer that year I was a married man with my new wife, living in a small rented house in the moderately fashionable Gilmore Place, off the Lothian Road.

For a year we carried on more or less as before - the same drinking friends; the same pattern of weekend eating and drinking; the easy punctuation of rugby weekends with the lads. One or two of the crowd were settling down, and not all were allowed to continue the full schedule of weekends. The norm was subtly changing around us, and if we slightly uncomfortably noticed it, we didn't discuss it.

By the time I was approaching 30, the pattern was changing inexorably. As friends settled down, the social drinking became more moderate and tended to be only on Friday and Saturday nights. As age intruded, more of the rugby players found they couldn't cope with excesses on Friday so they became more moderate. Golf became a new social focus and a useful source of business. I entered my fourth decade with a middle-aged set of club memberships; a very "Edinburgh" business – that depended a lot on relationships with old friends and contacts; and an increasingly pressing need to make sense of my marriage. I managed to ignore that need.

What had worked easily and automatically at first didn't seem to work any more. The changing priorities of friends and their partners left us struggling like ill-adapted survivors from a previous age. Others seemed to move easily into the domestic and child-bearing process. We seemed to be stuck. The chat about schools and the ridiculous fees they charged seemed to us irrelevant and boring. We hadn't really thought out our future so we were left behind in the ill-fitting past.

The good old path of least resistance was no help to us. It did not include facing up to the problem. Nor did it allow an honest analysis of what was happening. For me it was easier to work harder at the business, and to welcome the evening meetings and frequent excuses for travel. For Pat it was easiest to go back to her fashion writing and her contacts in the world of glossy fashion magazines. She had modest success with pieces in the Edinburgh and Dublin papers, and didn't need to make much money from them. We rarely talked about children and when we did the issue was dismissed quickly on the grounds of career and "not the right time".

It actually worked quite well I suppose. We were pretty compatible and neither one of us was motivated to dig beneath the surface of our marriage. We probably had fewer rows than most, so were able to convince ourselves superficially that all was well. Pat was content for me to develop the auction business into a property development venture with our partner solicitor/estate agent. Money was available for the good dinners, the weekend trips, and the little self-indulgences that we both enjoyed. Any marriage guidance counsellor, with a very few questions about the frequency of love-making or quality of planning, would have identified that we were not a healthy prospect. Our exchanges in the evening, on those occasions when we both sat down in the house on the same evening, were about arrangements for dinner at the weekend; our different travel plans for the coming week; or the investment potential in that apartment in Leith that we both liked. It was easy, relaxed, sociable and agreeable. In effect we were *ideal flat-mates but useless husband and wife.*

So we drifted easily into what I only realise in retrospect was middle-age. I don't think many people admit to themselves one morning that they have entered that ill-defined phase of life. If only there were a more positive and attractive term for it we might all find it something to aspire to, and to look forward to. But we don't, and more or less reluctantly, debt by debt, wrinkle by wrinkle, habit by habit, we teeter remorselessly into that pejoratively named stage of life.

Business tended to compensate. We had more money along with more interesting and demanding business projects. For those like us who avoided the complication of children it was easy to allow the enjoyment of relative wealth to distract from noticing the negatives. Pat and I were particularly skilled at this – we didn't even mention children any more, and I suppose we both knew it was no longer a sensible possibility.

Chapter 17

Edinburgh: William

The "Cally" - William continues his story

The marriage and the increasing introversion seemed to come back like a hazily remembered illness to William. His initial uncertainty about facing up to the sad story of his interpersonal incompetence had given way to a sense of relief and a sense of perspective. Like a mountain climbed and survived, it was only when looking back at the sight later, and from a distance, that the picture of what had been accomplished was easily grasped. He was finding that the calm recording of the events, and the relatively dispassionate narration of the history, allowed him to look back at it with a feeling if not of pleasure, at least with satisfaction at having survived it all. So in a spirit of therapeutic confession, William continued to put into words the most painful part of his history.

The comfortable, superficial but companionable state of

existence that I subsided into with Pat in the 90s left me plenty of time and mental energy to think of the business. They say that Queen Mary the First predicted that when she died they would find the work "Calais" engraved on her heart. My equivalent even sounds almost the same. It was my brainchild for a development of apartments not far from our original marital house, not far from the old Caledonian Hotel, and nicknamed by my solicitor/estate agent partner in the scheme the "Cally" project.

It was a scheme like dozens of others in Edinburgh at the time. Banks were pretty relaxed about lending money if you had the right credentials. Between our golfing friends, the old school pals, and the cast-iron respectability of the Solicitor/Estate Agent partner, we had no problem raising the cash we needed. We each of course had to demonstrate our commitment by signing up for a percentage of the total cost, and I met this with a combination of cashing in some investments and signing over the deeds of the house. Pat wasn't totally happy with this, but I convinced her that the start-to-finish time of the project was less than three years, and the profit was going to mean that I could choose if I ever worked again – and so could she. The figures were fantastic and we had planning permission for the asking.

Everything went moderately according to plan. Building costs were high and unfortunately we had tied ourselves to stage payments that effectively meant the builder at each stage could hold the gun to our head and threaten to walk away, as all his costs to date were covered. This wasn't too big a problem as the profit in the scheme left plenty of room for manoeuvre – as the builder had calculated – and in the heady mood of the time we could afford to be philosophical about it.

Towards the end of year two the whole thing was looking good. We had the pre-release brochures printed and there was plenty of interest even though we were being cagey about prices of the apartments. We reckoned that given the rate of increase, the later we declared the price the higher we could pitch it. We even invented a couple of delays in the release as prices were escalating at 15% per year in the city centre.

We could have released all the apartments for sale in the spring of 2000, but waited until the autumn. We told the queuing buyers that we were "snagging"; then getting the landscaping right; and finalising the legal work.

In the meantime, Sandy our solicitor/estate agent partner had hosted a beautiful young research student from Aberdeen University who was doing a post-graduate project. Sandy was always susceptible to the charms of beautiful young women, and when she arrived in his office asking to spend a month or two seeing how the system worked, in exchange for helping with basic office administration, he simply couldn't refuse. Her thesis in fact involved comparing final contract outcomes in the Scottish system of house-selling with the outcomes in the rest of the UK. In Scotland an asking price is published, and interested buyers submit their sealed bids to the solicitor. No-one knows what the others are bidding, and the highest bid wins. No gazumping, no messing about, on the given date the deal is done.

An obscure piece of work by a Japanese professor of Economics in the USA had trickled into the awareness of some UK academics. His work was later to become very public when many big-name and supposedly ethical companies in the US fell foul of his calculations.

He looked at the issue of stock options awarded to executives in US companies. The basic data was all in the public domain. Executive "x" awarded 150,000 shares on "y" date when shares were valued at "z". What he showed through his statistical analysis was that either there was some super-human prediction of share movements going on, or, and this was the devastating alternative, companies were retrospectively and illegally choosing the date the award took place. They could look back and pick a date when shares were at a low value, use that as the award date, and the executive made a welcome profit when he cashed in the shares at a market high point. They probably thought it was impossible to prove that this was being done. They were wrong. The economist showed that the accuracy of the choice of date and value was thousands of times better than the most expert analysts could achieve. Statistically it was not believable that the companies were doing anything other than the retrospective and illegal choice of date.

Who would have thought that this was relevant to my life, my project and my survival? Well unfortunately the attractive student from Aberdeen had a canny supervisor who read the US stories and began to think. He realised that the Scottish house-selling process, combined with the close involvement of Solicitors and Estate Agents could tempt unscrupulous operators to "fix" the system.

What would a buyer give to be able to know just exactly how high to pitch his sealed bid? The answer turned out to be something of the order of £10,000 on average, but that wasn't uncovered until much later when the police became involved. Using his disarmingly attractive summer placement student to do the data-gathering, he simply compiled his comparison of the winning bid with the next highest bid and analysed the results firm by firm. He found that in two firms there were more instances of the winning bid being less than 1% above the next highest bid than could be accounted for by chance. Statistically it was not believable that it was purely coincidental.

The results were presented formally to the Procurator Fiscal at the start of September, and leaked to the Scotsman on the same day. Our launch of the apartments was due at the end of the week, and we had some substantial repayments to the bank due within weeks.

Sandy at least had the decency to come clean with me. He rang me at home early on the Tuesday morning as his phone had started to ring incessantly. We met in his Range Rover at the airport carpark, and he confessed that for years he had been fixing the bids. Not on every property obviously, but when a friend of a friend tipped him the wink and a substantial envelope of cash, he would ensure that their bid was just high enough and no more. Totally illegal. Despicable. He said he needed time to think so was going to "get off-side" for a while. What he actually did was to run – he left the country an hour after we spoke and before the police had time to take action to stop him. He hasn't been back since, and we haven't spoken.

What followed was as irresistible and as inevitable as the grinding of the legal process usually is. Because Sandy's licence was suspended his firm couldn't operate as an Estate Agent even in his absence. Not that there would have been any customers anyway. Because he was my partner in the Cally project, I couldn't sell any of the apartments. I couldn't make the payments to the bank, and since they knew what was going on they wasted no time in foreclosing on the debt. That meant they were able to seize the company assets, which included the unsold Cally apartments, various details like the office furniture and fittings, and in the end the deeds to our house.

I was bankrupt, disgraced, and untouchable, even though I had nothing to do with Sandy's downfall. He had squirreled away the cash and was surviving somewhere cheap and sunny, while I picked up the pieces. Except there weren't any pieces left in Edinburgh.

It is hard to describe the feeling of injustice and bewilderment that I suffered. My inability to show my face in the golf club, rugby club, my usual pub, our favourite restaurants or even on the street, plunged me into an almost catatonic depression. I couldn't leave Edinburgh until it was clear that Sandy's misdeeds were in a separate business from mine. All I had done was trust a business partner who amiably and smilingly ruined my life.

Pat showed admirable devotion and constancy – to her own well-being. Rather than staying to support me through the business and *social horrors that followed, she was in Dublin by the weekend, having managed to make sure her best jewellery, clothes and paintings were in Dublin and out of the reach of the bailiffs in Edinburgh. She had always maintained her bank account in Dublin so that also was safe.*

She went to the small flat we had maintained in the cheaper but still fashionable end of Ballsbridge. Not a mile from the hotel where we had our original and fateful coupling. It was owned by the two of us really, but for tax reasons was in Pat's name. She sportingly let me know that I could use the spare room if I needed to get out of Edinburgh, but only until "I got myself sorted".

I stayed with my by then elderly as well as disapproving mother in Edinburgh until the end of December. All the legal processes still had some way to go but for practical purposes I no longer had a business, a home, nor a friend in Edinburgh. Yes, old friends who didn't see me in time and bumped into me on the street were considerate and consoling.

"Sorry to hear about the bother Sandy landed you in. Never did totally trust that bugger. And you're left with the mess. Bad luck, bad luck. Must get together for a drink – busy this weekend. Will give you a call." And off they scurry to avoid the contagion.

My mother alternated between her Scottish Presbyterian days when she couldn't resist her taunts of,

"I always knew your 'path of least resistance' would end like this,"

and her vaguely motherly days when she would do her best to comfort me with,

"Sure we're all right together here. We have a roof over our heads and what more do we need."

It was a far cry from my Cally millions that were going to see me to a comfortable retirement.

We saw Christmas and Hogmanay through together, and a

dreamlike experience it now seems. I'm sure I was in a state of severe psychological trauma, and not really able to think straight. I adopted a plodding, minimalist survival process, where I watched TV, ate, drank, slept and repeated the process.

In January Pat came to see me and must have been moved to some feelings of guilt. She packed up my few belongings and dragged me back to Dublin, but emphatically to the spare room, and "let's be clear about this", for a short time.

To her undying credit she really helped me to get back on my feet to the extent that I am. She was taking her own work more seriously than ever before, she had to. But every morning and every evening she chivvied and bullied me. She made phone calls for me and organised distant old friends for me. It probably literally saved my life, and by the summer of 2001 I was in a way back to where I had started. I was a willing runner for resurrected friends and new friends in the Dublin auctioneering and antiques world. I had to borrow their cars to go to auctions, but still had an eye for what to buy. Best of all I started to have that buzz again from the firm little roll of notes in the pocket. I had forgotten how much more immediate and more obviously stimulating and motivating it was than a set of figures in a set of accounts.

When Pat was sure I was functioning again, and making enough money to survive, she quietly but firmly separated herself from me. I found a bedsit in Sandymount that I could afford, and agreed, in exchange for a gradual and unofficial buyout of my share of Pat's flat, that I would sign the papers she had prepared for the uncontested and irretrievable breakdown of our marriage.

Single, and starting all over again at 45.

Chapter 18

Lavinia

Dublin: Hermione visits Lavinia: December 2005

Lavinia wiped the tiled walls of the kitchen to make sure they were completely clean, then stuck the wet prints to the walls using the natural adhesion of the moist glossy backs on the shiny tiles. She loved this moment, for the bright kitchen lighting gave the first really good view of the completed prints. This was the moment when she knew, without any doubt, which were due to be framed, which would be filed, and which would be binned.

This was a good batch, they all looked worth keeping, but the one that was most eye-catching was the night-time scene in Kapi Creek. Her eye studied each of the prints as she settled down with a strong black coffee. They were a potent reminder of the week on the Lycian coast – a week that had affected her more deeply than she knew how to explain. Perhaps it was the unexpected historical resonance of the area – so many scattered bits of evidence of past civilizations just lying there to be stumbled upon. Perhaps it was the intense delight in the physical sensation of sailing. When she had planned the holiday she had been attracted by the romantic picture of sitting on the yacht in the evening, sipping a cold drink, and looking like a seasoned member of a privileged elite. That had certainly lived up to expectations, but what had captivated her was the multiplicity of physical and sensory experiences that all seemed to work in harmony when the yacht heeled to the wind and started to pulsate with life as it cut through the water. Yes it was hopelessly idealised, and demonstrably slower than the powerful motor-cruisers that she had learned to disdain. But as Alex has said, it was one of the most accurate ways of recreating the experience of the ancient people who lived on that coast, traded along it, and transported even St Paul on his travels. The speeds, sensations, problems and delights were mostly the same – providing you ignored modern conveniences like GPS and diesel engines – but once sailing you were part of an almost timeless human experience.

Her reverie took her back to Gocek where they started and finished the holiday. One of her photographs had captured the strange incongruities as they sat in the little Palm Café in a dark street some way back from the bustling main street.

There was a rusty old upright Coca-Cola fridge against the outer wall of the café, all the advertising slogans in an unfamiliar tongue. The fluorescent light from the fridge illuminated a rickety glass-walled cabinet that stood at the edge of the pavement and displayed what was left of the day's bread. She could still see in the photograph the mixture of plain long loaves along with the delicious flat-breads that were so good with their mezes. What she wouldn't give for some of that yoghurt and watercress; and the tender baked peppers; not to mention those cheese rolls.

On the road behind the bread cabinet was a rough wooden crate, which at first she thought was full of large apples, but then realised it was full of enormous ripe pomegranates. The photograph had also caught a local man sitting astride his moped, but it had missed that strange and dangerous looking departure when his wife climbed side-saddle onto the moped behind him, while his 5-year old son stood on the frame between the rider and the handlebars, and the family rode off into the darkness with no helmets, no lights, and no fear.

She hadn't been able to capture the rest of the scene and regretted it still. They had been sitting at an outside table under the vine-leafed canopy looking out at the dark street past the bread cabinet, the pomegranates and the little wall of planted flowers in their painted tin cans. It was beautiful in its simplicity. On her left hand had been the brightly lit windows revealing the interior of the café, and it was this she most regretted failing to capture. The room had been large and rectangular. High on one end wall was a television that no-one seemed to be watching. Round one table was what she assumed was the café-owner's family, with three daughters who in Ireland would probably have been described as at the 'awkward age' of early to mid teens. The mother, wearing a headscarf, was holding the latest addition to the family – a very chubby baby boy with a scattering of dark hair, a happy round face, and a big pair of blue stretchy pants over his nappy. The baby was passed from person to person. Conversation seemed to flow without break all the time that Lavinia sat outside as an admiring spectator.

At a separate table a boy of about ten sat with a set of chess pieces arranged on the table in front of him. Eventually his father came in and the two played a serious and competent-looking game of chess. When they finished, Lavinia realised the chess-board was a cheap sheet of plastic, which the boy rolled carefully and slid into a tube along with the chess pieces.

The walls of the room facing her had two doors leading to the family accommodation, while the end wall opposite the television had been decorated with a strange array of pictures. There was a serious looking man in a formal business suit, who Alex explained was Ataturk, the father of modern Turkey, whose portrait was virtually obligatory and who was almost universally revered. There were some faded black and white family photographs – looking like wedding parties, and there were coloured prints of distant places. They looked like the prints of Italian lakes, Swiss mountains and foreign cities that could have been calendar pictures from years gone by. The slightly drooping cardboard and the fading of the colours suggested to her that this is exactly what they were. But what a scene! She wished she had been able to capture on film the palpably close family atmosphere; the simplicity of the décor; the serious and respectful behaviour and expressions; the unquestioning shared caring for the baby. And people thought of this as a backward and uncivilised culture!

Her warm reverie was interrupted by the distinctive

ring on her doorbell that announced her sister Hermione was visiting. Lavinia would have cursed if she was that sort of person, but she was still only partly successful in breaking free from the old constraints, so she emitted only a groan.

What was Hermione going to say about the party? What on earth would she do if Pat were with her? This last thought meant that Hermione was greeted with a smile and a look of relief as Lavinia opened the door and found her sister alone.

"O God, let me in and give me some coffee," was the sisterly greeting. Hermione obviously hadn't found as effective a therapy as Lavinia's darkroom to dispel the after-effects of the party.

"Coffee's ready, and I hate to say it but you look as if you need it."

"Need it? I'd kill for it." Moments later Hermione clutched the cup between her two hands as if she didn't trust herself to use just one. She took a sip, breathed deeply, put the cup back on its saucer and lifted her sunglasses from her eyes to restrain the hair on top of her head. "And talking of killing, I suppose that's what you want to do with me?"

"Well actually I was rather afraid that you would blame me for it all!"

"Why on earth would I do that?"

"Well I suppose it was my failure to warn William that led to the whole debacle. I was so embarrassed for him, for you, for Pat, for everybody, that I think I went a bit overboard with the champagne."

"You didn't force us to drink it. We are all

consenting adults, but yes, that moment when William dropped his glass is burned on my memory for ever. I'll never, ever forget the look on his face. That really was probably the most excruciating moment of my life – beats even wetting my pants on stage in that nativity play when I was six."

"I'd forgotten that," laughed Lavinia, greatly relieved both at Hermione's frame of mind and at the injection of humour into the situation. "I really had meant to tell William but things were tricky. I suppose I did put it off, but there were two new people there which meant it was hard to disappear with William, Anyway, I ducked it, and I'll never do that again."

"I hope you won't have to. But honestly Lavinia it was my fault. The whole idea of publicly announcing my "gay partnership", as the freaks in the office are calling it, was stupid. I should have forced Pat to meet quietly with William and tell him in private, but you know how flamboyant she has become. It's as if discovering her real sexuality has opened up her whole life. She is just totally unstoppable now. The way she dresses; her confidence; her noisiness; it's incredible.

"But don't you think that if you add her drinking to that list it maybe indicates a bit of insecurity and uncertainty? I really think you'll have to slow her down and get her to talk quietly to William. Get her to take a break from this supercharged act of hers and relax a bit. If she doesn't she'll come to grief in some way before long."

"You're right, and I know it. Perhaps I can use the party as the trigger for forcing her to do a bit of an adjustment to her behaviour. I don't want to lose her and I know she's still afraid that if she slows down she'll fall off. Maybe it's fear of finding that this is just as big a mistake as William that means she can't look down – has to keep charging on."

"What about poor William? You probably know him better that I do. How is he going to feel today?"

"You're right my darling do-goody Lavinia. You always were so good at looking after other people. That's why you haven't looked after yourself yet. But yes, William. You know when I first met William when he came over from Edinburgh he had such a hang-dog and beaten look to him. He has been looking so much better. How long is he in Dublin now? Is it three or four years? I think he has just improved beyond recognition. And you know what – I think you might be part of the reason why."

"Oh don't be ridiculous! I'm awfully fond of William and we get on really well, but there's no romance in it. He never talks much about Edinburgh, in fact he dismisses the subject if anyone else raises it. I suspect there is a story there, but I've never felt I could get to the bottom of it."

"Poor William. He was always so gentlemanly, so amiable, and for someone dealing in antiques and auctioneering so gullible. It's as if all his critical faculties were absorbed by his work – and he really is good at it you know – but the sort of insight, knowledge and general canniness that he obviously uses in the business just evaporate when it comes to his personal life and his relationships."

"What's that got to do with the scandal? I can see that his inability to spot that he was married to a suppressed lesbian would follow from that total blind spot – but what about the scandal – come on..”

“I'm surprised you have never winkled it out of William or me before now, but….”

“I only know him a short time don't forget. It was your idea to suggest him for the book club and it wasn't the sort of thing to ask at the first meeting, and it never seemed the right moment since. There I go again, putting off something important because I didn't find the right moment!”

“OK well here goes. He was apparently the totally innocent, in every sense, victim of an absolute rogue of a business partner. He had been quite, in fact very, successful and was on the verge of making an absolute fortune in a property development thing, when his partner was disbarred or whatever they do to solicitors for taking backhanders to fix prices. The bastard had enough put away in offshore accounts that he could run and hide in Spain, leaving poor trusting William with bankruptcy and disgrace. On top of that it was the last straw for Pat. I'm sort of proud about what she did, but also sort of edgy. It was a horrible moment to make the break in their marriage, but she did rescue him from his mother, and you've no idea the strings she pulled and favours she begged to get him functioning again. You know she was virtually destitute too, and was having to resurrect her old career, but she took on William at the same time bless her.”

“I can see that you could take that positive view of things, but wasn't she really rather a rat abandoning the marriage just at that time?”

“I asked her that but perhaps a little less politely. She really does believe that it was the best thing to do. The way she describes their existence in Edinburgh – well honestly – it's like one of those excruciating Alan Bennett sitcoms. I don't suppose he'd like them called that," Hermione giggled, obviously feeling relieved to be having a sisterly chat rather than a painful post-mortem.

"I can't really picture it though. William is always so proper and polite."

"But that's exactly it! They very properly and politely shared a house and to some extent shared a life. But they were far too polite and controlled to ever talk about the difficult stuff. Children for example. Do you realise they weren't able to be honest enough with each other to work out why Pat didn't want children? William is such a pet, but such a totally ineffective coward when it comes to anything to do with real personal relationships. Pat knew that they shouldn't go on together, that it wasn't right for either of them in the long term. She decided that if William recovered from the bankruptcy and a year later was hit by his marriage breaking up, it would just finish him. Better to get it all over in one fell swoop – then he could start rebuilding his life on a more realistic basis. I really do agree with her."

"Yes," agreed Lavinia thoughtfully, "I suppose it was better that way. But all the same, poor William. I'm really surprised in a way that he did survive it all. I don't think I would."

"When you think about it all it's actually easy to excuse his rather pompous ways and his awful dress sense. It's not as if he is a tough little cookie who could just get through it all and say "Fuck you" to the world."

"Hermione! Your language really is getting worse! I

don't think I know anyone else who uses language like that."

"Oh yes you do. They just keep it wrapped up because you project such a proper nun-like atmosphere. Swearing in front of you is like swearing in front of the Mother Superior."

"How can you say that! I'm not at all prissy… "

"No I didn't mean it – that came out much less cleverly than I meant it. But you are so polite and proper it does keep people generally behaving in a similar way."

"Do you think I'm showing any signs of getting better? Do I mean better? Maybe I mean worse? You know what I mean."

"Yes I think you are showing signs of behaving less well, which is better. I can't believe you're making me get my head round this after what you did to my poor brain yesterday."

"Consenting adult?"

"Yes, OK. But anyway, back to William. If he keeps going the way he is I think he's going to become a very attractive older man. He has improved so much, and if he gets his money sorted he'll move out of that horrible little Sandymount bedsit and you'll see – he'll be one of those mature eligible bachelors that rich widows prey on."

"Hermione you are incorrigible. I think that all that business about Brenda that came out in the heat of the moment will have knocked him back three years. I didn't know he had a sister - I presume she's in Edinburgh too?

"No, she lives up near Belfast. Did what Pat did in reverse I suppose. Met a guy from the North at university, and moved over from Edinburgh shortly afterwards. I don't know much about her apart from the odd scathing comment from Pat. Pat couldn't stand her. I suppose the superficial progress of Brenda's marriage, nice house, two children, just looked such a contrast to Pat and William's childless existence – which that old biddy of a mother never failed to point out when they had family gatherings. Can't you hear the tight-assed Edinburgh accent "Isn't it naice to see the bairns! Ach they just make the family don't they. Isn't it naice Pat?""

"No wonder she had it in for Brenda."

"But she really didn't have it in for William. She knows she shouldn't have told those 'William and Brenda' stories. That's just how it worked out. She is absolutely wretched today. When I left she was still refusing to get out of bed. Groaning and cursing herself. I thought I'd leave her alone for a bit."

"What about William? Should we do something?"

"Just be good humoured about it next week at your book club. I presume it's still going?"

"Yes, I should see him next Thursday."

"He's OK. He'll probably have an abject apology from Pat before then, so I think you'll see him back to his buoyant old self, yellow sweater and all. Just pray that he doesn't combine it with those awful pink chinos. I think I prefer the jeans with the creases."

"They are so wrong somehow aren't they! Don't worry, I have a little plan."

"So you are interested!"

"No I'm not. I just have a little thought about sorting out his style. In fact I think it's quite a good idea."

"No doubt I'll find out about it in the end. But look

at these photographs! I'm so slow today I hadn't really stopped to look."

Hermione walked round the kitchen, stopping and cocking her head at each of the prints while Lavinia sat quietly hoping that she really liked them. Hermione asked about the location and then remembered the sailing holiday, and everything fell into place. She completed her tour of the accidental exhibition and then went back to the moonlit shot of Kapi Creek.

"This really is very good you know. I think I could get this printed in the paper. Next time we're doing a travel piece about Turkey or the Med I'll drop a hint. Would you mind?"

"Oh Hermione! You've made my bloody day!"

"Lavinia!"

Chapter 19

Turkey October 2005

Alex and Maggie on board

They slipped the mooring ropes from the rusty quayside rings and motored gently out of the harbour into the sheltered expanse of Skopea Limani, the 12-mile wide bay that protects the towns of Fethiye - the ancient Telmessus - and Gocek, on the south-western coast of modern Turkey.

After picking their way through the boats at anchor they reached open water, where they turned directly into the wind to hoist the mainsail. It flapped noisily at first, but as they turned to allow the sail to fill, the flapping stopped, the noise disappeared, and the yacht heeled gently as the force of the wind pushed on the strong white fabric.

They were just as much at the mercy of the winds and weather as the pre-Christian traders, and later the pirates, who had sailed these waters. And just like a walker or a horse rider, they were travelling at a pace that the ancients recognise. The shape of the hills; the pattern of the morning and afternoon winds; the autumn risk of a sudden thunderstorm; all created the same conditions that St Paul sailed through on his way from Myra to his eventual shipwreck.

Alex stopped the intrusive diesel engine to reveal the seductive sounds of water chuckling happily past the bow and along the side of the boat. It was a transformation from a noisy mechanical progress through the water to a more basic use of the elements. It was also a transformation in time. It left them feeling more in tune with their surroundings and having more in common with the travellers who for thousands of years had used those same winds to cross that same stretch of water. It took the same time today to sail from Gocek to Fethiye as it had when Alexander plundered his way through.

They were leaving the smaller of the two towns – Gocek – and were planning to visit some quiet anchorages before risking the bustling Fethiye with its market later in the week. They looked just like all the other tourist yachts enjoying the late-season sun.

They turned due south, eased the sails a little, and set a course for a sheltered inlet on the north of Kapu Dag, where they knew they could spend a safe night, and where they could enjoy a view where neither modern buildings nor roads were visible. Centuries ago, the area had been a haven for pirates, who at first eluded even the fleet of the Roman Empire, and made this coast one of the most dangerous in the ancient Mediterranean.

Kapi Creek looks at first like a perfectly formed miniature fjord. But unlike a true fjord the narrowing stops after two-thirds of the length, and the inlet broadens into a sheltered basin that gives the best shelter for miles around. Clean blue water leads to a rocky shore, giving way to the unmistakable green of olive trees, and to the honey brown of the dried grass that the goats and cows nibble. Crosswise at the head of the inlet is a rickety-looking wooden jetty, whose underwater supports are pine trunks not much thicker than a domestic Christmas tree. Nailed on top of these irregular trunks are planks of bleached wood, recovered from other building projects and sawn not very precisely to size. It is picturesque, tempting and popular. It provides the perfectly natural rendezvous, as yachts coming from the Greek Islands in the Aegean use it as a peaceful refuge from the strong winds that drive them along the Turkish coast.

Alex confidently predicted that as they sailed into the inlet a figure would appear on the jetty. He hoped it would either be Mehmet or one of his cousins to help them tie up to the jetty, greet them with effusive Turkish kisses to both cheeks, and tell them what wonderful food they would have that evening. It was a landfall that never ceased to please, and a harbour so perfect that they could spend hours sitting and gazing at it. It seemed a sacrilege to spoil it.

As they came into the inlet they dropped the sails, tidied them away, and prepared the mooring warps. In Turkey it is the norm for yachts to approach the jetty in reverse. This means that they end up with the open cockpit right by the jetty, and the bow facing back out to sea. It allows easy socialising and a perfect ringside seat for whatever evening promenade may be taking place. It also focuses attention on the jetty and on the land. Fewer people notice what is happening out in the bay.

Alex reversed carefully back to the jetty, and as predicted Mehmet and his cousin Ishmael caught the stern lines and held the yacht steady as Alex secured the lazy line to the bow cleat. He made fast the two stern lines, checked that all was well, and stopped the engine. Alex stepped nimbly onto the wooden boards and greeted Mehmet and Ishmael with genuine affection. They hugged him in return and joked about when he was going to make babies with Maggie. A little embarrassed he turned the chat to eating that evening and the two cousins went off laughing. Mehmet winked as he left.

Alex swam out from the boat to the centre of the inlet and lay spread-eagled on his back, feeling the chill of the water on his overheated head, and listening to the little cracking and popping noises in his ears. The salt content of the water was high, so his buoyancy made it easy and relaxing to lie as if on an endless waterbed.

He worried quietly about the mess he was in. He hadn't meant to be mixed up in anything illegal, but one thing had led not just to another, but to an irresistible avalanche. At 52 he should have known better. Anyone seeing the slightly jaded businessman arriving from London would have thought him respectable and reasonably well off. In fact he was more than a little jaded. And he was virtually broke. His well-used deck shoes, fashionably faded blue linen shorts, and old Musto sailing shirt gave no clue to the disastrous state of his finances and the threat to his freedom. He worried about having dragged Maggie unwittingly into the mess.

They had met last year, both nursing thundering

hangovers, and both taking refuge in the classics library in London University. There in the quiet tower building in Malet St, Alex was pursuing his hobby of digging out accounts of the English gentleman-explorers who had mapped the ancient cities and treasures in his favourite corner of the old Ottoman Empire. Maggie was trying unsuccessfully to find material for a book that was obstinately refusing to be written. She was recently 40, and her long dark hair was tied back to reveal a strong sunburned face, with dark but bloodshot eyes. How many love affairs have started with the line,

"Excuse me but you wouldn't possibly have a Paracetamol would you?"

They had scarcely been apart since. Her book was temporarily abandoned as she tried to help Alex build up his two businesses – chartering in the summer and consultancy in the winter. Both knew it was going to be tough.

After swimming Alex dried off lying on the swimming platform at the stern of the yacht, sometimes reading, sometimes absorbing the scene around him. He let his right foot dangle into the cool water beside him.

As he looked back towards the land at the head of the inlet, the scene started on his left with a conical hill, rocky and with scrubby bushes. On the top of the hill a red Turkish flag was flying in the wind. It was the signal that all was well. No Jandarmes or Coastguards were prowling. Allowing his eyes to drift down to the right, the scrub gave way to olive trees, and then at the head of the inlet was the wooden roof of the little taverna. It was open on three sides, with a large rectangular chimney built into the centre of the roof – a reminder that early and late in the year a fire in the big open fireplace was a welcome sight. Directly in front of him at the head of the inlet were the semi-submerged remains of an ancient house, and on the honey-brown shore some goats and a couple of cows picturesquely posed and give scale to the scene.

As smoke drifted from the wood-fired oven, and smells of cooking teased his appetite, Alex relaxed with a scene that seemed as many years as it was miles from London.

He was wakened from his reverie by a shadow falling over the book he was almost reading. He looked up and saw Mohammed, the eminence gris of the family who ran the taverna.

"Merhaba Alex Bey."

"Merhaba Mohammed. Nasilsin?"

"Iyiyim"

"Alex Bey. I have a message for you again. Can I speak to you?"

"Come on board." Said Alex, seeing that his old friend looked uneasy.

Mohammed stepped onto the stern of the yacht and the two sat facing each other across the cockpit table.

"Alex I know you a long time. It none of my business but you know what you doing. People say to meet them in middle of bay at 10:00 tonight again. I not know this. I not see this. Nobody see this. Alex why you do this?"

"Mohammed I'm really sorry. I hope this is the last time. You know I don't want to do this. I can't tell you the whole story but believe me I don't like it any more than you do. Let's just keep it like it is. The less you know the better.

As I say, I hope this is the last time. I'm really sorry to do this but I honestly don't have a choice."

"Alex you my friend. I trust you. I don't like these men. You be careful. I go now."

And with that he was off, taking his troubled look and his strong shoulders with him, but leaving Alex with a heavy rage that he couldn't do anything about. The serenity he had experienced earlier was shattered. His anxiety had returned in full measure, and he threw the book down as he knew he couldn't hope to concentrate on the story while worrying about the night ahead and then the weeks to come.

Maggie reappeared on the jetty having walked up the hill for some land exercise, and joined him in the cockpit with a quizzical look on her face.

"I thought you'd be relaxed and enjoying yourself this week. No charter customers to please, just ourselves, and there you are looking as if you have the cares of the world on your shoulders. What's the matter love? There's something you need to tell me isn't there?"

"Sorry – didn't mean to look downcast – I'm not really – I do love this place and I do love being here with you."

"That's not what I asked and you know it."

"Look there is one little thing that is a hangover from times gone by that I don't want to involve you in. It's better if you don't know anything about it, but every now and again it just pops its head up and bites my bum. My personal black dog. It isn't anything that affects you and me, and you have to believe me that you are better just not knowing about it."

Maggie's face darkened, she leaned forward and looked him very fiercely in the eye,

"I know there is something not right. I know it dates back to before my time but I think I have a right to know what it is because I've given up a lot for you, and I'm giving everything I've got for you. I'm not holding anything back and you know it. Alex I know you think you're protecting me from something, but I don't know what way your mind works if you think you really are."

"Maggie this is really killing me. I can't tell you and it's because I love you and want to protect you and you're going to have to believe me."

Maggie leaned even closer.

"OK then. Let me tell you what I know already, so you'll see you aren't actually protecting me from very much. If I took the trouble to go back to the log book I could find dates for about 3 other visits this year to this bay when you have had a visit from Mohammed, looked like shit afterwards, and disappeared for a while in the dingy later that night."

Alex's eyes were widening as he realised how obvious he had really been.

"I'm not totally stupid you know. Each time that happened was not long before a trip back to London – two of them were our planned trips but the other one you came up with an excuse at short notice for flying back and you were on edge until you made the trip. I take it I'm warm so far?"

Alex nodded numbly.

"You're a hopeless liar, and you're also hopeless at hiding things. I'm really surprised the customs people haven't pulled you in. You looked so guilty on the two trips I made with you. You fussed over your bag, tried to look nonchalant, tried to joke and chat through customs, so you were obviously carrying something."

Alex despite his long-term suntan was looking pale and shaken.

"The other part of the jig-saw is that creepy Greek guy in London."

"How on earth did you figure that out?" whispered Alex.

"Wasn't hard. There was a phone call from him the first time we got back to London, and you disappeared for about 3 hours that evening – you had to tell me where you were going because I answered the phone. I didn't hear the call the other time but you were gone for the same length of time that same night, and you were odd about talking about where you had been. Two and two definitely made four. And you were so relieved after you had been to see him – presumably to get off your hands whatever you had been carrying since picking it up here."

"You're in the wrong job. And so am I obviously. I'm really sorry. Shit. The only thing you don't know is why."

"And that's what I'm really looking forward to hearing."

"OK, let's go below and I'll tell you the whole story if you can bear it."

They stood up and hugged in the most heart-felt, relieved, loving embrace that Alex could remember.

They left the yacht at 20:00 to eat in the taverna. Walking arm-in-arm along the jetty, they both felt a closeness that was born of sharing everything – even the shameful history of the last 18 months that Alex had not been able to share with anyone. He felt a temporary relief that lightened his heart even though he knew it was only going to last a short time. As they walked slowly towards the stony open area where the tables were populated by a couple of dozen other sailors, Alex confided,

"I don't know why I feel so relieved. It's been more of a pressure than I realised to have that secret area that we didn't talk about."

"I know, I know. We'll sort it all out."

"Sorting it out is a different matter, but it's the feeling of stopping hiding something that is such a relief. I was quite clear that I was hiding it so that I could protect you – but in retrospect maybe that wasn't even very realistic."

"You make life so hard for yourself sometimes. And you really are useless at hiding what you're thinking. Let's eat and then maybe we can think what to do about tonight."

"Look, don't imagine there is anything we can do. I've just got to get on with it, and the sooner it's over the better."

They crunched their way across the stones to the table that Mehmet was pointing them towards.

"Tamam Alex?"

"Tamam Mehmet. Tesekkurler."

"Bir she deyil Alex. What do you want to eat? Madame first!"

"Thanks Mehmet. What do you have tonight?" asked Maggie, still not really able to adjust to the idea that the list tonight was the same as last night and the same as it had been in May."

Mehmet ran through the usual list of lamb shish, meatballs, lamb-stew, fish-stew, fresh fish, kalamari, cheese-rolls…..

"What fresh fish do you have?"

"Sea-bream and barboun."

"I'll have the sea-bream."

"I could have written the script for that," laughed Alex. "And I'll have the cheese-rolls please."

"To drink?"

"Oh let's have a bottle of Chankaya tonight."

"Tamam Alex," confirmed Mehmet before striding up the steps to the kitchen to start organising their food. He shouted loudly to his cousin in the bar to bring the wine and some water. No time wasted.

They sat back and watched their fellow-diners as first the drinks, and almost immediately afterwards the plates of mezes, started to arrive. They hadn't ordered them as they knew they were automatically part of the meal. They leaned forward and looked at the little dish of spicy tomato puree, the delicious yoghurt with watercress and garlic, and the usual salad. Tonight there was also a little plate of fried aubergine complete with the strong garlic dip that took the uninitiated by surprise. Alex poured the water and then two glasses of the chilled white wine. They raised the two glasses of wine, and looked searchingly into one-another's eyes as they said the ritual "Sherife."

They looked like two lovers making up after a fight

as they continued to hold one another's gaze, and Alex reached out with his free hand to grip Maggie's left hand tightly.

"Kissy kissy tonight Alex," laughed Mehmet as he delivered the basket of bread to the table.

"Lucky man Alex. Maggie you come to me when you are tired of him. I make you very happy."

They laughed and had to break the intensity of their exchange to cope with the mischievous Mehmet. Alex tore off a chunk of bread for Maggie and they turned their attention to the food. The bread was almost crumpet-like in consistency, yellowish in internal colour, and with a rich brown crust which still smelled of the pine-scented wood that had burned in the oven that morning. The simple basic honesty and wholesomeness of the bread and mezes was like a soothing hand to their intensity. They sat back more easily in their chairs, munching the bread dipped in yoghurt and scooping up with their forks the green water-cress that had probably been growing in the little vegetable patch that morning.

"It's hard to believe in the nastiness of the world when you're sitting here," breathed Alex. He sighed and tore some more bread. "I'm just going to relax and pretend I'm as carefree as everyone else here – for an hour or so."

"As if!" challenged Maggie. "Just enjoy the food but don't try to bluff me. I know you're not going to relax till about this time next week when we are back in London – but anyway – I do love being here with you."

They looked up through the overhanging pine branches to the already dark sky. There was still a little light left from the day, and the stars were gradually emerging into the darkness, the brightest first. Each time they looked up more were visible – countless, mysterious specks of light in a dark unimaginable scale of distance. It was a backdrop designed to make human beings register their puny insignificance in the visible universe, and to help put today's worries into some sort of perspective against the infinite. It wasn't working as well as usual for Alex.

At 21:45 Alex and Maggie returned to the yacht. They exchanged the usual farewells to Mehmet and the others, still busy serving the tables. As a gesture of trust they always refused to let Alex pay his bill in the evening.

"You pay tomorrow," was the indication that he was a favoured customer and friend. The visitors on the other tables watched quietly and wondered how this English couple had achieved such favoured status.

Maggie went below so that she could avoid contact with anyone walking along the jetty who might ask or just wonder where Alex was. She filled the kettle with water and lit the gas - after remembering to go up to the gas locker in the cockpit to turn the tap which Alex had safely closed after breakfast that morning. She stood in the galley staring at the neat cupboards but her eyes were unfocused. For several minutes she didn't move, then her eyes came back to reality and she started ritually setting out the cafetiere and the coffee cups. She shook her head crossly and put the cafetiere away again. Rummaging in the cupboard she found a box of Camomile tea and extracted a tea-bag. They would have enough trouble sleeping tonight without any extra caffeine.

She went to their cabin and shook the duvet. She

lifted the discarded t-shirt from earlier in the day and examined it critically before putting it back into the "wearable" pile in the wardrobe. Living on a yacht demands a high degree of neatness and good-housekeeping, otherwise squalor takes over with inconvenient speed. She lifted the novel she had been reading last night and went back to the galley just as the kettle started to whistle. She turned off the gas and promised herself she would turn it off at the cylinder later. She lifted a plastic box of biscuits from the deep trough-like shelf behind the cooker that kept the contents in place when the boat was at sea.

Maggie nibbled one of the crisp little sultana biscuits that were Alex's favourite. It was dry in her mouth and she put it down. She went to the guest cabins and checked them for tidiness – unoccupied this week - so they were bare except for the folded sheets, duvet and towels that were ready for the next clients. Nothing to tidy away. Nothing needing to be done to keep her fidgeting hands busy. She sat on the comfortable settee at the saloon table, and opened the book. Once again her eyes looked unfocused and she stared pointlessly at the steam still rising from the kettle.

She put the open book down on the table and shuffled over to the chart table. Alex's neat log-book was open on top of the chart. She read his entry for today and saw that he had remembered to enter the barometer reading every few hours. She smiled wryly at the order and efficiency with which he had written their passage plan for the day, even though it was such a well-travelled route that he didn't even need to look at the chart. Nonetheless, there were the distances and the course to steer; the departure time; the note about the wind and weather; their arrival time; and finally the barometer reading from just before dinner that evening. She held the log-book and studied the neat handwriting as if admiring a ancient manuscript, or re-reading an old love-letter. She flicked back through the log-book and tried to find the entries for the significant occasions that they had been in Kapi Creek earlier in the year. She found an entry at the end of May – a few days before their flight back to London in the first week of June. Nothing seemed different about the entry. The usual passage plan, weather notes, barometer readings, and record of arrival time. As usual Alex had noted at the start of the week who was on board, so that wasn't repeated each day. She flicked back a couple of pages and tried to picture the people whose names were neatly listed. There had been two couples that week, but she couldn't remember anything significant never-mind suspicious about them.

She leafed forwards through book and found another entry at the end of July – the one just before Alex's unscheduled flight back to London, which had left her to run the yacht with Alex's friend Tolga, who sometimes looked after things while they were away. She ignored the almost weekly entries for Kapi Creek, focusing only on those that preceded a trip to London. Again she read the entry looking for some sign of significance. She expected a red asterisk or an unexplained letter in the corner, but could find nothing. She was about to move on to look for the September entry when she realised that the observation "dolphins in the bay" appeared in both entries. She flicked back to the May entry, and there it was. "Dolphins in the Bay." She didn't actually remember ever seeing dolphins in

Kapi Creek. They were quite frequent outside the busy inlet, and almost reliably seen across at the headland on the other side of Fethiye Bay, but she was sure she hadn't seen them in the anchorage. She flicked forwards again to the middle of September – the week before their scheduled trip back to London to take care of the usual boring bank and house issues. She let a little laugh of triumph escape her lips. "Dolphins in the Bay" again in September. She had found his little secret code for these clandestine meetings.

Her moment of triumph was interrupted by the sound of the dinghy bumping gently at the bow of the boat. She could picture Alex tying the painter to the pulpit, and then hoisting himself up onto the bow using the lazy-line as an extra foot-hold. She didn't have the strength in her upper body to emulate him, and always had to take the dinghy to the stern to come on board. She fondly felt a little pride at the strength and agility of her lovely man. She pictured him looking around to ensure all was well before walking silently along the side of the yacht to the cockpit. Her expectation was interrupted by the faint squeak of the hinges of the anchor locker at the bow, and then the solid thud as the lid closed again. She knew his hiding place now as well as his secret code.

Alex stepped gently down the companionway steps into the saloon, looking tired and tense. He spotted the logbook in Maggie's hands and raised his eyebrows.

"Any dolphins in the bay tonight?" she asked innocently.

Despite himself Alex laughed and pulled her close in a hug that spelt infinite relief to be with her, as well as love, admiration and just plain joy at being able to share the

Jack Dylan

secret at last.

"You are such a clever old thing."

"Hey not so much of the 'old' if you please," she laughed.

"I don't know how I'd survive without you. I really don't."

Maggie forgot to make the camomile teas. She forgot to turn off the gas tap in the locker. But they slept wrapped on one-another's arms until the heat made them sleepily roll over to their respective sides of the bunk.

"Don't worry love, we'll be OK," she whispered.

"I hope so. I really hope so."

Next morning Alex woke at his usual early hour. He stroked the dark hair straying over the pillow beside him and sighed gently with the mixed emotions of the two opposing sides of his life. He ached for the time when he could have the simple joy of being here with Maggie, and could put behind him the ill-fitting, gut-gnawing anxiety of the "little favours" he had to do for Katharos. He prayed that this was the last one but felt helpless as he knew that each favour left him deeper in hock to the unscrupulous Greek. He couldn't escape the trap. But everything he did snared him more and more securely. God, he hated the mess.

He slid as quietly as he could out of the bunk and relieved himself in the heads, pumping the waste quietly into the holding tank that was obligatory in the Mediterranean, but strangely not normal round the UK. For the thousandth time he puzzled at the stupidity of the authorities who allowed tens of thousands of yachts to discharge their waste in the marinas and harbours round the English coast.

He flipped open the porthole glass and looked out through the narrow slit at the early morning dampness left by the cool of the night. Another clear sunny day in prospect. Alex slipped into the easy morning routine that required little thought and provided a soothing comfort from familiar repetition. The comforting feeling of routine was as insubstantial as the evaporating dew, but like the dampness it was real while it lasted. He slid back the companionway cover and climbed the steep steps into the cockpit. His routine look around the deck confirmed that everything was in order, but the towels and swimming costumes pegged to the guard-rails were still too damp to bring inside. He opened the cockpit locker to reach the gas supply and was surprised to find it was already turned on. He wondered at his slip from the safe routine.

Going back down to the heads, he had his wake-up face wash before reaching quietly into the cabin to find a clean t-shirt and shorts. He dressed quietly in the saloon, then sat at the chart-table for the daily start of the entry. He noted the barometer reading, the same as yesterday morning, but left blank their destination for the day. It should be across to Fethiye to say farewells to friends and contacts before the flight home at the end of the week, but he was reluctant to plan the trip to the noisy and crowded marina. Perhaps there was time for just another night in quiet little anchorages and they could get to Fethiye later to say their farewells and make plans for the winter. He'd see later.

Alex filled the kettle, although it was already almost

full, and lit the gas. He set out two glasses, two mugs, two plates and two knives. The breadboard, bread-knife, butter and fruit completed the basic preparation. An orange for him and an apple for Maggie – what could be simpler. Checking the brass clock on the bulkhead, he saw that it was well after 8:00 so he turned the gas low, and climbed back to the cockpit to make his way ashore. He went gently along the planking trying not to disturb the late sleepers in the other boats, before climbing the stone steps to the little shelter where the wood-fired oven produced a batch of the crumpet-like village bread each morning. He was early, and watched as Ishmael slid the metal oven door to one side so that he could reach in with his long hook-tipped pole to rearrange the bread tins.

The fire was re-kindled each morning from the embers of the previous evening. Ishmael scooped out the ash and encouraged the remaining wood into fresh flame with the addition of some dry logs. The fire burned healthily for an hour before he transferred most of the burning material into the second oven, leaving only some large solid smouldering logs in the oven that was going to be used for baking. The thick walls of the old oven maintained the heat very efficiently, and probably never really cooled down completely from start to end of the tourist season. The plate-like dough-filled bread-tins were slid into the hot oven and only required about twenty minutes to cook. The mixture rose quickly in the heat, and the smouldering logs combined with the solid heat of the oven to produce a crisp smokey-flavoured crust over the dense spongy bread.

Alex nodded a greeting to Ishmael, who nodded

quietly as he continued to concentrate on the bread. A couple of minutes later, he scooped out the first half-dozen tins and expertly flipped them over so that the crusty bread fell onto the tiled workshelf to cool.

"Kac ekmek, Alex?" he asked Alex.

"Bir, lutfen," Alex replied – only needing one loaf for himself and Maggie. He was handed the loaf with a bit of cardboard to avoid burning his hand, and he skipped triumphantly back down to the yacht smiling broadly in anticipation of the hot bread.

On board again he made the coffee, carried all the plates and mugs to the cockpit, and on the saloon table sliced the first crusty edge from the still-steaming bread. Maggie emerged from the cabin as he did so and slid an arm around his shoulders – leaning her sleep-rumpled hair on his back.

"Morning," she murmured, kissing the back of Alex's neck before stepping into the heads to get herself ready for breakfast. Alex sighed contentedly, and still smiling, carried the bread to the cockpit where he sat back to admire the view once again. The sun was already making its presence felt, and he thought about raising the bimini, but decided it was worth enjoying the heat for another hour or so.

He poured the orange juice and coffee, peeled his orange, and enjoyed the flavours of his habitual breakfast. As he ate he pondered the plan for the day – a lazy sail or a business-like departure for Fethiye? He decided that a swim and an early lunch in Kapi would allow them to sail briskly over to Fethiye in the afternoon. It seemed a good mixture of pleasure and responsibility.

Maggie joined him in the cockpit, and helped herself

to juice and coffee, then sat back sweeping her hair from her face. She let her gaze roam over the calm bay and the neighbouring yachts, where few people were yet organised and no other bread had been fetched from the oven. Her eyes came back to Alex.

"I love this place," she murmured quietly. "Have you a plan for the day yet? I'd love to stay here for a while before we go back to reality."

"Your wish is my command. I thought we really should be in Fethiye tonight so that tomorrow and the rest of the week isn't a rush, but we don't need to leave until after lunch, so you can have a thoroughly lazy morning if you want."

"Watching the dolphins?"

"Why did you have to mention that? I was enjoying a quiet morning forgetting about harsh realities. Sorry, didn't mean to snap."

"Is this really the last time Alex? What's to stop him making you do it again and again?"

"Let's not talk about it up here. But you're right. I hate to admit it but I, sorry we, will have to think of something. Can't imagine what."

"OK, let's leave it for now. But not for ever. I'm not going to let this worry kill you – which it will in the end."

"We'll survive. I'll talk later about it, but for now just enjoy that magic bread and make the most of the last morning in Kapi till May next year. I'm going to read a book, then I'm going to go up the hill to see if I can get the photograph I want for the website you tell me I need to have."

"I'll come with you. I'm going to swim later but a

walk would be good first. Anyway, if you top up that coffee please, I'll sit and supervise the coming to life of Kapi Creek for one last time this year."

They both sat back with their coffees, watching the other crews emerge into the sunlight and inevitably pause to gaze around the bay. Half an hour went by as the various nationalities of crews talked in their respective competing languages over cereal, drank their tea, and listened to skippers organising their day. Before long Maggie was stifling her comments as charter yachts began to leave the jetty. One nearly caught the lazy line in his propeller motoring away too quickly, another trailed long mooring warps astern as disorganised crews gradually learned what to do. Most motored away from the jetty at unreasonable speed, not yet having learned that the most experienced yachts generally looked the most relaxed and unrushed, as they slipped gently and under calm control away from the jetty and into the waiting breezes.

That night in Fethiye, Alex and Maggie were securely moored in their berth in Ece Marina. Maggie bustled round the yacht and then disappeared to the luxurious shower block that was part of the marina experience. By 7:30 pm she was sipping her gin and tonic in the cockpit as they planned their evening activities.

"Let's go to the Locanta tonight," she begged.

"That's just what I was thinking. Anyway we need to say goodbye there and make sure they are going to do the same deal for us next year."

All the local restaurants depended on good relationships with the permanent crews of visiting yachts, just as much as the couriers from the package holiday companies. Most visitors took the advice of their courier or skipper about where to eat, as they were often uncertain about the food and the local customs. The lead crews from flotillas didn't spend any money all season as the competing restaurants fed them free of charge so long as they remembered to shepherd their customers to the right place. The same applied to the bars and night clubs – where good relationships made for cheap living. Alex didn't bother with the clubs and bars, but he had a good relationship with Bulent, the Locanta manager, who made sure that Alex and Maggie could always find a table and paid remarkably little for their food.

"What about the marina people?"

"Already sorted. While you were contributing to the serious water shortage in southern Turkey I paid our fee for tonight and managed to get the rate for next year agreed – so all is well, and it really was worth making the trip. They'll give us the good berth near the office again if they possibly can, and they aren't raising our price for another year. Well worth the visit."

They nibbled their pistachio nuts, sipped the gin, and chatted quietly about the shops they wanted to look in and the route they would take to the restaurant. As usual they debated the visit to Bulent's cousin's carpet shop. Should they buy one this time? Nearly half their charter visitors did, and Alex always worried about the excess baggage charges they were going to have to pay on the way home, on top of the surprisingly high prices for carpets rugs or kilims. As usual they decided not to buy anything but to pop into the shop on the way back to the boat so that they would keep the relationship with the carpet seller fresh and warm for next season.

The rest of the week passed peacefully with visits to Gemiler Island, Sarsala, and Tomb Bay before finally tying up for the last time that year in their berth in Club Marina. The warm feelings and friendly farewells at each stop jarred painfully with the nagging anxiety about the package in the anchor locker and the hazards of carrying it through customs. However Alex allowed the warmth of the late sun to push the worries of chilly Gatwick from his mind most of the time. He finally packed and prayed that he would be safe again from discovery, but his tense smile, his sweaty back and his nervous jumps told Maggie that he was more nervous than ever before on the journey.

"I reckon it is a matter of probabilities," he confided to Maggie. Do it once and there is a good chance you'll get away with it. The next time the risk increases. Do it every week and you are bound to get caught. This is my fourth this year. I think I need a gin."

They were sitting near the back of the charter plane as Alex ordered the drinks and tried to concentrate on his book. It was no use. He couldn't concentrate and he couldn't sleep, so he fretted and fussed and generally annoyed Maggie all the way through the four hours from Dalaman to Gatwick.

"At last," she groaned as they stood to queue for the exit from the plane. "I thought that would never end. I couldn't sleep at all."

"Nor me."

"Exactly. That's why I couldn't. Anyway – home in a

couple of hours."

"I'm actually quite looking forward to Clapham! What a thing to say. Never thought such words would leave my lips."

"It's all to do with the company you keep."

"You're right. It's you I'm really looking forward to."

Alex slipped an arm round Maggie's shoulder, as she cleverly took his mind away from his guilty conscience, and transformed his appearance into that of an impatient and preoccupied lover.

Chapter 20

Lavinia: Dublin 2004

The first book group meeting

"So who'd like to start?" asked Lavinia in a brisk businesslike tone.

No-one spoke. Steve studied his notes carefully; Sinead blew her nose and fussed with the tissue; while William looked absently out of the window at the fine autumn colours that already lined the visible road.

"Would you like me to begin?" asked Lavinia, fearing that this was going to be one of those catastrophes that featured in her worst nightmares. She had floated the idea of the book-group to each of those present and all had responded with caution. Steve really wasn't sure if it was his kind of thing. Sinead wasn't sure if she had time, given her accountancy course commitments. William didn't confess it but really read very little apart from the antiques magazines and the Irish Times – particularly the racing section. But they all agreed to give it a try.

"Well let me get things rolling," Lavinia bravely continued. Steve picked up his cup and saucer, thinking he would much prefer a mug with its reduced rattle potential. Sinead chose a clean page in her notebook and sat pencil poised like the efficient secretary she was trying not to be. William yawned and didn't make eye contact.

"First of all I have to confess that I haven't finished it yet, so I can only talk about my reaction to what I've read so far."

There was a murmur of support and an easing of anxiety round the small group, none of whom had made it past the first few chapters.

"I think it can be very funny in parts, but I'm finding it really hard to get to grips with."

The atmosphere eased further, as Lavinia seemed to voice what they had all feared they would be the only one to say.

"I somehow feel that the student character is Flann himself, and he's painting a picture of the sort of aimless, self-indulgent, work-avoiding wastrel that most older readers expect students to be. But then he goes into all the mock Irish epic poem style and I get a bit lost. I even feel a bit awkward about him making fun of the folk heroes we were brought up on."

"I'm so glad you said that," sighed Steve. "I know we're all supposed to think this is a classic example of modern Irish humour, but I'm finding it hard to connect with. I love the 'Pint of Plain is Your Only Man' poem, but then I suddenly find I'm lost with this Pooka character, and frankly I've felt like giving up."

"I've found exactly the same," chimed in Sinead,

who could sense that a rebellion against persisting with the book might be on the horizon. "I know my father used to find O'Brien's column in the Irish Times absolutely hilarious, but when I tried it I didn't really get it the way he did."

The discussion continued among those who had valiantly tried to get into Flann O'Brien's 'At Swim Two Birds', and they shared their reactions to the scenes and language that they had found amusing.

"William, you haven't said much yet," said Lavinia trying to include William without putting him on the spot too much. William by now was more comfortable that he wasn't out on too much of a limb, so he was able to confess,

"To be totally truthful, I've picked the thing up about six times in the last two weeks and within a few minutes given up. I don't really find the story comprehensible, and I don't get the references to the Irish myths and legends that you all seem to know"

"Perhaps I didn't make a very good choice for our first book," worried Lavinia.

"On the contrary," responded William, ever more confident now he wasn't going to have to actually discuss the content of the book. "On the contrary I think it has been really useful because everyone has had the same problem. It has given us all the chance to share an honest reaction and find we're pretty much in agreement."

"But I feel as if we should persist with it," Sinead could see the direction that William was going, and her personality, training, and self-discipline had never allowed her to give up on a book she had started.

"I think it might be good to switch to something we can all get our teeth into, and then maybe come back to 'At Swim Two Birds' later. It would be a shame to drop it completely, but maybe there is something that we could get going more easily on." Steve was trying to be a diplomat, allowing everyone to satisfy their preferences, but maybe not just yet.

"OK, I think that's a good idea. We'll come back to 'At Swim Two Birds' when we have got into our stride, as it were." Lavinia was glad of the potential solution.

"Could I suggest," began William, still buoyant from his reprieve from exposure as a philistine, "that we each suggest a book we have read that we think would be good for the group to try." A sudden panic overcame him halfway through the sentence as his mind blanked for the name of any book he had ever read. His worst fear suddenly came true.

"Good idea William. I think it would be very practical as a way forward. So why don't we start with you, as you are probably already decided on your suggestion." Lavinia innocently called his bluff.

"Catch 22," blurted William, unable to remember the author, never having read it, but sure at least that everyone would have heard of it and would probably think it worth reading if they hadn't already done so.

"Good choice," supported Steve.

"But do tell us why you chose it," Sinead blithely punctured William's rising confidence.

However, you don't succeed in William's business without a good combination of always being able to find something to say, and being a reasonably convincing bluffer.

"Well it's such a classic really. Everybody uses the phrase 'catch 22', it's part of the language, and it's such a long time since I read it I'd really like to revisit it."

"Right William. That's one good suggestion. What about everyone else?" Lavinia was enjoying her role in leading the group, and had recovered from her momentary panic when it seemed as if her first choice might have brought the group to a stuttering standstill before it had taken off at all.

They shared suggestions, compared their rationale for choosing, and enjoyed a relaxed, unthreatening chat about their likes and dislikes. Lavinia excused herself when she noticed the time approaching 9:30, since they had agreed to stop at 10:00. She emerged a few moments later from the kitchen with a tray, a bottle, and four glasses.

"I say!" William rubbed his hands at the sight of the bottle of Veuve Cliquot. "I say, what a splendid idea!"

"This isn't going to be a regular feature," cautioned Lavinia, "but I thought we should celebrate the launch of our little group." She passed the glasses and expertly popped the cork on the bottle, using a linen cloth to grip and retain the cork.

"I think you've done this before," laughed Steve, impressed by the style and panache of his hostess.

"Oooh," squeaked Sinead, who had never drunk really expensive proper champagne before.

They toasted each other, their group, and their already promising friendships. The night was judged a great success, each of them relieved in their different ways that their worst fears were not going to be realised. Lavinia was relieved that she didn't have an embarrassing flop on her hands. Steve was relieved that the others seemed not too stuffy. Sinead was relieved that she was valued for her English literature degree, and was listened to in connection with something other than office accounts or biscuit recipes. William was the most relieved of all. It was perhaps the champagne that did it. And not just any old champagne. Somehow the choice of Veuve Cliquot seemed so right for Lavinia. He liked her style; he hadn't been rumbled; and best of all he was basking in the fact that they had accepted his suggestion of the next book to read. "There's a trick or two in the old dog yet," he thought happily to himself as he grinned his way back to Sandymount from the leafy loveliness of Lavinia's apartment – he was feeling quite literary just then.

Chapter 21

Dublin: summer 2006

Sinead

Sinead, at 32, was thirteen years James' junior. She had joined Lavinia's reading group because she was ambivalent about abandoning her arts degree and background for the harsh-seeming world of accountancy. No-one had explained to her class of convent-school girls that going to university to study an arts degree wasn't an end in itself. They all had vague ideas that careers would follow, but unlike the few who opted for social work, or catering, they didn't have a clear perception of what the career might be. It was sufficient success to achieve the grades and get the offer of a place in UCD, or for the more adventurous, in TCD. The challenge, the excitement, and even the fear of going to study at one of these famous institutions overshadowed the need to think any further ahead. Questions of what to do after university were drowned out by the more pressing questions about where to live; how to live; what to wear that first day; what to say to the male students who just as nervously, but with more bravado, would surely crowd the student bars and coffee shops. It was all too preoccupying to leave much room for longer term plans.

Sinead's first year at Trinity had felt like an accelerated learning course about life. She moved into the women's accommodation in the legendary Trinity Hall in Rathmines. It seemed safer than finding a bed in an old-fashioned student digs, with who knows what sort of landlady. Her parents approved, and Sinead found herself thrust into the company of a hundred similarly excited girls from every sort of background. There were relatively few other convent educated girls as they had mostly gravitated to the more traditionally Catholic UCD. Those who had faced the disapproval of the Mother Superior and applied to Trinity felt a little braver, a little more emancipated than their more obedient and malleable friends. For the first time Sinead was experiencing girls from Northern Ireland; from England; from USA; and in single or small numbers from all corners of the world. To her inexperienced eyes, they had exotically different skin hues, accents and names.

Sinead had opted for an English Literature course, which seemed safe, as she had always scored well in the subject before. Throughout her first year she learned to read and to write in a far more critical way than the prescribed school teaching had allowed. She was introduced to authors and styles of writing that took her tentative convent-taught insight, expectations and confidence, and shook them like a blanket exposed to a hurricane. All she thought she knew about what was permitted to be written was suddenly redundant and laughable. She by turns felt prim; shocked; liberated, and even titillated by the unabashed sexuality of Nabokov, the raw rough rudeness of Behan, and the sad, doomed desperation of Hughes and Plath.

Little wonder she found herself in a turmoil of uncertainties when it came to life outside her lectures and the library. Gradually able to loosen her thinking and her expression in the weekly essays, she struggled to permit herself a matching freedom in her social life. She gravitated despite herself to the safety of the less adventurous inhabitants of the coffee bar and the dining hall. While inwardly angry with herself, and cursing the ingrained caution that curtailed her exploration and self-expression, she still walked to the seat kept for her by similarly constrained friends. Was it a process of unconscious socialisation that ensured the girls at her table were more plump, less fashionably dressed, and less likely to attract the attention of male students? Sinead longed to be at the tables with the languorously confident jeans-clad English girls, who had an air of comfort with their bodies that was foreign territory to her nun-taught self-consciousness about anything remotely sexual. She noticed that her friends from similar backgrounds either remained intact within their social and sexual caution, or went overboard in denying it, rebelling, and adopting an extravagantly explicit sexuality. There didn't seem to be a moderate middle way for the products of her safe education and conservative catholic family wrapping.

While the emancipated girls made plans for sharing flats in their second year, Sinead clung to the institutional safety of the Hall. As first year ended, with the satisfaction of surviving the year, and the cosy comfort of her social equals, she still fretted at the failure to achieve any romantic adventures to whisper to her old friends at home. She opted for the mysterious hints and suggestive silences when pressed for the embarrassingly missing details.

Second year followed the same depressingly monocultural path at first. But Sinead's determination to undo the tight constraints of her past pushed her to experiment a little. She decided to skip the routine daily safety of the coffee coven, and took herself nervously to the college bar. It wasn't long before she was rewarded by a male approach.

"How's that essay on Eliot?" was the easy opening from a spotty youth with an English accent and a dangling cigarette. She had forgotten how inseparable the cigarettes were from the bar. Despite the health warnings and the shortage of money, most of the inhabitants of the college bar seemed to be able to buy their packet of Silk Cut, or their cigarette papers and tobacco.

"Nearly finished it I think," she replied in as confident a voice as she could muster, suddenly even more aware than usual of her unstylish cardigan, her positively frumpish tweed skirt, and those sensible shoes her mother insisted on buying for her.

"Lot of bollocks really," tested the spotted one, who was just as much a product of his schooling, his family, and his peer pressures as any convent graduate. Plenty of bad language, one or two pints at lunchtime, and the flourishing of roll-your-own cigarettes, were the badges of struggling maleness, which needed just as desperately some romantic and sexual experiences to bolster the fragile self-image.

"Is that what you're going to write?" she surprised herself by asking.

"Yeah. Why not?" The uncertain bravado persisted.

"Well I don't think you'll get too many marks for it, unless you can back it up with some literary arguments."

"Yeah, well, I'll have to see if I can think of some won't I," said the lamely retreating youth.

"Did you really not like it?" Sinead decided to help him along.

"To tell you the truth I haven't really read it yet. Bloody thing's due in tomorrow and I don't know what to write."

"I've got some notes you could borrow if you're really stuck," she found herself offering. She hadn't thought it out, she didn't fancy him at all, but some philanthropic recognition of another inadequate soul prompted her gesture of kindness and support.

Unfortunately Sinead had limited insight into the mental gyrations of male prisoners of hormones, peers, and bar-room expectations. The average ex-boarding school male had been finely tuned to read sexual meanings and possibilities into every innocent word, look, or gesture.

"What are you doing later?" made perfect sense as a response in the mind of the testosterone driven hopeful. To Sinead it was illogical, bizarre, unwelcome, frightening, and strangely welcome all at once.

"I'll give you a hand with the essay if you like," made perfect sense to her charitable nature. She didn't know that it could possibly be heard as an open invitation to a sexual encounter of the fumbling embarrassed kind, carried out in the darkness of the stairwell to someone's rooms in Botany Bay. The furtive, tongue-pushing, roughly inexperienced grasping of her breasts, which led to an alternating sequence of exploring hands slipping up under her woollen jumper to feel the shape of her white innocent bra, grasped by the wrist and forced to retreat, only to be replaced by a hand lifting her skirt and running up her cringing thigh.

"Stop it! I mean it!" she whispered urgently.

She rejected the next invitation from the spotty undergraduate to help him with an essay. Sitting quietly in her room she knew she wasn't desperate enough to tolerate his unattractiveness, his beery smoky breath, and the juvenile inadequacy of his range of social responses. It didn't take her long to work out that the attention she attracted from him was entirely lustful. He saw her as a potential conquest – his long-awaited ticket to the camaraderie of the knowing looks and smug self-satisfaction of the sexually experienced. Her brief encounter was enough to persuade her that she should bide her time.

As the end of her degree started to loom, Sinead was devastated to find how few career opportunities there were for her. The so-called milk round of employers visiting the university in spring of their final year provided a harsh set-back to her increasing awareness of the need to do something. The awareness had always been there in the background. In the early days of university, conversations sometimes drifted into career plans. In first year it was easy to be as vague as most of the other students. In second year it was increasingly difficult to completely ignore the question. By third year it was as if the student body was undergoing a self-determined amoebic split into those who knew what they wanted to do, and those who had no clear path. Socially and academically the groups mixed and interacted, but by final year it was easy to discern which students had identified their desired career path and which were wallowing.

The wallowers developed sophisticated coping mechanisms. As a group they displayed mutually supportive disdain for the business-studies, engineering, medicine, and dentistry students, who generally knew what they were heading for.

"Well really," went one particularly comforting line, "it isn't as if we were in a training college. This is a University for goodness' sake – supposed to be an education broadening the whole person, not just preparing you to do the books in some boring office."

They could all nod and agree with the warm, vaguely worthwhile nature of a broad education. They agreed on the necessity to experience the world more fully before settling in to some career that would present itself when the time came. The Gap Year companies were flourishing as more and more were drawn by the prospect of travelling the world, and innocently working in some cynically disguised money-making scheme that was posing as a voluntary project with altruistic intentions.

Sinead in her sensible shoes kept her feet on the ground. She took the failure to get past first interviews in the milk round as a valuable piece of data. If she wasn't attractive now to all these big companies was she going to be any more attractive a year later? She lowered her sights and enrolled in a secretarial course made more palatable by being called 'Business Administration'. Most of the other students were graduates like her, facing the reality of the relative uselessness of their degrees. They were able to conspire together to find consolation in their shared experience. They agreed that they were the practical ones who would be able to demonstrate their competence, and would be recognised as people with organisational and managerial potential. In the meantime, learning to file, to create business letters, to master double-entry book-keeping and to share time on what was in 1996 a scarce resource – the college computer – was a demeaning but necessary stage in life.

Sinead by her late twenties had almost abandoned her optimism about finding either the right job or the right man. She lived in a flat she shared with three similarly aged, similarly disappointed women – who of course referred to one-another as 'the girls'. She had been in three secretarial and administrative jobs, two in small Dublin companies whose promises of future prospects were as thin as the boss's receding hair. She had finally managed to secure a better-sounding job in the university administration department, where she felt more at home, more respectable, and dangerously settled.

She became one of those sensibly skirted and stoutly shod untouchables, who gravitate together and repeat the cycle from their early student days of adopting a social grouping and habit that is at the same time comforting (because they are all in the same boat) and totally self-defeating (as they become less and less likely to attract a romantic advance from a male). She became one of the habitual spinsters who sequester themselves in their favourite corner of the coffee bar and share their home-made biscuits. It didn't take long for the first knitting bag to appear, that final step that seals the spinsterhood identity, and ensures that approaches from males will be impossible. The knitting bag is an inviolable symbol that shrieks 'no males at this table'. It only takes one person in the group, but as soon as the step is taken, all those who persist in advertising themselves as adherents to the group are lost souls in the romantic lottery. Their number is no longer in the hat. Their age is immaterial as they might as well be senile. They descend into the strange social ostracism of the untouchable spinster, and carry the badge that every man recognises as he turns away. 'The Girls' are a life sentence.

For some unaccountable reason, all this started to become clear to Sinead. To be more accurate, for some reason Sinead allowed her conscious mind to perceive and understand what she knew was happening. It was clear at some level to all the participants, and they all had their preferred strategies for ignoring, denying, or confusing the issue.

Something in Sinead's psyche wouldn't allow her to deny the process any longer. Perhaps it was something she read; perhaps it was the businesslike straightforwardness that she had learned to cultivate. When she applied it to an appraisal of herself on the eve of her thirtieth birthday she felt a bursting frustration and disappointment that at last transformed itself into an energetic determination to 'do something'. Too often the frustration and disappointment had cried out only to be drowned in comforting swathes of avoidance. Too much comfort food; too many escapist books; too many retreats to the mutually-supportive sharing of sisterhood littered her last few years of apathetic acceptance of her status.

She looked around with a new intention. While not wanting to ditch the friendships that she had built up at work and in the flat, she knew that she needed to inject some radically new elements into her life. Sinead was good at her job. Despite her traditionally arts oriented education, and the complete absence of scientific instruction, she had found that she was good with figures. She was able to see sense in columns of numbers, quickly estimate relationships, and intuitively spot errors in calculations. More surprisingly she had found herself attracted by the logical simplicity that lay behind the apparent complexity of the computer programmes they used. She had quietly become the person that others turned to for advice when the software surprised and baffled them. She could format documents better than anyone in the office and was the only one who could set up a spreadsheet faster than the supposed experts in accounts. On top of all that of this she knew fundamentally and without a doubt that she could do more. She could organise, and was frustrated by the inability of those who were paid to organise and manage to do just that. So she did a lot of it herself.

With a sense of resolve and belated self-appreciation, Sinead made an unusual visit to her distant friend in the student careers office.

"Look I know you are here to advise students, but I need some advice and you are the obvious person to ask."

An hour later, easily, positively, and with growing excitement Sinead had found that her reputation as a very competent organiser, administrator and 'person who gets things done' was well established. 'Build on your strengths' rang in her ears, and had made the choice of a part-time accountancy course an easy one. She couldn't believe it was so simple to take the first step. When she started the course she was even more pleased to find that she already had a lot of the information and expertise because of actually keeping books and helping her managers and accountants to prepare reports and find solutions to the perennial need to make the numbers add up. Two nights each week and every Saturday morning, Sinead excelled, blossomed, and made the strides in confidence that she had vaguely thought she could.

Her mother wrote to her to ask her to make contact with the daughter of an old friend who had recently died. Sinead didn't know her mother's friend, although the name was familiar from Christmas cards at home as a child. She once would have shied away from making the contact, but perhaps because she now had something she was more proud of, something to say for herself about her career, she made the call and arranged to meet the recently bereaved Lavinia.

"Oh it's so funny to meet someone who knows all those people I've heard of. I can't believe that you are one of those names from the Christmas cards years ago. You had a sister…."

"Hermione," prompted Lavinia, "and well might you ask what on earth possessed my parents to come up with those names. I sometimes think that the names they gave us made a lot of things in life inevitable – some impossible, some inescapable."

"I can imagine," sympathised Sinead, not sure if she should be politely disagreeing but unable to stop herself.

They chatted easily and amiably over a Saturday afternoon coffee and sticky bun in Bewley's. They each recognised in the other a spirit they couldn't put a name to, but they agreed, found they intuitively understood the other's feelings and point of view, and to their mutual surprise were glad they had met.

Chapter 22

Dublin: August 2006

William and James at lunch

William walked almost jauntily down Grafton Street. The lunchtime crowds were bustling as queues formed in Bewleys and in all the competing cafes and snack bars down the famous shopping street. The smirk on his face betrayed his excess of good humour, and his benevolent air drew the hopeful attention of the supposedly homeless magazine-sellers. Avoiding their clutches he swung left into Suffolk Street, and glancing briefly at the musical instruments on display in a shop window, he strode purposefully to O'Neill's bar on the corner.

"You're looking very pleased with yourself," challenged James as he nodded to the barman and pointed to the Guinness tap.

"Well yes, I suppose I am," agreed William, "But not without good reason I'm happy to say."

"So what is it this time? A win on the horses? No,

too early in the day for that. A coup at the auction? No, too early for that as well. I give up, you'll have the pleasure of putting me out of my misery."

"I'll let you suffer until that pint arrives, but I'll give you one clue. You are right about the financial angle – nothing else guaranteed to put a smile on a man's face."

"Oh, I don't know about that," laughed James. "I am reliably informed that intimate relationships with persons of the opposite sex have been known to result in the occasional inane grin."

"Short-lived gratification of the baser instincts, old boy." William shook his head. "They are short-lived and are guaranteed to be followed by grief and tears. Weeping, wailing, and a sore willy are all you get from the opposition. Believe me, I'm one of the walking wounded back from the battle-front."

"So the good humour is the result of the gratification of your true love, your everlasting relationship with your wallet?"

"You make me sound like a shallow, soul-less mercenary. I'll have you know that this tough exterior hides a sensitive and vulnerable spirit."

"You must be the first antique dealer in history to have a sensitive and vulnerable soul. Without exception your colleagues are a grasping greedy crowd of money-grabbing charlatans."

"Have to keep body and soul together," said William with undisturbed equanimity, taking the first sip from the creamy pint. "And I do admit that most of my colleagues in the trade had a scruple-ectomy at an early age."

"Scruple-ectomy? While you have just had a triple

scruple by-pass?"

"Exactly. Scruples and finer feelings intact, but not always indulged."

"That's handy. Could I have one as well?"

"I'll introduce you to 'old mother necessity', who dishes them out free of charge. You've just had too cushy a life and never needed to engage in the baser forms of trade. Mind you the banks, your old employer included, are becoming just as bad as the loan-sharks. They invent charges for everything; they'll soon be charging us for the privilege of charging us."

"Don't laugh, it'll happen. Did you read in the paper that in the UK, BT has introduced a 'payment processing charge'? Whatever whiz-kid thought of that has probably been promoted already. Can you believe it? Charging you to accept your money?"

"That is good. It's so far-fetched you couldn't really believe they'd have the nerve to do it. But the phone companies are great at that. Did you read about the mobile phone company that rings people when they are out of the country to sell them international packages? The really brilliant wheeze is that all the time the customer is listening to the sales pitch, their phone is clocking up the extortionate roaming charges. One chap twigged this and asked them, "Who is paying for this call?" And the girl actually said, "Well, you are sir." Fantastic!"

"OK. You're well down that pint now. Time to tell me what has you looking so pleased."

"OK," smiled William, "It's really quite simple. Today is the day that Pat made the final payment to buy out my share of the old flat. Without lifting a finger I have money in the bank, freedom in my bones, and a song in my heart."

"As good as that is it?" laughed James.

"No, better. Really better by far than a poke in the eye with a burnt stick, or whatever you used to say."

They ordered another pint each, moved down the steps to the now-uncrowded lunch counter, and continued their good humoured celebration. James laughed with William but envied him. His own finances were as bad as ever; his sense of failure as cripplingly intense as ever; and the certainty of the descent into despair that almost always followed a lunch-time session loomed greyly in the eyes despite the laughter. His eyes laughed less than his mouth. A skilled observer would have noticed how quickly the laughter muscles round his mouth dropped their smile and resumed their serious aspect. Just as telling was the way in which his eyes resisted the instruction to smile. Cover the lower half of his face and you wouldn't have known he was smiling or laughing at all. William didn't notice this. His own good humour carried him blithely through lunch and into the early afternoon.

Their conversation turned to other friends, and William quizzed James about the others in the reading group that Lavinia still hosted.

"She really is quite a character," confessed an admiring James. "I don't know where she gets the energy to take up new interests and to do so bloody well at them."

"Her photography, do you mean?"

"Yes, that's the best example. When I first joined that group she hadn't even started it. Now she's virtually a professional, and planning to exhibit."

"What about the others in that little group? Whatever happened to that very proper South African?"

"Simon, you mean. He's apparently doing fantastically well. Lavinia told me she came across him at a formal do in Trinity a few weeks ago. They're trying to persuade him to stay on there when he finishes his research. Apparently an absolute genius in his way."

"But does he still dress in those dreadful M&S basics?" asked William unkindly.

"And why not?" countered James, conscious of the label in his own jacket and hoping William couldn't see it.

"Steve's quite a character too isn't he?" William rambled on, oblivious to James' discomfort. "Apparently some publisher has paid him a retainer for the book he's writing. Quite unusual for a first book."

"That's Lavinia again. Her knack of spotting the talent in people and encouraging them really is quite something. Wish she'd spot some talent in me and encourage it," muttered James wistfully.

"Must have done. She thinks out everything she does you know. She wouldn't have invited you without a reason."

"Felt sorry for me I think," tested James, hoping that William would deny it.

"Well I know she felt sorry for me. All that business with her sister and Pat. God, I still break out in a sweat when I think of that party."

"That must have been tough. Can't imagine how I'd feel if it happened to me."

"Talking of which, any new relationships on the go?"

"No such luck," lied James, who had actually met the

same person twice and was starting to hope that things were changing. For the first time the smile on his lips was genuine, and for the first time the eyes joined in, as he let himself indulge in a secret little reverie about his next date with the only person who seemed not to mind that he was poor, jobless, and a bit of a twit. Had William been at all observant he would have noticed the faraway look, the relaxing of the face, and the unaccustomed faint air of optimism in his friend's face.

Chapter 23

London: November 2005

Alex gets a warning

The Golf spun out of control and slammed backwards into the solid brick wall. The old woman with her limping spaniel watched as the headlights spun towards her then away. Finally they lit her face, wide-eyed and with her free hand involuntarily raised to her mouth, as she flinched at the solid impact. The sound of broken glass tinkling on the pavement seemed to continue for an unreasonable length of time, as, hand still raised to her open mouth, she saw the car settle at an angle across old Mrs Goldberg's new brick wall. The headlights continued to shine and dazzled her view. She couldn't see past the lights to see the interior of the car.

Mrs Byrne tip-toed hesitantly towards the car, talking to the dog all the time apparently to reassure it, but in reality to calm and reassure herself. As long as she kept comforting the dog she could ignore her fluttering heartbeat and the tremor in the hand still raised in front of her now active mouth.

"There, there, Teddy. Don't you worry, we'll be alright. Let's just have a look to see if he's hurt. There, there, Teddy. Just stay beside me and you'll be alright."

The silence in the street seemed shocking and unreal after the noise of the crash. The distant drum of the traffic a few minutes away on Hampstead Hill seemed muted. She was aware of the ticking noise of metal cooling, and jumped slightly as a final piece of glass fell noisily to the pavement.

"Come on Teddy. Daddy would have known what to do wouldn't he. He'd have a look and then get Mrs Goldberg to phone the police." So she kept tip-toeing closer to the front of the Golf, finally edging round out of the glare of the lights to see the interior of the car.

Just as she reached the driver's door, she heard the delayed reaction of the neighbourhood, as doors opened and people started calling questions to one-another about the violent disruption of their peaceful television-watching. The first more curious neighbours arrived at the scene just as Mrs Byrne crumpled to the ground beside the whining spaniel.

"Take your time Mrs Byrne. Have another sip of tea and tell me what happened." It was a young policewoman, sitting, notebook ready, on a chair beside the A&E bed.

"What happened to Teddy?" the old lady urgently wanted to know.

"Don't worry about Teddy. One of your neighbours is looking after him till you get back."

"What happened to me?"

"They think you just had a little faint with the shock of the accident, and you bumped your head when you fell. You'll be a bit sore but I'm sure you'll be home tonight."

Mrs Byrne lay back on the pillows and took a deep breath.

"Is he dead?"

"No. He's very lucky. He just has some bruising and shock. But we need to find out what happened."

"Oh he looked like a corpse when I saw him. He was white as a sheet – and that blood running down his face. And he was just staring. Those eyes – that's why I thought he was dead. Just sitting there still strapped in. Eyes open. Not moving. White. And all the blood."

"Don't get yourself agitated Mrs Byrne. He's fine now. They'll keep him in for observation but let him home tomorrow probably. Now you tell me what you saw and heard."

"I was just walking Teddy, that's my dog, oh and I hope he's alright. And there was a crash. That young man's car was spinning across the road. And then the bang. I was sure he'd be dead."

"He was lucky that the impact was at the rear, so the seat and headrest protected him. But did you see him before he started spinning – was he going very quickly?"

"Oh they all go too quickly down that road. But I don't really remember seeing him before he was skidding."

"Now I want you to think very carefully about this. Did you hear a bang or a crash before you saw him skidding, and did you see another car at all?"

Mrs Byrne closed her eyes and tried hard to remember what she had seen and heard. The trouble was

she was usually so wrapped up in her thoughts and memories as she walked with Teddy that she often arrived back home without noticing anything that went on around her.

"I might have heard something. I looked up before the crash I know. But I don't know if was the sound of him skidding or just the lights spinning. Oh – do you think someone else hit him? Is it one of those hit-and-run accidents?"

"It might be Mrs Byrne, in which case it isn't an accident. But we won't know until the car is properly examined." PC Devenish didn't think it was correct procedure to share with the only witness the claim from the Golf driver. He was down the corridor in a similarly curtained booth. His staring eyes and shaking hands weren't just because of the shock of the accident. She had seen frightened people before and she knew that the driver of the Golf was very, very frightened. She was taking seriously his claim that something big had rammed the rear corner of his car. He was maintaining that it must have been a simple hit-and-run, but that didn't explain why he was so frightened. Mr Fox looked to her as if he had something to hide, but she couldn't put that in her report. She had suffered enough taunts about 'feminine intuition' in her short career with the Met, and she was going to play this very straight. Unless the witness could remember something significant or the engineers could see some obvious evidence of ramming, she would just have to record it as an unsubstantiated claim from the driver. A case like this wouldn't justify the tv-style forensic examination that could prove or disprove his story. She hated those CSI programmes that left people expecting amazing results from forensic evidence. They didn't realise how hard it was to justify the expense of even the simplest forensic tests.

If Alex Fox's story was true, there should be evidence of a first impact somewhere about 50m before the final crash. The trouble was that her Sergeant had already been on the radio urgently asking her to get back to the station to help with yet another 'domestic'. Unless she had more than the driver's word her story would be treated with laughter, and her credibility would take another dent. Unless Mrs Byrne could volunteer an eye-witness statement that pointed to a double-impact she would be best to adopt the usual cynical attitude of her male colleagues. She would have to report that the driver claimed he had been forced off the road, but in the absence of corroborating evidence the likelihood was that he had made an error and crashed on the greasy bend. 'Excessive Speed' was the going to be the usual cover-all box to tick in these circumstances.

.

Chapter 24

Alex and Katharos: Nov 2005

Threat? What threat?

"Calm yourself Mr Fox. I should be angry that you make such foolish accusation. But I know you have big shock. Why would I do such a thing? You are my valued associate. We do good business. Just a little more business from you then we are both happy. It would only make sense for me to do this terrible thing if you were not my associate. But that is not so, is it Mr Fox?"

Alex was sitting again in Katharos' plush back room. The Greek was spreading his hands in a calming gesture, and denying all knowledge of the incident. Yet Alex could hear the threat in the denial. The words and the syntax seemed on the surface to be saying one thing, but the implication beneath the words conveyed a threat that he didn't feel like ignoring.

"Look I'm sorry if I'm being unreasonable, but I want this business to end. I'm not able to cope with the stress of it. I've promised Maggie that there will be no more, and you promised me that October was the last."

"What can I say Mr Fox. My other associates are very pressing. There is a last little series of deliveries in the coming year and then I promise you it will be my wish as well as your wish that we bring our business to an end. What is the American phrase?"

"Quit while you're ahead?" suggested Alex.

"Precisely Mr Fox. That is what we shall do. Don't forget that this year you are 'ahead' with twenty thousand pounds, with no tax record, no bank transactions, and no way of tracing it. At least not if you are fair with me Mr Fox."

The threat again. The man had Alex over a barrel ever since the first encounter, and Alex knew that the scheming manipulator would have laid a trail that ensured Alex was trapped, enmeshed, and unable to disobey the continuing series of 'requests' for deliveries as he quaintly termed them.

"So let us drink a little toast Mr Fox. Take some of this excellent Metaxa that my cousin sends me and drink to one more year of mutually profitable association."

"To the end of this whole business," toasted Alex grimly as he wondered how he would tell Maggie he had failed again to bring an end to the enslavement.

"Come come Mr Fox, I think you will enjoy the cash again next year. It means after all that you continue to live a life that most people envy."

"If only they knew," muttered Alex, "If only they knew."

Katharos beamed and enjoyed another rich

combination of Cuban tobacco and Greek seven star brandy.

The Golf was judged a write-off by the insurance company, so it was Maggie's even older Polo that was transporting Alex from Hampstead to Clapham. He reviewed the last week that had brought him to visit Katharos for the second time. After arriving back in London at the end of October, Alex made the usual phone-call to Katharos and visited the Greek that night. The package was, as instructed, concealed in the well of the boot, in the centre of the spare wheel. Not a very sophisticated hiding place, but enough to keep it safe from prying eyes. Alex had placed it as usual in a Tesco plastic bag, as the package itself, bound in duct tape, seemed to shout its illegal status. Carrying it from house to car was less conspicuous in the ubiquitous bag.

Alex had parked as usual in the brightly lit driveway and handed the keys to Iannis Junior as he followed the older man into the recesses of the Hampstead house. Their conversation had been more brittle, more difficult that usual, as Alex had arrived fully primed by Maggie to refuse point blank to carry out any more "deliveries". ("Smuggling, Alex, that what it's called. That's what they'll charge you with," still rang in his ears.)

Katharos had as usual taken his refusal to co-operate in much the same way as a parent listens to a toddler's announcement that they are never going to bed again. It was as if the Greek didn't need to waste his time and energy arguing. He knew the next steps in the dance and he could predict the outcome.

Alex realised again that the everyday rules of truth, lawful behaviour, and open meanings just didn't apply. Why had Katharos not handed over the normal bundle of cash to pay him off? At the time the story about his "associates" wanting to examine the delivery first had seemed odd. It had never happened before. Alex felt so ambivalent about accepting the money that he hadn't argued. He almost felt better not accepting it - so he didn't think hard enough about it. But now, a week later, with his neck still aching from the crash, it all seemed obvious. It was frightening that Katharos must have had the non-fatal but salutary attack planned in advance. He knew how unhappy Alex was in his part in the smuggling chain, and had arranged a little reminder of the forces Alex was dealing with. Of course he wouldn't have wanted the £5,000 cash to be found in the wrecked Golf – too many complications and questions. The implied threat was all that was necessary. Katharos didn't have to be explicit about it, he could continue to act out the supposedly civilized little charade in his obscenely plush, falsely respectable Hampstead home. But he could rely on Alex perceiving the threat and continuing to play his part. He thumped the wheel of the Polo with the heel of his hand in frustrated impotence.

Far from easing the problem as he had naively and romantically imagined back in Kapi Creek, Maggie's involvement was becoming an extra pressure and anxiety. What could he tell her? If he came clean about the full extent of his suspicions and worries, that would only serve to exacerbate the pressure from Maggie to make an end to it all. But unless she understood the threat he felt, how could he explain his continued involvement in the coming year. Damned if he did, damned if he didn't. He decided to leave it to Maggie to make the running. If she didn't push it, he would let her stick with her preferred view that the accident had been a simple hit-and-run, the other driver probably having been drinking and therefore not willing to risk being involved. He would let her hope in the meantime that Katharos had accepted his declaration of no further collections. It was quite truthful to report that he had delivered his verbal ultimatum exactly as planned. If Maggie could delude herself into thinking that a serious accident fifteen minutes later was a coincidence then so be it. He would deal with the problem in May next year when the next request arrived from Katharos.

In the meantime he needed to find a replacement car and to get his mind back into the world of business and consulting. The winter was going to be moderately busy by the look of things and Alex decided he would immerse himself in the old routines and forget Katharos till the man inevitably phoned him late in April to issue his next 'request'.

"Well? How did it go?" Maggie demanded as soon as he was home.

"The usual supposedly civilised charade," said Alex almost listlessly throwing the envelope on the coffee table. He didn't look at it and didn't want to touch it, but he knew that he would be using it the next day to supplement the expected insurance settlement for the Golf, and to form the reassuring little reserve of comfort-money that would tide them over the inevitable delays and gaps in payment for his consultancy work.

"How did he react this time?" persisted Maggie.

"Just the same. He didn't argue. But it's almost as if what I say is of no consequence. Believe me, I laid it on the line just as we had planned, but it feels like a damp squib. It's like you dealing with one of my tantrums. You don't quite believe it but you know it's good for me to get it off my chest."

"He'd better believe it," insisted Maggie, with a look of fierce determination and a blaze of righteous zeal in her eyes.

Alex felt like the powerless pawn in a game of chess in which his wishes had no value, his preferences were irrelevant, and his room for manoeuvre non-existent. So he did what men all over the world do to end a discussion. He threw his arms round Maggie and whispered "I love you."

Chapter 25

Dublin 2006

James and Sinead

When James was invited by Lavinia to join the group he was a little worried about spoiling the comfortable mood that he imagined already existed, but he knew that another couple of people would make it less vulnerable to occasional absences.

However his first experience of the group was sufficiently stunning to leave him in a state of confusion and uncertainty about continuing. Lavinia's idea of a social event had been so thoroughly exploded by Hermione's arrival and Pat's behaviour that James wasn't sure he could cope with the aftermath.

However Lavinia rang him, having sensed the probable panic, and persuaded him to excuse her catastrophe. He was taken by her argument that the kindest thing for William would be to carry on. If everyone deserted him after his extreme embarrassment it would be even worse. So James duly presented himself every second Thursday for Lavinia's increasingly enjoyable sessions.

Until he realised that Steve was gay, James had wondered with an unaccountable feeling of disappointment if Sinead and Steve were more than just friends. He picked up in conversation how Steve had been involved in helping Sinead with what the others called her 'new image' and her shopping. So far as James was concerned Sinead didn't need any help. But he hadn't seen the pre-Steve style, he reminded himself.

It was with a mixture of excitement and panic after the first half-dozen meetings that James realised one of the main reasons for his enthusiasm for Lavinia's group was that he would see Sinead. He was disappointed to quite an unexpected degree when she was absent. In fact it was this reaction that made him realise that at some level in his bachelor brain, 'something was going on.'

He thought she was amazingly attractive. Not in the scary way that the girls in the racing crowd were attractive. They and he had instant clarity about the mutual mis-match. Sinead was different. Her face was comfortably attractive. Not so brittle, artificial, and threatening as the others he used to meet. Her dark hair was always clean and shining, and he loved how she somehow wasn't precious or self-conscious about it. She wasn't really very slim, but somehow she suited that, and her clothes always looked fashionable but at the same time comfortable and practical.

He was a bit in awe of her combination of English Literature degree with her current accountancy studies. His long-forgotten General Studies degree and basic book-keeping certificates felt just as irrelevant as in reality they were. She had an air of quietly and unfussily doing something with her life. He realised that he probably looked at her too much, and would have to stop himself doing that.

But she looked interested when he spoke. There was an encouraging, genuinely interested smile when she looked at him. She often agreed with what he said and helped to make it sound intellectually worthwhile. When he said that something read as if it was not based on the author's experience, she would jump in with some literary arguments to back up his elementary comments.

James however was firmly stuck in the frame of mind where close relationships with women didn't work for him. He was too scarred by old emotional damage, too afraid of the uncontrollable helter-skelter of emotions and potential failures to allow himself for a moment to dream or to imagine that in reality a relationship with Sinead was possible. He allowed himself to fantasise, but it was strictly in the realm of fantasy, with no potential connection to an actual future reality. He enjoyed the warmth of the feelings she created in him, but didn't even consider risking spoiling the present with an inevitably clumsy move to take things further.

Sinead, meanwhile, had found the relationships with Lavinia, Steve and William liberating and mind-expanding. It was as if they each in different ways gave her insights in to other lives and other privacies.

Lavinia had unexpectedly become a warm supportive friend, with whom she could talk about anything. It was her conversations with Lavinia that were most perspective-changing. They allowed her to see her other lives with a clarity and comprehension that was both disturbing and confirming. She could see how right she had been to take the bold step of starting the accountancy course, and with Lavinia's encouragement she could believe more actively in the future career she could have. When she described the work relationships with 'the girls' and confessed the frustrations with the others in her flat, Lavinia didn't make her feel stupid or incompetent. She made her see them in a warmer and less frustrating light. She saw the patterns in her life and in the others' lives for the scripts that they were. She and Lavinia shared the same great, overwhelmingly and delightfully exciting task. When they were together they could understand and encourage one another in what they were doing, which was a bit like sitting back from the play in their directors' chairs and deciding to manipulate the script. They were deciding that they had the power to stop following the next inevitable lines and the predictable stage direction. They were no longer prisoners of the script that had been unwittingly handed to them by parents, neighbours, schools, churches, and the whole oppressive history of who they were and where they lived. It didn't have to just trundle on as it had been doing. They genuinely felt that the mind-opening insight into what they could do was real. It was liberating, but it wasn't fanciful.

Lavinia helped her believe in the changes that she was making and helped her to be less limited in her vision. She helped Lavinia to be realistic and practical. They worked well together and what made it delightful was that they knew it, and they loved each other for it.

Sinead's relationship with Steve was different. She

first of all didn't think that any of 'the girls' and certainly none of her flat-mates had any real insight into or contact with the gay parallel universe that surrounded them. For whatever reason, she and Steve were immediately at ease with one another. It was Sinead and Steve who exchanged eye-contact most during that first tentative book-group meeting. It was she and Steve who compared notes afterwards and uncomplicatedly agreed to meet for a drink between the formal meetings.

She found that Steve reacted easily and with a light, amused but uncondescending style to her naïve questions about the gay way of life in Dublin. She knew vaguely that some bars were known as gay bars, but had no insight into the intricate networks of contacts that formed an instantly accessible social scene for gay men in the city. He laughed when she asked about gay women, for it was then a much less developed and much less accessible network.

Steve was able to tell her about life with his mother. He found in Sinead a listener who could fully understand the contradictions, frustrations, and warmth of that relationship. Steve's mother was a widow who had seen her life shaken from one script to another with a cruelty that might have killed a lesser woman. Without self-pity of any sense of resentment Steve described the unexpected transformation of his life from the comfortable wealth and social connections due to his father, to the free-fall from grace that followed his death. With the death crumbled the façade that had been plate-spinningly maintained. Foolish investments, bad luck, worse timing, and a flawed personality had left Steve's father maintaining a front he didn't confess even to his wife. It was only when they met his solicitor after the funeral that Steve and his mother realised that they were in effect destitute. There was no house to sell, it was already owned by the bank to cover old debts. There were no more investments. There was literally nothing but debt.

Ten years later and Steve was sharing a neat little terraced house with his mother, and they were both doing work that they had never imagined they would have to do. Sinead could have cried in her empathy for the overwhelming waves of disaster that seemed to have engulfed the mother and son, but somehow she knew that such self-indulgence on her part would spoil the relationship with Steve. He didn't want her sympathy. He allowed her to see inside his life as part of the two-way process that built the bonds, enriched the understanding, and strengthened both participants.

William was different. Sinead couldn't stop herself smiling a little when she thought of him. Normally she would react strongly against the pomposity and what she always thought of as fake Anglo-Irish style. Bur there was something so innocently transparent about William that it was amusing rather than offensive. At first Sinead felt guilty about being amused, but quickly realised that it was almost a conspiracy with William to react in this way rather than a conspiracy against him. He colluded in maintaining the amusing fictions and stances. It was as if his style of dressing was not so crazy. She felt an unexpressed wink of collusion with William at the over-the-top datedness of the occasional cravat, the yellow jumper, and the pressed jeans. At some level she felt that he too had been let into the secret about writing one's own script, but that he was enjoying playing along with the script as it was.

Sinead had really laughed and relaxed the first time she unthinkingly and unpremeditatedly punctured one of William's pomposities. He often made statements or put forward views that were obviously fabricated on the basis of quickly picking up what other people had just said. He had a funny knack of sounding quite pompously self-opinionated, but at the same time self-parodying. When Sinead unexpectedly said,

"Really William, I don't think you've even read it," and immediately put her hand to her mouth in shock at what she had just said. William paused only for a moment and then laughed,

"You're absolutely right, old thing. Totally bluffing. Thought I was getting away with it!"

And they all laughed because they all knew, and because it was all right.

And that left James.

When James first joined the group she didn't really know what to make of him. He was of a type outside her experience. His family was a familiar Dublin name, and she expected the well-schooled politeness and propriety. She didn't expect the vulnerability and sadness that oozed from his smoky blue eyes. For the first few sessions he seemed hesitant, not used to giving his views, or perhaps not used to having them listened to. When she quizzed Lavinia about him she realised that James' and Lavinia's families would have known each other over the years, so it was natural that James was part of Lavinia's wider social network. She heard about James losing his job in the bank, one of an older generation and style who didn't seem to fit in the new order that was marching through all the old family bastions of nepotism and privilege in the city. No wonder he looked a bit bewildered. Somebody had changed the rules of the world and he'd found himself left behind, with no seeming role in the forceful new Ireland. It didn't seem fair to Sinead and she instinctively wanted to help him.

The help she found she could give him was to encourage him in the reading group. When he tentatively suggested a possible view, usually at Lavinia's prompting, she made a point of trying to help and support him. She realised he watched her in anticipation of some support and encouragement. It was becoming another symbiotic arrangement and it was good for both of them. She felt better for helping him and also felt richly appreciated if not by words at least through warm eye contact. He felt encouraged, and because of the positive response to his comments he became more and more likely to express a view without waiting for someone to prompt him. It was an unusual experience for him, and one that gradually overtook the years of negative reinforcement he had received during meetings in the bank.

Sinead knew that he was more than ten years older, but when she realised that the thoughts she had about him were actually of a fondness and hopefulness that was beyond the normal social reaction, it somehow didn't matter at all. She routinely met Lavinia for coffee, and uncomplicatedly met Steve for a quiet drink, but she didn't see how she could prompt such a thing with James.

Lavinia laughed delightedly when Sinead confessed the strange mixture of feelings that she was experiencing, and at once wanted to engineer something that might actually allow these two inexpert and tentative people to get together.

"I know what I'll do," she enthusiastically proposed to Sinead. "I'll tell James that you and I are meeting for coffee, invite him, but I won't turn up."

"Don't you dare," exclaimed Sinead, terrified at the prospect. "I won't turn up either and the poor man will be all on his own."

"What about the three of us meeting but I'll need to leave unexpectedly early?"

"No, this is pathetic. I, or rather he, should be able to get things started without you having to act as matchmaker."

"It's just a question of timing really. I'm only trying to help you along. I'll stay out of it if you want."

"Oh, I don't know. He doesn't look as if he would ever have the nerve to ask me out, but I don't want to feel it is set up. Promise me you won't do anything unless I ask you to."

"Of course, I promise, but I'm ready and willing to help if you ask. I'll be watching."

"Thanks Lavinia. Let's just see how things go on their own. Better not to complicate them."

*   *   *

"James?"

"Yes, this is he."

"James, it's Lavinia."

"Hello Lavinia. What can I do for you?"

"Well actually James, this is a bit tricky, I'm starting

to think I shouldn't have phoned. I don't quite know how to put this." Lavinia had of course planned every move of the conversation.

"I'm afraid you'll have to spit it out Lavinia now that you have started. You can't leave me hanging."

"Perhaps you'll be cross with me for interfering. I really shouldn't I know."

"Lavinia will you please tell me what you are talking about."

"Well if you insist. It's rather personal and totally secret. You must swear you will never, ever, tell anyone about this."

"Lavinia you have to tell me." James was intrigued, worried, out of his depth, but experiencing a vague uncertain excitement and hope that surprised him. He didn't dare really frame the hope that was flickering but waited for Lavinia's next words.

"Promise me."

"Yes, I promise not to tell."

"Cross your heart?"

"Lavinia!"

"It's about Sinead. And you mustn't, mustn't tell her I've said anything."

James felt slightly giddy. His face flushed, he could feel the redness engulfing his face and neck. He sat down on the dining room chair and waited, oblivious to everything in the world other than the silence on the telephone line. The lunchtime news was quietly continuing on the radio. His soup was cooling and developing a congealing layer of something semi-solid looking.

"Lavinia?"

"Yes James?"

"Please tell me about Sinead." It was the question that Lavinia had been steering James towards all along. Now she could honestly say to herself and if necessary to Sinead that James had asked her point blank.

"It's just that I've been watching you two, and I know it's none of my business but you obviously like each other a lot. You exchange more glances than anyone else, and you both make the other smile a lot."

"Really? I didn't think….."

"Well I do think. And I know that, without meaning this unkindly, neither of you is very good at taking first steps in relationships."

"In my case that is something of an understatement."

"So I just thought you might need a little prompting, or a little confirmation that you should get on with it."

"Oh…."

"James?"

"I don't know what to say Lavinia."

"To me or to Sinead?"

"To either of you."

"Well you can say either 'thank-you' or 'mind your own business' to me first."

"Oh, thank you Lavinia, I really do appreciate this."

"And in that case you can ring Sinead and suggest that the two of you meet for a coffee – no better to meet for a drink, after work, her work that is, she finishes at 5:00 so you could meet her in one of those nice little places off Grafton Street."

"When should I phone her?"

"Next week. Not this week. She'll suspect something

if you phone too soon."

"Oh thank you Lavinia. I don't know what to say. But thank you."

James didn't think to ask why telephoning this week would have made Sinead suspicious. His mind was in too much of a daze to reach the obvious inescapable conclusion that Sinead and Lavinia had been talking about him. He was too overwhelmed with a strange heady mixture of panic and anticipation to think straight.

Chapter 26

Dublin 2006

James and Sinead together

"What would you like to drink?"

"I'm not sure. What are you having?"

"I think I'll have a gin and tonic."

"That sounds nice. I'll have that too."

James ordered the drinks at the bar, leaving Sinead to sit at the little round table in the corner of the Bailey. It was 5:30, and not busy. There were a few tourists at another table, a few students chatting in a desultory way at the front, and a couple of solitary men reading their papers and sipping occasionally from their pints of Guinness. From time to time someone slipped outside for a cigarette, Ireland having taken an early decision by European standards to ban smoking in public buildings.

"Here we are," said James, trying to sound casual and confident.

"Mmnn, thanks."

"Well, here's to crime," he toasted for no particular reason.

"Slainte," toasted Sinead, understanding completely how bizarre and inappropriate words could pop out when you least expected.

"You must tell me about your work in Trinity. Somehow we never get to find out things like that when we're all chatting about books."

"Oh, I don't want to bore you. It's very basic admin. I don't think you'd want to know about all the details."

"But I would, honestly. I'd like to be able to picture what you do and what the office is like."

And so the seemingly innocent factual questions and answers conveyed between them the desire to be closer; the irresistible urge to confide in each other; and demonstrated the unpractised awkwardness of the mature romantic.

They spent an hour together before Sinead said she had better go, as the girls in the flat would be expecting her to eat with them. James was disappointed that there was no more time. He had started imagining candlelit dinners within minutes of Lavinia's phone-call. But he told himself to be patient. He had after all invited her for a drink after work. His disappointment made him bolder and without planning he said,

"Let's meet again next week, but why don't we go to eat somewhere?"

"Oh let's," agreed Sinead without hesitation.

They parted awkwardly outside the Bailey. Neither of them was bold enough to touch, but both of them were physically primed to touch or even to kiss. James clumsily put his hands in his pockets, Sinead clasped her bag as if expecting a robbery, and they parted reluctantly and uncertainly.

"See you on Thursday then."

"Oh yes. See you at Lavinia's. Thanks for the drink."

"A pleasure. Bye."

"Bye."

They walked off in opposite directions: Sinead to catch a bus back to her flat in Rathmines, James to go in the opposite direction for a moment just to ease the awkwardness. He was still in a state of something approaching hyperactivity, twitchingly ready to do something but not knowing what. He was happier than he could remember being for years. His grin was more genuine, spontaneous and uncontrollable than he could cope with. So he couldn't go home to his lonely-seeming flat. He felt a man of the world; a chap just coming from a secret meeting with his lover; a romantic hero; a Lothario.

James strolled nonchalantly into O'Neill's.

"Pint of Guinness please."

"You have a win on the horses or something?" asked the barman cheekily. Not reacting to the extravagance of the drinks order, but to the unusual extravagance of the happy grin on the face of his usually doleful customer.

"Something like that," admitted James, a little taken aback by the observation. He was secretly pleased that he had such a positive air, which was obvious to others, but he wasn't used to such man-to-man informality, so he withdrew a little clumsily to a far corner of the bar.

On Thursday they met at Lavinia's book group, and again were blatantly pleased to see each other, but pointedly avoided any physical contact. Despite separate resolutions made by each of them, they simply couldn't avoid looking at each other and smiling, as if there was a special bond of communication that was as exciting as it was resistant to being hidden. Lavinia didn't need to be told that her plotting had worked. She was unselfishly delighted for them and was so focused on the signs and signals between them that she was oblivious to the amount of attention William tended to give her. This wasn't surprising, as she took the lead in the discussions and kept an eye on the time, so people naturally looked to her more than anyone else. But she had been missing the soft wistful air that came over William when he watched her and daydreamed.

Chapter 27

Turkey May 2006

Maggie writing

"I hear a gentle sound of water lapping against rocks, which sounds quite different from water lapping on sand or on shingle. I hear the high-pitched singing and chirruping of birds high above me. There are distant male voices in a language I don't understand, but they sound matter-of-fact rather than argumentative or emotional. I hear the gentle rhythmic creaking noise of ropes taking the strain and relaxing; taking the strain and relaxing, as the slightest swell rocks the boat and pulls then relaxes; pulls then relaxes, on the iron rings on the jetty. I hear the distant but increasing beat of a simple engine on a local boat. How do I know it is a simple engine on a local boat? It has the noisily discernible separate percussions of a single cylinder engine rather than the smoother sound of a multiple cylinder engine. It is poorly silenced, in fact it is making a terrible racket, which means it is a local open boat rather than a more expensive and probably foreign-owned motor boat or yacht."

Maggie was exercising her writing brain just as she had been taught to do years before. She was examining her senses one by one and using the experience to enrich the descriptions of the scenes she was writing about.

"What do I feel? I feel the heat of the sun on my ankles and feet, as the low morning sun cuts its path under the shade of the bimini and under the cockpit table. I feel the hardness of the seat pressing through the thin cushion on the backs of my thighs, and the squishy give of the cushion round my bum as I move slightly from side to side. I feel the hairs on my head moving slightly as a breeze from my left-hand side ruffles the water and disturbs my hair. I feel the cooling effect of the breeze on my left shoulder and arm as I sit writing here.

"What do I smell? I smell smoke. I smell two kinds of smoke. There is a prickly-smelling wood-smoke from the oven, not harsh enough to be termed acrid, but pungent enough to be identified as coming from the pine-wood gathered in the hills behind the taverna. More superficial and temporary is the tobacco smoke wafting over from a nearby yacht, where the teenager seems to have been banished from the cockpit to the bow to indulge, if not enjoy, his rebellious morning cigarette. I smell a faint aroma of fish. It comes and goes so much that I can't be sure if it is there at all. Perhaps it is because I know the little fishing boat is at the end of the jetty that I think I can smell it. There is a freshness in the air of the breeze that is wafting in from my left, a freshness that isn't quite an absence of smell yet can't really be defined. Is it fresh pine-needle smell, is it ozone? That's no good – that's me projecting what it might be rather than simply reporting on my senses. I can smell a faint perfumed smell from the sun cream that I used earlier. Perfumed isn't good enough – if I had used the old coconut oil it would have been easier to describe. I'd need to be a perfumier to identify the clean, hygienic-smelling and deliberately inoffensive scent.

"What do I taste? That's harder. I taste the after-effect of coffee in my mouth. It is still bitter but pleasant, solid tasting in contact with my tongue, still discernible on the roof and back of my mouth. I think I can still taste the combination of butter and honey on the crisp-edged bread, and the oily sponginess of the bread itself – I can remember a hint of saltiness in it but I can't still taste that. What I can't taste is toothpaste – forgotten to do my teeth again – too keen to get started with my writing.

"OK, nearly finished. What do I see? Always the easy one to do, except there is so much. I see distant hills and mountains, still hazy with morning mist, gradually emerging as mostly green, but higher up grey, in the slanting morning sunshine. I see sea, not just a single entity, but a series of patterns differentiated by the breeze and the reflections of land. Close by it is a series of little parallel ripples corresponding with the breeze that I feel on my skin. The ripples disrupt the reflections of the other yachts nearby, and of the trees that seem to be growing out of rocks on the curving shore of the bay. I see a less-rippled, mottled band of water further out. The early morning breeze convected by the heating of the land isn't affecting the surface out there yet. It looks to be a lighter blue than the rippled water, catching the reflection of the sky and in places the reflection of the green, grey, brown hills in the distance. I see the nearby trees, some impossibly fresh lime-green; others darker pine; some the very darkly saturated green of the mulberry and other bushy growths. In between there are occasional olive trees. Not the regimented and orderly planting on the distant hills, but the random scattering of olive green between the pines. I wonder is that the remains of a more orderly planting, or the self-seeded, bird-dropped pattern of nature? I'm sure birds don't eat olives so they couldn't be seeded through bird-droppings – bloody big birds they'd need to be.

"I see the jetty, wood planks whitened by the sun, smoothed by countless feet and deck shoes, hammered into place with now-rusty nails that leave their pattern of spreading brown stains on the bleaching wood. The iron rings on the edge of the jetty look like the work of the village smith. They have the ribbed surface you see on the steel reinforcements before concrete is poured – probably a cheap source of off-cuts of steel, fashioned by the smith into hoops for the jetties, and secured by similarly village-fashioned little iron strips, a raised section forged in the flat to allow the ring to fit in place. The whole assembly is seemingly held in place by nails rather than bolts, but rusting securely into place so that the grip is probably nearly as good."

"You still scribbling away?" interrupted Alex rudely.

"Just about to finish I think," came the mild reply. The mood of satisfaction and pleasure was too good to be dissipated by the unwelcome interruption. "In fact I think I might just stop there. It's really just some limbering up exercises rather than carrying on with the story."

"How on earth do you do limbering up exercises

when you are writing?" asked an unsympathetic Alex.

"Oh I'll explain sometime," said Maggie, in such a calm and satisfied mood that she wouldn't rise to Alex's usual taunts.

"I've been trying to describe this place – you know – a bit like a verbal photograph. Sometimes I think it is the sensations other than sight that really bring a place to life again. When you're sitting in grey old Clapham in the winter it isn't just the sights you need to recall, it's the sounds, smells, and feel of the place. Photographs only do the visual bit."

OK I'll admit that given current technology there isn't much point in smelling a photograph, but surely the photograph acts as the prompt for all those other memories?"

"Yes, you're right. A good photograph will really do that for me. But the average holiday snap gets looked at for about two seconds before being passed on to the next person. That isn't long enough for all the associations to come back to life. I want to have words that I can savour, chew, and enjoy again later. Each description fills in another dimension in my little mental reconstruction, and it engages more of my brain than just looking at a photograph."

"OK, we'll test it in darkest January in Clapham. A nice bottle of wine, some mezes from the deli, and I'll happily test your theory."

"I look forward to it. You can show me your photographs and I'll make you lie back with your eyes closed and listen to my descriptions."

"Mmnn," said Alex with a mischievous grin.

"You know exactly what I mean." Maggie closed her

notepad, picked up her pencil and glasses, and pretended to huff down the companionway to the saloon below. The smile on her face betrayed the fake huff, and belied the stern tone of voice. She too could imagine just how that evening in darkest January in Clapham might work out. And she liked the idea very much indeed.

It was late May. They were moored in a little bay in Skopea Limani about ten miles from their base in Gocek. Alex had completed his rendezvous a couple of nights previously, and they were now preparing to take their paying guests back to Gocek for their flights home. Apart from the nagging worry of his illicit cargo Alex was happy. The fact that he could be totally, blissfully, uncomplicatedly and almost solvently happy made the underlying worry all the more annoying. He cursed and fumed internally when he thought of the extent to which Katharos was screwing up his perfect enjoyment of life. He had Maggie, whom he appreciated, loved, adored and enjoyed. Physically, mentally and in some vague way that he supposed people labelled 'spiritually', he felt relaxed and in tune with her. An involuntary sigh escaped as he thought again of how good life could be after Katharos: the summers on the yacht pottering around Turkey and Greece; the winters picking and choosing the consultancy work that he did. He planned to earn enough to keep them ticking over, but not being driven so much that he resented the work. It sounded ideal. Too ideal.

Chapter 28

Alex: August 2006

London – A letter from Dublin

The winter season in England had gone as well as Alex could have hoped. He had managed to maintain a steady stream of work except for the long gap from mid December to mid January. Maggie had settled into her fairly undemanding role as part-time secretary, and helped Alex organise himself and his work. She fielded phone-calls when he was away from Clapham, and took over all the bookings of hotels and equipment. More significantly, she picked up the threads of her own writing and happily devoted about three hours each morning to her laptop in the kitchen.

"No, you're not going to see a word of it till it's finished," was how she rebuffed every inquisitive enquiry from Alex.

"Chicklit, then, is it?" didn't go down too well as a taunt, but he knew only that she was enjoying the process and was generally in a humour that related directly to the number of words completed each morning. He teased her about her addiction, and about the negative affect of any failure to meet her self-imposed targets.

All was calm until the third week of April, when Maggie answered the phone and heard the unmistakable torture of consonants that announced Katharos the Greek. He seemed to hang on to his Greek identity through the caricature of Greek-accented English. Maggie suspected that he enjoyed the play-acting that had become an engrained part of his personality since his days probably as an apparently obsequious waiter in the West End taverna. He apologised for disturbing her and asked when he might speak to Alex. Maggie found herself telling him that Alex would be home that evening, and cursed herself for failing to confront the man who was the main threat to their happiness and well-being. However her failure – her realisation of the impossibility of confronting this politely threatening ogre, left her less strident in her complaints to Alex as he complied again with the rendezvous, collection and delivery arrangements dictated by Katharos in May and in July.

The periods in Turkey were the same mixture of delight with the surroundings, mingled with annoyance and anxiety at the illicit activities on behalf of the Greek. Alex developed a comforting theory that the packets he collected were in fact innocuous, and that Katharos was engaged in a subtle game that rendered Alex trapped but in fact in no danger when he carried the packages. This unconvincing hypothesis did not bear scrutiny. He did not allow himself to test it by slitting open one of the elaborately sealed parcels. But the comforting mental escape route sometimes gave him an illogical and disproportionate relief from the otherwise oppressive anxiety.

The chartering business was healthy that year, so without the pressure of guests every week, Alex and Maggie entertained enough groups to make the venture seem worthwhile. They were covering their costs, making a modest profit, and enjoying an enviable life-style.

They arrived back in the heat of London at the end of July, feeling pleased with themselves and full of optimism about their partnership and the business.

But in August an envelope arrived at the Clapham flat. It was belatedly forwarded from Alex's old office and it contained an artistic and innocent bombshell.

Chapter 29

August 2006: London

Alex opens Lavinia's letter

Alex picked up the envelope and examined it carefully, rather than opening the inviting tear-off strip. It had a Dublin postmark, which was unusual in itself, and it was one of the high quality data-post envelopes that kept the contents safe from damage in transit, even through the ordinary mail. He hadn't ordered anything from Dublin – perhaps Maggie had – but it was addressed to him – a present perhaps?

Maggie walked in.

"What have you there?" she wondered aloud.

"Don't know. It's come from Dublin. You order anything?"

"No, nothing. What a pity we can't open it to see what it is."

"What? Oh very clever. I'm just enjoying speculating for a minute, savouring the expectation, making the most of the mystery. Thought you'd be quite into that sort of thing."

"Oh stop teasing and open the thing will you."

"No, I think I'll wait until tomorrow," he laughed.

Maggie deftly whisked it from his unresisting fingers, enjoying the tease and the childish fun. She turned her back to him and protected the prize with bent back and jutting elbows as she tore the perforated strip and extracted the contents.

"Oh, I knew she fancied you! You didn't tell me you had been in touch."

"Who, for goodness sake?"

"Luscious Lavinia, your Molly Malone, she of the dark hair, dark eyes, and adoring gaze."

"Yes I did mean to tell you about our steamy affair conducted exclusively through mail packages. What is it?"

"Here's the letter – I'll read it.

Dear Alex,

This is a belated letter to thank you for the spectacular holiday last October. In every way it was the holiday of a lifetime I had promised myself. You and (Maggie?) were so good to me. So patient with my incompetence and so good at teaching.

You will probably remember that I took millions of photographs. "How could we forget?" I hear you saying. Well it wasn't a total waste of time. Some of them were picked for an exhibition – I must admit my sister's assistance in publishing one in the Irish Times may have helped - but the good news is that they are going to be featured in one of the UK national Sunday papers. Five of them are going into a section on the "magic of monochrome". They are all from that magic trip with you. I can't thank you enough.

I enclose a print of my favourite shot – from Kapi Creek I think. It is my thank-you to you for creating the possibility of the photographs.

Please do look me up if you are ever in Dublin.

Very best wishes

Lavinia."

"Please look me up indeed! I told you she fancied you."

"Let's see the photo then. Maybe it will test your theory about words being better than just visual images."

Maggie slipped the glossy photograph from its protective sleeve and held it up to Alex.

The effect on Alex would have gratified her if she had showered him with a thousand of her elegantly emotive descriptions of Kapi. He reached out a hand to steady himself on a kitchen chair. His complexion paled and his mouth opened, but no sound emerged. His eyes eventually closed and he unsteadily lowered himself to sit on the chair.

Chapter 30

Dublin 2006

Sinead and James

Sinead was having many positive effects on James. He was a man more relaxed, positive and confident than he thought he had ever been in his adult life. The years in the bank seemed in retrospect like a long-drawn-out nightmare. He had always known that he was used as a properly spoken low-cost front man with a certain type of customer. He had no real authority, so he wasn't allowed near the really important clients, but there were many of the bank's personal customers who liked to deal with Mr Findlater, impressed by the manner, accent and name of this ever-polite and obliging official. More perceptive customers quickly realised that he had virtually no authority and preferred to deal with a senior person, but for years it had suited the bank to continue to employ people like James who personified the old style and ethos of the institution. It had become increasingly clear that he was tolerated as an anachronism by senior managers, but the slights, the put-downs, and the impatience of the younger breed had damaged James in a cruel and stressful way. It was just what he needed now to have a warm, supportive, loving woman to start to rebuild his self-confidence and instil in him the belief that he had something other than a once-useful accent and demeanour to offer the world.

Sinead started to help him to think about what he was going to do with the rest of his potential working life. He was subsisting on the paltry interest from his redundancy money on top of the basic State benefit, and it wasn't going to last.

"You're intelligent, polite, well-dressed, well-connected and able to do loads of things," Sinead reassured him.

"But I don't want to go back to a job where I'm laughed at behind my back, and go home feeling generally useless."

"You don't have to, James. I'll help you think about the sorts of work you'd like to do and I know someone who'd help you with applications. I just know you'll feel better when you're back in a job, and this time one that you enjoy."

"Oh, Sinead,"

"Oh, James."

They looked lovingly at each other and James reached out to hold Sinead's hand.

"I do love you, you know."

"I know that, and I love you too, so don't forget it, as I wouldn't fall for anyone who wasn't a bit special. Just because those horrible people in the bank put you down for years you've started to believe it. I'll be hurt if you don't start believing what I tell you."

"Oh I do, I do. It's just so hard to believe I could really do something that I'd enjoy and that someone would pay me for."

"We're going to start with a list of your positives, then we're going to start looking for jobs that could make use of them. It's just a matter of trying to apply a bit of business sense to the problem."

Sinead was indomitable. She was finding her own confidence so much greater than it used to be, that she felt sure she could share some of it with James and heal the wounds that he picked at in his mind without her.

She tackled him like a business project, and before long they were setting targets for polishing his cv; for identifying the top three types of jobs he would want; and for completing an application each week.

To his surprise James found that the feeling of making progress was reinforcing of his improved humour and confidence. It wasn't just the final getting of a job that would make him feel better, it was the little steps along the way that had almost as positive an effect.

.

Chapter 31

Dublin Sept 2006

Lavinia organises Alex's visit

"Can everyone come for drinks on Saturday and then go somewhere for dinner?" Lavinia proposed to the group one Thursday a few months later.

"I have just heard that someone I know from London is coming and thought you'd all like to meet him."

William's face fell.

"He's actually the skipper from that yachting holiday I went on last year. I sent him one of the photographs a couple of weeks ago and said if he was ever in Dublin to give me a call. I didn't honestly think he would – it's just one of those things you write isn't it – but almost right away here he is. I'm a bit taken aback and frankly it would be great to make it more of a social occasion."

"Maybe the chap wants you to himself and we'll just be in the way," tested a nervous William. He had been quietly allowing his distant but warm feelings for Lavinia to become part of his mental furniture. It was quite a safe, unthreatening but pleasurable thing to allow himself to admire Lavinia from a distance. After his battered psyche's experience with Pat he felt safer not actually doing anything about the feelings - they were fine as a low key, almost proprietorial feeling. To his surprise, they were suddenly being brought into the relative open by this unwanted intruder from some other part of Lavinia's life.

Lavinia laughed.

"I don't think Maggie would have much patience with that. So far as I could see he is devotedly attached to his 'mate' in both senses of the word. Whatever has motivated him to take up the offer it certainly isn't a romantic intention."

William relaxed, and became aware of just how strongly he had reacted. He wondered if others had noticed and glanced round Steve, Sinead and James, who were all looking slightly oddly at him.

"Well I think the least we can all do is give you a little moral support," he blustered, trying to make it a group issue rather than the personal drama it had been.

Steve looked at Sinead with raised eyebrows. Sinead blushed, as if any reference to relationships was bound to uncover what she blithely thought was her secret. James looked at William and wondered, but he wasn't very good at this sort of thing. Lavinia didn't notice. She was a little in awe of Alex, didn't know how they would get on when they were in her world rather than Alex's, and for some unaccountable reason wanted the security of numbers her little group could give.

"This Saturday night?" checked Steve.

Sinead and James exchanged glances to check with each other that they would both go.

"Yes I know it's short notice but he's really taken me by surprise. Says he's coming for some boating event but I've no idea what it is."

"I'm fine," volunteered William, and the others joined in, making it a full group.

"Just promise me that Hermione and Pat aren't making a special appearance," joked William.

"What a good idea!" laughed Lavinia.

"Oh no please. I don't think I'd survive it," pleaded William.

It was the first time he had been able to actually make a joke about the previous year's event. There was a general air of relief that at last it had achieved the status of a safe subject to joke about.

"Let's say 7 o'clock here, then we can book a table at Delaney's which is easy walking distance. And by the way I'm paying. We'll make it a sort of celebration of my photographs if that doesn't sound too self-praising."

"No, no, no," came the murmurs from the group. No-one sure if they were protesting the issue of Lavinia's modesty or the issue of her paying. It suited James to leave it vague as he selfishly loved the idea of a meal at Delaney's that he didn't have to pay for.

"So that's settled then – just smart casual, but see you here at 7:00." Lavinia was used to laying down the law with this group.

Chapter 32

Dublin: September 2006

Alex meets the book group

It was in a positive mood that the five gathered at Lavinia's on Saturday.

"Well Alex, how does it feel to have your feet on dry land for a change?" William felt he was close to the yachting fraternity. He had never sailed but felt a certain affinity for what he perceived as the nattily blazered and well-heeled crowd who frequented the Dun Laoghaire and Howth yacht clubs.

"Well actually I'm fine – rather in between things. I've been back in the UK for a few weeks now, and not due to go out again till the start of October."

"What happens to the old tub while you're back in Blighty then?" William was showing himself to be an absolute master of an inappropriate style of language that owed everything to his firmly ingrained stereotyping and very little to the world that Alex inhabited.

"Hopefully she's earning a little money for me with bareboat charters while I sit out the heat in more northern climes."

"It sounds awfully exotic to have a yacht in the Mediterranean," joined in Sinead, genuinely impressed that anyone could have Alex's life and still seem a friendly down-to-earth sort of person. "Is it as exciting as it sounds?"

"It has its moments, but I suppose I take it a bit too much for granted half the time. It's when we have groups on the boat and I see their reaction to the places we go that I'm reminded of just how lucky I am."

"I suppose that was me, wasn't it?" laughed Lavinia, recalling her wide-eyed reaction to the scenery and the unique perspective from the cockpit of a sailing boat.

"Well you certainly took full advantage of the photographic opportunities," said Alex, turning the conversation to the display of black-and-white 10 by 8s on the wall.

"Oh, I just loved the place, and couldn't resist the light, and those jetties. They wouldn't be allowed here but they fit in so well to the unspoiled atmosphere of the place."

"Wait till they join the EU and a few inspectors start cleaning up the place."

"What a thought." Lavinia was horrified at the prospect of standardised EU regulations changing the style and atmosphere of the taverna jetties in the little bays she had fallen in love with.

"I don't imagine that's going to happen for a few years yet," James flexed his confidence in a way that he wouldn't have risked a year earlier. "I reckon there is such a lot of work to do on the Kurdish issue and the human rights problems before there is any mission of accession."

"You're right," agreed Alex. "It's still such a different world there, and I don't want to see it go the way Greece has gone. Prices are sky-high there and somehow the ubiquitous Euro takes away a bit of the romance. I know it simplifies things but it also makes for too much sameness. I don't want to see the same brands in Gocek that I see in London and Dublin."

"I agree," said Steve, who up to then hadn't found the yachting chat easy to get a foothold in. "I think the way McDonalds and Starbucks pollute the civilised world is terrible," he continued, "and the supermarket chains are just as bad."

The chat continued easily as Lavinia topped up the drinks and made sure everyone was involved. Alex was the natural centre of attention and managed to amuse them all with his poking of fun at the hierarchies of yachting participants in the Mediterranean.

"Well at the top you have the owners of the mega-yachts, which are only yachts in the American sense of the term – no sails, a bit like liners really, with every conceivable comfort on board. The owners of those don't talk to anyone. They arrive on board by helicopter and so far as anyone can see rarely leave their pampered world. Down the scale a bit you have the big Sunseeker, Cranchi, and Feretti cruisers – I'm talking about the 50 to 100 foot boats costing a few million. The owners of them only talk to owners of similarly sized boats. We see them in places like Kapi and Gocek where they actually do step ashore, smoke cigars, and parade themselves, strutting like fat peacocks within a few yards of their boat so that no-one can fail to realise who is the successful man, and yes it is always a man who owns the monstrosity. They usually have a professional crew, a skipper, hostess, and deckhand, so the owner can pose at the controls from time to time without actually knowing the first thing about seamanship."

"Come the revolution they'll have to go." Steve wasn't entirely joking.

"The funny thing is they never look as if they have any fun at all," continued Alex. "They can only get into the bigger harbours, they are fast, insulated, air-conditioned, and generally speaking the people on them have to spend such a lot of time preening, posing, and worrying about how they look that there's no time to actually have any fun."

"Don't they even swim?" asked Sinead incredulously.

"Some do, most don't – not good for the hairstyle."

"Oh, my favourite saying was that aging Istanbul businessman with the huge Sunseeker," chipped in Lavinia. "He must have been 55 at least and weighed 18 stone, but the girl who I thought must be his daughter turned out to be English, and not averse to a bit of improperly intimate contact. She swam for a couple of minutes and the fat old man kept shouting at her, 'Get your head in the water, get your head in the water, your ass knows it's swimming but your brain doesn't.'" Lavinia imitated the man's American accented English, which somehow allowed her to use the words with impunity.

They all laughed at the thought while Alex continued.

"Then you come down the pecking order to the

actual sailing yachts which again have their hierarchy, partly to do with size but overwhelmingly to do with owners versus charters. The owner of the 50 foot yacht will check out the skipper of the neighbouring 44 foot yacht, and if he sees a charter flag he'll just exchange pleasantries. If he sees no charter symbol or flag, they'll be inviting one-another for drinks and comparing the cost of marinas. If the owner next door happens to have too small a yacht, he'll fall somewhere between the other two, not quite a social equal but worthy of reasonable respect."

"It all sounds horribly snobbish," worried Sinead, as if the glamour of the world he described was a little less wonderful than she had hoped.

"I suspect every social system sorts itself out like that," Lavinia didn't want the glitter to be scrubbed off too thoroughly.

"So where do you fit in all of this?" James bravely asked the centre of attention.

"Ah, good question. Because I have a reasonable sized sailing yacht and because I'm the owner, at times I'm safely in that upper echelon of the middle group. But I'm afraid that I let the side down by taking paying guests, and worse still I charter the boat out when I'm not there."

"This reminds me of Monty Python, or was it the two Ronnies?" laughed William.

"I bet it was "That Was The Week That Was" you're thinking of. John Cleese and the two Ronnies lined up and saying 'I look down on him' because of whatever it was, and poor little Ronnie at the end with nobody to look down on. 'I know my place,' - that was his line at the end."

They all joined in the merriment although only the

older members of the group had actually seen the sketch.

"So who do you look down on," persisted James.

"Well actually I hope I don't look down on any of them, except perhaps those big motor yacht people who think they are at the top of the pile but don't enjoy themselves at all. But in the scheme of things that I was describing the easy answer is the group represented by little Ronnie, the people everyone can conspire to look down on, and they are the flotilla crowds. We all groan when we see a noisy crowd of inexperienced flotilla boats coming in, because inevitably they are loud, they are almost always incompetent, and they are entirely unaware of either failing. So yes, I suppose the bottom-feeders are the noisy English flotillas. Very unfair really, because everyone has to start somewhere, but at least they don't realise their place in things."

"Sorry to break things up but we'd better be going," Lavinia interrupted the sociological exposition.

As everyone gathered their various jackets, bags, phones and other impedimenta, Alex quietly drew Lavinia aside.

"Sorry to be a nuisance, but my mobile's flat and I've promised to ring Maggie. Could I possibly stay behind for a couple of minutes and use your land-line. I'll catch up with you in a few minutes."

"Of course – I know you'd like a little privacy. I showed you where Delaney's is earlier so just pull the door behind you."

The noisy group jostled down the stairs, into the evening air and set out for dinner.

"Sorry to interrupt….." Lavinia was starting to say as she burst into the flat minutes later. She was about to explain that August showers had caught them by surprise and she had returned to fetch umbrellas.

The telephone was sitting unused on the kitchen shelf. The living room was empty – so recently the scene of good-humoured socialising. Lavinia paused, then thought he must be in the cloakroom, but the door was open and the room was dark. She could see a light upstairs and without pausing for thought tip-toed up the stairs. She could faintly hear William and the others in the hallway below.

The light came from the open door of the darkroom that she had proudly shown Alex earlier. Her ring-binder of neatly filed negatives and contact prints was open on the table and Alex was quickly leafing through it. She saw him stop and slip a strip of negatives out of the folder, holding it briefly up to the light. As he did so he caught sight of Lavinia staring at him through the open door.

"I think you have some explaining to do," she said in more of a steady and challenging voice than she felt. "What the hell do you think you are doing here?"

At that moment William came striding up the stairs having heard Lavinia's outraged challenge. Without pause he put supportive hands on Lavinia's shoulders from behind and took in the scene.

"This had better be good," he grimly added to the challenge.

"Lavinia, I think you should call the police." William still hadn't adjusted to calling them the Garda.

Alex slumped forwards as if his bonhomie, strength and self-assurance had suddenly been switched off.

"I'm sorry Lavinia. I really am. I didn't mean to….. Oh God this is such a mess."

Chapter 33

Dublin: September 2006

Alex explains himself

"So you are telling me that this Greek guy really would do something life-threatening if he discovered that there was evidence of the delivery route?" William was absorbing, and trying to get clear, the muddled story that had been emerging over the delayed dinner. Once they had seen that Alex was obviously distraught, full of remorse and apology, they decided to continue the investigation over dinner. Alex wasn't eating much.

"I know it sounds far-fetched, but he organised a little demonstration of his ruthlessness when I tried to back out of doing the deliveries this year. I ended up in hospital and my car was wrecked. I have not the slightest doubt that if anything threatened his well-being, I'd be dead."

"What on earth did he do?" James was fascinated and not a little in awe of the whole story.

"Last year, after our last trip, actually the one Lavinia

was on, I tried to insist that I would do no more. He is hard to describe. He didn't threaten me at all. He maintains this false air of politeness and civility. But within minutes of leaving his house my car was rammed very expertly by someone, and I was catapulted into a wall. When I put it all together later it was obvious that it had been planned. He knew I was unhappy, and knew I'd try to back out. So he organised a little non-lethal demonstration for me which he has never explicitly acknowledged but cleverly made sure I was in no doubt about. I know it all sounds implausible, but honestly and truly I believe he is an absolutely ruthless and unscrupulous gangster. I don't doubt his willingness or his ability to hurt me or God forbid to hurt Maggie. I've been living in fear of him for two years now, and I know this may not seem rational, but I just knew that as soon as I saw that photograph, I had to stop it being made public where he would possibly see it. It isn't rational I know. How could anyone make all the links between that photograph and his sleazy operation – but believe me it seemed real to me."

"I can't believe I've caused so much trouble," Lavinia started to say. She felt her initial outrage completely swept aside by her sympathy for the obvious state of distress that Alex was in.

"Lavinia, this isn't your fault. So don't blame yourself. Alex, I think you are going to have to trust us, and explain how the whole thing started. If I can help you I will. But I need to be clear just what has been going on and how you got yourself into this mess." William was emerging from the evening as the clear thinker, the one with a voice of surprising authority, and was effortlessly taking the lead. The others waited for his questions and for his direction.

His experience at the hands of his crooked partner in Edinburgh had left him more realistic about the nasty side of apparently normal business life, and more able to think clearly about how to help the shattered Alex.

.

Chapter 34

London: September 2006.

Katharos briefs Alex

"Mr Fox. We need to talk. I think that you are going to your boat again soon?"

"Yes. I'm going in a couple of weeks – should be there most of October."

"I'll see you next Monday night Mr Fox. You will join me for a little drink and some mezes. We have things to organise."

"What time do you want me?"

"The usual of course Mr Fox. Come at eight o'clock. I will be waiting for you."

Alex hung up the telephone with a sick feeling in his stomach. The process was starting again. He had no choice but to go through with it, but he was cross with himself for seeming such a willing and compliant participant.

Maggie looked across at him.

"That was him, wasn't it?"

"Yes – his master's voice. He speaks and I jump. I'm so sick of this. I really wish it was all over."

"He has promised that this is the last time hasn't he?"

"Again – yes. Although he has never given me any reason to believe it when he says it. But there maybe is some logic this time in wanting to quit while he's ahead."

"What if you just sold the boat?"

"I've thought of it so many times. It seems the obvious way out doesn't it. But so far I've reacted against it because it would mean he was changing an important bit of my life. I don't want to give him that much power, and I know, I know, he already has it. It just seems symbolically the ultimate concession if I let him force me to sell up."

"I suppose there isn't really any benefit anyway. There would be nothing to stop him threatening you with exposure for everything you have done up to now, and forcing you to simply charter a yacht to do the same thing again."

"Exactly. He has me trapped whatever I do. The thing I really can't understand is why I didn't blow the whistle the very first time that he called. If I had gone to the police right at the start there must be a chance that they would have believed my story about being set up. But once I complied with his instructions wittingly, I was sunk. And he knows it."

"Easy to say that now, but you thought it was one trip and then you'd be clear. Besides, you were in the middle of all the mess of marriage break-up and you were really short of money. I don't think you were analysing things too well at the time."

"Nice of you to take that sympathetic view. But I can't imagine the police or customs being just as understanding."

"Too late to think that anyway. Let's just get this last trip over and done with. If he makes any more demands then you should sell the boat, refuse to be blackmailed, and if necessary go to the police yourself."

"Yes, one last time. How many is that now?"

"This time it really must be."

"OK. One last time and then we can stop worrying."

Alex was struggling to be positive, fighting the waves of despair that threatened to overwhelm him, and physically swallowing hard to avoid the sickness in his stomach getting out of control. He was more nervous than ever. His sleep was disturbed virtually every night. He knew he was drinking far too much in an attempt to blank out the nagging fear, and knew every morning when he woke hours before time to get up, that the drinking was making him feel worse rather than succeeding in its anaesthetic purpose. He woke each morning with a recurring feeling of panic. The dreams that he could remember seemed to have themes of chasing and desperate evasion. They always ended with him trapped, no more escape routes, the inevitability of capture about to overwhelm him. He always seemed to waken without the consequences of capture becoming clear. His dreams stopped short of his pursuers killing him, torturing him, or whatever it was they intended to do. The horrors were of the endless pursuit; the desperate running; the missing of trains or flights; and the sinking feeling of the impossibility of avoiding whatever it was that was about to engulf him. He woke momentarily relieved that it was only a dream. A split second later the reality of his worries swept away the relief, and he found himself drawing his knees up into a foetal position in a pathetic and unconscious reflex action.

Alex had developed an ulcer. He started to feel pains in his stomach at night and at times during the day. Being generally healthy, it took him time to acknowledge that it was something other than indigestion. Maggie forced him to go to the doctor, and the diagnosis was straightforward. Pains that increased with time since his last meal; reaction to spicy foods; general state of anxiety; it looked classic to the GP. He was put on a regime of antacid and soothing tablets, and his diet was altered to avoid the greasy and spicy foods that exacerbated the problem. But the glasses of wine and the 'nightcaps' of whisky that he increasingly couldn't avoid, negated the beneficial effects of the drugs and he was getting worse by the day.

Alex drove gingerly to Hampstead on Monday evening. He was superficially calm, but his stomach was giving the lie to the appearance. He drove through the gates and the floodlights came on as usual, though the September evening was far from dark enough to justify them.

The familiar routine followed, as Alex was led by old Katharos into the plush, over-upholstered room at the rear of the house.

"Good efening Mr Fox. Good to see you. I can assure you that this is the last time that our activities will be necessary. So you will please not raise unnecessary difficulties in this last errand for me."

"You know how I feel about it. The sooner it is over the better."

"Exactly Mr Fox. Another couple of weeks and it is over."

Katharos busied himself with the glasses of Metaxa. The dishes of accompanying nibbles were already spread on the table. Again Alex wondered about the domestic arrangements in this strange, slightly alien house. Was there a wife quietly sipping gins in the kitchen after ensuring her husband had all he needed? Were there domestic staff hidden out of sight? He didn't expect he would ever know, and didn't really care. Despite himself he was eager to grab the fiery glass of Metaxa and to feel the numbing warmth that affected his stomach as well as his head. He accepted the glass from Katharos, and responded to the gesture to pick up the little plate and help himself to some food. He picked a stuffed vine leaf, some olives, and some feta cheese, avoiding the tempting little cheese and spinach pies with their fatty pastry and ulcer-teasing spiciness.

They settled themselves in the plush red armchairs, each provided with a little table whose leather insert was protected by a neat lace doily. Again Alex wondered about the domestic touches and who was responsible for them. He sipped the brandy, and waited while it temporarily eased his stomach pain, before forking a portion of the stuffed vine leaf and chewing the lemony-bitter green-ness. Katharos as usual seemed to be in no hurry. While giving the impression of being unhurried, he actually wasted little time. His lumbering movements and ponderous delivery made for an atmosphere that had the pace firmly in Katharos' control. But Alex knew from experience that the business was actually dealt with quite quickly, and his dismissal would follow without delay.

"I need to tell you about some changes to the arrangement this time Mr Fox." He paused to sip his brandy, and looked ruminatively at the plate of food that was now balanced on his knee, reserving the little table for his glass and for the enormous crystal ashtray where his part-smoked cigar lay waiting.

"My associates have become worried that the arrival in Gatwick is not as safe as it used to be. While we have never had any trouble in the past, we have decided that this time a different route will be used."

"But I already have my tickets booked to come back through Gatwick at the end of the month. It will look odd if I change my usual arrangements."

"This need not concern you Mr Fox. In fact your role is a simpler one this time. We do not want to disturb the existing arrangement where you pick up the package. That is well tested and we do not need to disturb those who are meeting with you there. You will go to Kapi Creek as usual and our friends there will tell you at what time to make the rendezvous."

"What night do I need to go there?"

"Just the usual Mr Fox. Your habit is to arrive there on a Monday night I think, and only to return later in the week if our friends ask you to do so."

"OK. I can do that. We will have a party of four on the boat next week. I fly out with Maggie on Thursday, and the four arrive on Saturday. We can be in Kapi on the Monday and Friday if necessary."

"I think that is the best idea. You should plan for both. The delivery will be made on the Monday night as usual, but it will be important for you to be in the area at the end of the week also."

"What are these new arrangements?"

"Those making the delivery to you will not need to know any of this. Their sole concern is to make sure that you receive the package safely on Monday night. So far as they are concerned their role ends there, and you will carry on as usual. However, later in the week, on leaving Kapi Creek on the Saturday morning, you will make a short stay in Tomb Bay, perhaps for a visit to the tombs, whatever you think. You will tie up next to a Greek registered yacht called the Rodos, and while you send your guests ashore, you will transfer the package when requested to the crew on the Rodos."

"What if it isn't there? What do I do with the package?"

"It will be there Mr Fox. There will not be any problem. You will need to be there early in the morning I think if you are going to return your guests to Gocek on Saturday?"

"Yes, we like to be back in the marina late morning so they have time to pack and get sorted before leaving late afternoon. However as long as we are in the Marina by 3:00 pm there is still time to do everything. I can be in Tomb Bay by 11:00 am on Saturday. There won't be many other yachts around – they generally arrive late afternoon and Saturdays are quiet anyway. I'll take the group there for a look at the tombs and an early lunch before motoring back to Gocek."

"The Rodos will be waiting for you in Tomb Bay. If there is a change in plan someone will speak to you. Do not forget that we have many friends in the area. Your movements are well known to me and I can ask that someone contact you if necessary."

The threat as usual wasn't really explicit, but Alex was clear that Katharos was warning him that any unusual activity on his part would be noticed. If Katharos was able to organise a violent lesson for him in a leafy London avenue, how much more easily could he organise a 'message' in the relatively unsupervised waters off the Turkish coast.

"And that's it? I don't carry the package back to London this time?"

"You will be relieved to know that your responsibilities end in Tomb Bay. You do not need to know anything further."

"But why are you changing the routine? Have you heard that I am being watched? Is there some danger that I need to know about?"

The implications of the change of plan were worrying Alex. His agitation increased the more he thought that the Greek's network of informers and 'associates' might have raised a worry about Alex's trustworthiness. While logically he might have been relieved that he had to cross no borders with the illicit package, the deviation from the normal routine worried him and his grumbling stomach underlined the physical reality of the worry.

"Calm yourself Mr Fox. It is simply a precaution in case we have become too lazy about the route to London. It need not concern you at all. I thought it would make you happy that your responsibility was so limited on this occasion."

"It does. It does, of course, but I do find the whole

process a constant worry, and I'll be glad to get this last trip completed. This is the absolute end. I can't do it any more. My health is suffering from the stress of it, so I'm getting to the point where no matter what you threaten me with I just can't do any more."

Alex hadn't meant to say all of this. It just burst out of him with the emotion born of the tension and worry that had accumulated over the previous two years.

"I think you are not yourself, Mr Fox. It is not my way to 'threaten' as you put it. We have had a mutually profitable association for the last two years, and it is drawing to a natural close. Let us not be uncivilised about this please."

The charade continued. Alex's stomach was really paining him now. He wanted simply to get away and be done with the whole business. He promised himself that there would be a spell of total relaxation once this final delivery was complete. The complications of the handover to the Rodos needed a little thought, but that was for later.

"I'm sorry. One last delivery as you say. I will expect the usual message in Kapi when we get there."

"Just so, Mr Fox. My friends will tell you the time. And you will be in Tomb Bay on Saturday morning?"

"But why Kapi Creek the night before?"

"It is just a precaution Mr Fox. The delivery to the Rodos must be on Saturday morning, so it gives us a second opportunity to deliver to you if for some reason Monday night is not good."

"You mean if the Coastguard are out and about," Alex thought but didn't speak. He was also aware that specifying where Alex should be increased the ease with which Katharos could monitor his movements. It didn't matter particularly where he was on Tuesday, Wednesday, or Thursday if he could have his watchers ready to report that Alex was safely in Kapi on Friday and therefore ready to make the rendezvous on Saturday morning. It was a simple but effective precaution, and once again Alex was forced to admit to himself that Katharos was a deft and clever planner. He managed to stay out of trouble by thinking ahead, and having plans that could cope with the setbacks that he could predict. He did not underestimate the man, and he stopped himself from thinking further about the unscrupulous remedies he might have planned should he suspect that Alex wasn't playing absolutely straight with him. He did not doubt that they were in fact already in place, and that a signal from Katharos could precipitate a very nasty accident at sea, many miles from leafy Hampstead.

"May I wish you safe chourney, Mr Fox."

The time for dismissal had arrived. Alex was left with an unexpected change of plan that he had to welcome, but didn't understand.

"How will I be sure that I am dealing with the right people on the Rodos?"

"That will not be a problem Mr Fox. Leave the details to me. When the time comes you will be clear."

He was now walking down the hallway with the cigar-smoking Katharos half-a-pace behind him. Alex knew that if he slowed he would find the heavy arm on his shoulder conveying him towards the door and away from whatever secrets the other rooms in the house held. Just as he was reaching the front door and preparing to step to one side so that Katharos could deal with the security locks and release him, a figure stepped from the cloakroom on his left and reached out to unlock the door.

"Goodnight Mr Fox. I will be seeing you soon I hope." It was Iannis Junior waiting on guard at the door. He was conscious of an intake of breath from Katharos. As if he started to say something but decided against it. Iannis' eyes flicked to his father and the incipient smile disappeared. The unpleasant almost-sneer returned to the lips, and the defensive hostility returned to the eyes of the junior Katharos.

"What's going on there?" thought Alex to himself as he gratefully slipped out of the door and into the glare of the now-necessary floodlights. He let himself into the Polo, and had plenty to think about as he drove slowly back to Clapham and to Maggie.

He decided to continue to spare Maggie any of the details of the discussion. For some reason, perhaps based more on spy films he had absorbed than on any rational thought process, he still operated on the basis that the less Maggie knew the better. He knew that Maggie would put two and two together and make a large and worrying number if he told her about the change in plan. In fact it was just another detail that he was sparing Maggie. Compared with the total of the complexities that he was now hiding from her, this was an unimportant detail, but one that would disproportionately worry her. He resolved to continue to act as if this was an absolutely routine rendezvous and subsequent delivery.

Chapter 35

Gocek Coastguard base Turkey: 0200 hours 14th October 2006

Alex's guests en route to Gocek

The white Coastguard launch motored gently into the broad anchorage in Gocek. Anchor lights were visible on most of the yachts in the bay, and some of the large motor-vessels were still lit up as if electricity was just one more commodity to be flaunted. The Coastguard picked its way slowly through the anchored yachts, like a vigilant sheepdog shadowing the captive yacht. The journey from Kapi Creek had been painfully slow for the crew left on board, as the boarding party that had commandeered Alex's yacht motored back to the base in Gocek at 5 knots.

Following the boarding of the yacht, Alex was transferred first into one of the black inflatables, and then onto the fast Coastguard launch. The leader of the boarding party had instructions to secure the yacht, prevent any dumping of items overboard, and bring the entire party to the base where the crew could be questioned and the yacht searched. He explained to the two couples in perfect English that they were to remain quietly in their separate cabins, and await further instructions in Gocek. He politely but insistently requested their mobile phones, which he examined briefly and then dropped into his overall pocket. His pre-operational briefing had been thorough, so he was able to identify Maggie. Unsure of the extent of her complicity in Alex's activities, he apologetically, politely, but securely fastened her wrists with plastic cable-ties behind her back. She was seated uncomfortably in the main saloon, watched by a silent, dark-clad guard. Her arms behind her back, she couldn't sit comfortably, and she glared at the guard, who impassively watched her squirming discomfort with the air of one who had seen it all before.

"I demand to be told what is going on," Maggie repeated at intervals during the ninety minute voyage. "I am a British citizen and I am going to complain to the Embassy about our treatment."

The guard might have understood perfectly, but he gave no sign of it. So far as facial clues were concerned he might have been deaf. Occasionally when Maggie became more agitated, he said something harsh in Turkish and gestured backwards with his machine-pistol – ever ready in his right hand, and otherwise resting across his left forearm. It was almost sufficient discouragement to persuade Maggie to give up her protests, but her anger rose again a few minutes later and they repeated the fruitless cycle again and again.

"What have you done to my husband?" Maggie demanded, deciding that strict definitions of their relationship were irrelevant in the circumstances. "You cannot just board an English registered yacht and take away the skipper. There are international rules about this."

The guard looked bored but watchful. She might as well have been shouting at a tailor's dummy but she had to vent her anger and her frustration. It kept her panic and despair at bay. As long as she could shout and demand she felt as if she was keeping some sort of positive grip on things, perhaps just on herself. If she gave in she would quickly collapse in tearful hopelessness. She kept up the brave, outraged front, largely for her own benefit, and without any sign of progress.

In the bow cabin, Jack, the doctor, and his wife Patricia were whispering together. They were shaken and still suffering from the combination of alcohol and fear.

"I really need to go to the loo," pleaded Patricia. "I'm going to open the door and ask them if I can."

"I think you're going to have to hold on I'm afraid."

"I can't. Oh Jack, I wish we hadn't come," she wailed. She started to lose the calm self-control which they had all been surprised to find themselves maintaining.

"Oh all right, I'll see if I can get them to allow you."

Jack opened the door of the cabin a crack and found himself eyed warily by the guard who was standing watching the opening door. With quick gestures Jack pointed at the heads compartment and at his wife and put his hands together in a begging gesture. The guard shouted up the companionway to the cockpit, where the officer in charge was quietly watching their progress through the night back to Gocek. With surprising politeness he came down the steps into the saloon and addressed Jack, still holding the partially open door.

"Your wife may use the toilet sir, but the door must remain open at all times. If she does not want to use the toilet in these circumstances, I will find a plastic bucket for her."

Jack looked somewhat taken aback at the response, and turned back into the cabin to find a wide-eyed Patricia shaking her head vehemently.

"I'm not going to use it with those men watching," she hissed.

"Well do you want a bucket then?" asked Jack pragmatically but a little unsympathetically.

"No I do not want a bucket. Oh hell Jack – I'll have to do something."

The officer understood the general sense of the situation, even if he couldn't hear Patricia's urgent pleading. He unexpectedly relented on condition that Patricia did not flush the toilet. He opened the door to the heads compartment, and opening the cupboard beneath the washbasin, closed the sea-cocks for both the toilet and basin. With the hatch closed and watched from on deck, there was no other way Patricia could get rid of anything from her possession – so he reasoned that it was safe to allow her the privacy.

"I am sorry for the inconvenience," he announced, "but it is important that we bring this yacht to our base exactly as we found it. Please do not attempt to discharge anything overboard."

Patricia hurried past Jack and the two guards, casting a dubious glance at Maggie as she went. The situation had left the guests with a puzzle. They had been interrupted in the process of putting into words how wonderful they thought Alex and Maggie had been, so it was difficult to switch instantly to blaming them for the trouble with the Coastguard. But the more they thought about it the more it seemed as if some blame must lie with their erstwhile hosts.

"They knew Alex's name," Julie whispered to Bruce in the aft cabin. "It looks as if they knew exactly who they were looking for. So he must have done something."

"I just can't understand it," Bruce responded worriedly. "Why on earth would they have been mixed up in anything underhand? How could they afford to take risks in foreign waters with what was their livelihood?"

"Why do people ever get mixed up in crime?" Julie was now clear that that was the only explanation. "I hope they will know that we are just paying guests for the week and don't know anything about it."

"What do you think will happen in Gocek?"

"I was going to ask you that."

"Well I think that they'll take our details, and send us on our way. They are obviously treating Alex as the main suspect – he's been taken onto their boat, and it looks as if they are treating Maggie as if she's involved."

"They won't just let us go."

"No, they'll probably hold us while they do a search of the boat. It would be silly to let us go before that. But given that they'll find nothing in our belongings, I'd reckon they'll let us go before long."

"I don't know how you can be so calm about this. We're under arrest in Turkey. Don't you remember Midnight Cowboy? Do you know what the jails are like?"

"No point of getting ahead of ourselves. They must

let us make a phone-call in the morning. I'll get the British Embassy in Ankara. Or do you think we should phone Jamie and let him start agitating from back home?"

"I think the embassy should come first, but phone Jamie as well if you can. Get him to phone our MP whoever that is now. Phone the police at home. They're bound to have contacts."

"We're assuming that they'll let us make a call," said Bruce, "but I think we're relying on what we see in crime movies rather than knowing that rules about phone calls actually apply here."

"Oh God. Do you think we'll be locked up without anybody knowing? Oh Bruce. This is a nightmare. I don't know what to do."

"Let's make sure that they know we aren't linked with Alex and Maggie other than paying them for this week."

"I can't believe they've done anything. It will turn out to be some administrative error. Some forms not filled in or some licence Alex forgot to pay for."

"And they mount a James Bond style operation for some missing paperwork? I don't think so. Whatever they are after Alex for, it is serious. I just hope we can distance ourselves from them."

"What are Jack and Patricia doing? I heard Jack's voice. Something is going on out there."

Bruce opened the door a crack to look into the saloon. He could see the back of the guard standing over Maggie. He couldn't see past the bulky black figure but could sense that something was going on. He heard the heads door open and the guard moved slightly as Patricia moved awkwardly down the saloon to the bow cabin. He quietly closed the door, without the guard being aware of his actions.

"They've let Patricia use the loo. I wonder how they managed to persuade them to allow that?"

"Talking of which, I wonder if they'd allow me? All that wine is catching up with me. I feel totally sober now – amazing what a fright will do."

"Do you want me to ask them? I don't want to antagonise them, but if you need to go I'll try."

"I don't want to wait till we're in Gocek if that's where they are taking us. God knows what will happen there and I'd rather be prepared."

Bruce knocked the door loudly and then opened it again enough for him to attract the attention of the guard. With a weary air the coastguard shouted again up to the cockpit, and the officer appeared down in the saloon again.

The same warning was issued to Bruce and Julie as had been given to Patricia, and one by one they made their way to the heads, and an air of strained normality almost resurfaced. Julie looked at Maggie, who started to ask her if she was OK, but the guard abruptly intervened to put an end to communication between the different groups of prisoners.

They remained in the cabin for the rest of the journey, until they became aware of Turkish voices on deck, heard the change of speed of the engine, and finally the gentle bump as they came alongside a dock. After a few minutes the engine noise stopped and they waited expectantly.

Chapter 36

Gocek: 14 October 2006

Alex's guests on land

"Best be ready to go for a trip here," Bruce maintained his calm, matter-of-fact air. They decided there was no point in trying to pack their bags as it would all be searched anyway, so they packed their passports, travel documents and money into a day-bag, grabbed a warm jacket, and waited for instructions. Feet sounded down the companionway and an authoritative voice began,

"Ladies and gentlemen, please open the cabin doors and pay attention."

Jack and Bruce immediately opened their respective doors and looked enquiringly at each other. There was no sign of Maggie, who had been already taken from the yacht.

"I apologise for this disruption to your holiday. You will be taken ashore and we will have some questions for you. We also will need to search your cabins, but please be aware that everything will be safe. Please bring your personal documents and travel information with you, but leave everything else in the cabin. As soon as you are ready please join me on the dock."

Bruce looked at Julie and nodded, they exchanged wan smiles as they made their way up the steps to the cockpit and stepped across to the concrete dock. Jack and Patricia were moments behind them.

"Well what do you make of this then?" Jack muttered to Bruce.

"I'm going to try to phone the British Embassy as soon as possible, but I don't know what to expect here. Innocent bystander approach I think."

"Exactly old man. No idea what this is all about. Co-operate in every way. I've read about this – just be completely polite and do as they say."

"Don't you worry. I'm not planning to run for it."

The four were led up a floodlit gravel path to a functional-looking military style building; freshly painted stones along the path, metal outer doors, and an institutional corridor led them to a set of hard wooden chairs in the corridor. They were signalled to sit and wait. The bare light bulbs in crude old-fashioned wall fittings reminded them of their worst images of Turkish jails, but the clean corridor and the general politeness of their captors reassured them that they were not about to be locked up and the key thrown away.

A weary looking officer in a creased white uniform emerged from a door beside them.

"Dr Fulton?" he said.

Jack stood up and nodded.

"Would you and Mrs Fulton come in here please."

They entered the metal-desked office, leaving Bruce and Julie to whisper anxiously in the corridor. A young guard was posted between them and the entrance, but he stood at ease, gun in its holster, and stared fixedly at the wall with no sign of desire to talk.

"Your passports please Doctor." The formalities in the office began. The officer examined the passports, with their visas dating from one week earlier, and checked the airline tickets, insurance documents, and finally the copies of e-mails arranging the charter with Alex.

"May I see the bag please?" Jack handed over the day-bag and the contents were systematically emptied onto the desk. The bottle of water; the travel tissues; the sun cream; and the filofax that Jack took everywhere.

"Why were you in Kapi Creek twice this week Doctor?"

"I think it was just a handy place to be last night – we fly back to London today and Alex, the skipper, wanted to be a short distance from Gocek. We were all happy with that as we liked it the first time we were there, and it seemed a practical idea."

"Who suggested it?"

"Well the skipper of course. We discuss options each day, but basically we go along with what he suggests."

"Where else were you going to call?"

"Oh yes, I think we were going to stop in Tomb Bay to have a look at the tombs on the way to Gocek – nothing else – we planned to be back in the marina early afternoon I think."

"You have seen these tombs before?"

"No. We read about them and have seen pictures, so

it seemed a good idea to call in there."

"Tell me about your first visit to Kapi Creek." The officer seemed to be after something that Jack was unaware of.

"We just arrived in the afternoon – Monday it would have been – and did the usual things. We all went for a swim; we all sat around in the sun. Bruce and I walked over the hill to see across to the other side of the cape. We all had a drink on the boat before dinner, and then ate in the taverna. I don't remember anything unusual."

"Was Mr Fox with you all the time?"

"He didn't come with us for the walk. I think he was chatting to the taverna owner. He was on the boat the rest of the time, and ate with us in the evening."

"And he didn't leave you at all that evening?"

"He left the taverna before us," Patricia reminded Jack.

"What time was this?"

"What do you think dear? I can't remember precisely." Jack had hazier recollections of the details than Patricia due to the enthusiasm of his enjoyment of the Turkish wine.

"Well we probably ate about eight o'clock, and we sat on for a good while afterwards. If Alex left after the food it was probably some time between nine and ten."

"Did you see him again that night?"

"Yes, he was waiting for us on the boat when we got back – must have been eleven or so."

"Did he say what he had been doing?"

"Don't think we asked him. He had charts and the pilot book out on the table and I think we had a chat about where we would go for the next few days. That was the usual pattern."

"And did you see him meet with or talk to people other than the taverna owner?"

"Not that I remember. Now look here," Jack was starting to feel more confident, "we need to telephone the British Embassy to sort out whatever is going on here."

"There will be time for that later Dr Fulton. It is three o'clock in the morning. This is not a time for making phone-calls."

Jack didn't argue. He hadn't really been told if he could or couldn't make the call, just that it wasn't worthwhile at this hour. He decided to wait.

"If you would take your seats outside again please Doctor, Mrs Fulton." The officer gestured towards the door, and made no movement to hand back the documents or the rest of the contents of the bag. Jack hesitated, eyeing the phone which was now with his other belongings.

"Your belongings are quite safe here Dr Fulton, please wait outside."

They did as they were asked and exchanged shrugs and raised eyebrows with Bruce and Julie as they swapped places. After a seemingly interminable delay, which was probably only fifteen minutes, Julie and Bruce emerged from the office and took their seats again.

"What did he ask you?" Patricia whispered to Julie.

"Really just about why we were in Kapi, and who decided where we went. He seemed interested in Alex really. What about you?"

"Same thing. He's got our passports and phones."

"Ours too. Bruce asked for them and he was told to

be patient."

They sat mostly silently for 30 minutes while voices could be heard in other offices and in their interview room. There was evidently another door into it as no-one passed them in the corridor.

"Do you realise we didn't ask about Alex or Maggie?" Julie said guiltily to Bruce.

"I certainly do. Part of the distance we want to create. I don't want them to think we are linked in any way other than as customers."

"It seems, I don't know, maybe disloyal or something."

"You don't think it was disloyal of them to land us in the middle of all this?"

"I suppose."

The time dragged on.

Light started to appear in the sky before they saw more activity.

Two of the black-clad guards came noisily into the corridor, and seeing the four English captives immediately went silent. Their black overalls were dusty, their hands were still covered in the latex gloves they presumably used when searching. They looked tired and dishevelled as they knocked on the officer's door, and when summoned went in.

The four waiting English captives could hear voices which sounded like the two guards making a report and then being questioned. It lasted only a few minutes. The door opened again and the black-clad figures disappeared down the corridor and round a corner. Silence again.

"Ssh, he's on the phone," whispered Patricia, who

was nearest the officer's door. "He's reporting to someone I bet."

A minute later there was the single ding of the telephone receiver being replaced, the sound of a chair scraping on the floor, and finally the door opened.

"Please come in all of you."

They filed into the office, and could see their belongings laid out on the officer's desk. A closed manila file was alongside them.

"On behalf of the Sahil Guvenlik – the Coastguard – I would like to thank you for your patience and co-operation. I am sorry you have been inconvenienced. You are now free to collect your belongings and return to the yacht. I would ask you please to complete your packing right away, and bring your bags back to the building here. I will arrange for you to be transported into town where you can get some breakfast at a hotel and wait for the time for your flight."

They were all rather stunned by the simplicity of it. It seemed too easy. However without comment they did as requested, and made their way back to the yacht. They found it still under guard, but with no-one aboard. In their cabins they found evidence of every item having been moved and every storage place emptied. However nothing seemed to be missing or damaged, so they gratefully set about their packing with minimal fuss. They found themselves still whispering to each other in their respective cabins.

"What on earth is going on?" Patricia hissed to Jack.

"I don't know and I don't want to know. I just know that they are happy to let us go, so I'm going to get on with it before they change their minds. Where did you put my razor?"

"What about Maggie and Alex?"

"I don't think we can do anything to help them, and I don't want to get mixed up in whatever this is all about, so let's just keep our heads down and do exactly what they say."

Patricia reluctantly complied. As her own anxiety had receded, she had found herself worrying more about her new friends, who had seemed so normal, so straightforward, and, well, so English.

"I really think we should do something," she persisted.

"Let's get to the hotel and think about it," Jack insisted.

In the other cabin a similar anxiety and matching reluctance were evident. The upshot was that they emerged onto the dock with their bags packed and no mention was made to the guards about Alex or Maggie. As Jack struggled up the steps with the bag, Patricia guiltily scribbled a note to Maggie and Alex on the open logbook on the chart table.

"Hope you are OK. They are sending us home. Ring when you can. Patricia."

She salved her conscience with the gesture, and didn't consult Jack, who was intent on self-preservation and not entertaining any comradely ideas at all.

The bags were loaded into the back of what appeared to be a staff car, and they were driven by a young, silent cadet into the main street of Gocek, where the early morning sunshine revealed the humdrum daily activities. Shopkeepers were unlocking their shutters; the racks of souvenirs and clothes were being wheeled out onto the clean-swept street. Locals shouted morning greetings to one another. Another routine day in a quiet little town where nothing ever happened.

The four dragged their bags into the only real hotel in the centre, a small family-run establishment with twelve rooms and a tiny swimming pool. A feeling of disorientation was hard to shake from their consciousness. The horrors and anxieties of the night were still chronologically recent but felt disconnected and unreal in the context of the normality of the wakening town. They rang the tinkling bell on the counter and wondered how they were going to pass the long hours till their evening flight.

Chapter 37

Mugla Jail, October 2006

Alex summarising the story so far.

He thought back over Maggie's perception of the messy sequence of events that had led to their arrest. She could piece together the narrative from the fateful day when he searched out the previous owner of the old Mercedes SLC. He had described to Maggie the first visit to Katharos in London; the preparation for the Grand Tour with Liz; and the strained oddity of the visit to Katharos' supposed cousins in Thessaloniki. How did he fail to suspect that all was not as it seemed? In fact "as it seemed" was a strange term to use. With the benefit of hindsight he realised that it had "seemed" downright suspicious at the time. It was now annoyingly obvious, and it had been blindly stupid of him not to have paid attention to the clues that he was being manipulated.

The examination of the car by Iannis Junior in London, and the subsequent subtle messages between father and son had been obvious enough for him to notice. He had registered them at the time, but without real thought had decided to ignore them. The similar process in Greece, when he was obliged to hand over the car keys while he and Liz were kept out of the way for a day – it was blindingly obvious in retrospect. He could only excuse himself on the grounds that he was preoccupied with making the Grand Tour a success, and with the constant attention to the relationship with Liz. What a waste of time that had been. A swan-song. A deceptive spell of harmony which didn't survive the return to humdrum routine, and the intrusion of the years of hurt and deception. Maggie had not dwelt on that bit of the history. Perhaps she didn't like to pay conscious attention to her predecessor in his life, so hadn't analysed the sequence of events, nor chastised him for his early blindness to the steps in setting him up.

She concentrated instead on the time since her involvement. It surprised Alex that she hadn't been more resentful of the extent to which he had tried to keep her in the dark. It was another "if only". Perhaps she would have been able to persuade him to confront the issue rather than step by step, concession by concession, becoming more entrapped by each favour he was forced into carrying out for Katharos. By the time he had told her the whole story in Kapi Creek last year, he had built up such a history of misdeeds that he could not conceive of the possibility of going to the police or the Customs to admit his complicity.

Maggie had kept up a constant pressure on him to confront Katharos, and to say "no more". But each time he failed to do that she had loyally and forgivingly stuck by him. She had continued to give him the support he needed.

He felt stupid for having deceived her at the outset, and now even stupider for allowing himself to wade back into the mire of deception following the warning ramming of his car. He now found the failure to come clean about the Dublin adventure was almost pathologically bizarre. It had driven him further into the dark double-thinking world of secrecy and half-truths, where every statement had to be checked before it was made to ensure that it fitted with the authorised version of the truth.

At 8:00 o'clock Alex became aware of an increase in noise as the jail's daily routine ground into action. He heard the scraping slide of the barred hatches on the old metal doors, followed by the tinny clatter of breakfast mug and bowl being handed to each inmate. His own door-hatch opened noisily and a guard looked in from a safe distance before wordlessly proffering the unappetising bowl of bread and sour-tasting cheese, and the tin mug of lukewarm black Turkish chai.

He accepted the breakfast because there didn't seem to be any sensible alternative, and gingerly tried the bread and cheese. The cheese he decided was inedible unless he was absolutely starving, but the bread served a purpose in giving him something to chew and to keep his churning stomach a little quieter.

He paced about the cell, which allowed him only three unambitious steps in one direction and two across. He sat down again on the edge of the filthy bed. He paced again. His agitation was coming in waves, and increasing. The impatience to get his world in order and get out of this cell was becoming overwhelming. The rising panic over

Maggie was threatening to drive him to irrational shouting and ranting at the guards, or more probably at the bare unhearing walls.

Chapter 38

Arif

Iannis and Arif: summer 2000

Iannis Junior met Arif when he was on holiday on the Turkish coast. His father disapproved of this holiday visiting the historically hostile shores, but Iannis Junior ignored his father's annoyance and took off with some friends from the other restaurants in Marylebone. They stayed in a hotel by the beach in Olu Deniz – an area so picturesque that it featured in many of the colour supplement advertisements for Turkish holidays. They rose late in the morning and spent the afternoons sunbathing and swimming, watching the uninhibited girls from non-Turkish backgrounds, and preparing the way for later nightclub encounters.

Each evening the three friends showered and after-shaved themselves for the evening assault on the village night-life. The invasion of the inland part of the village, some way back from the beach, began at about 8:00 pm.

The friends made their way noisily to a cafe on the main street that sold Turkish food almost indistinguishable from the Greek food that Iannis was used to. They ordered beers and gyro pitas that came with onions and fresh garlic-laced yoghurt dressing. They laughed and teased one-another as the low-cost food and more expensive beers were swallowed and re-ordered.

By 9:00 o'clock the main street was beginning to buzz with the expectant holidaymakers as they moved from shop to shop and bar to bar. Groups of males and females tried to study one another surreptitiously. This ritual involved exaggerated laughter, whispers, pauses to examine irrelevant shop windows, and a general frisson of expectant excitement when eye met eye and glances were noticed and exchanged.

Between eleven and midnight the reconnaissance was largely over and people were settling on the nightclub that was to be their choice for the night. The decision involved a cautious checking of where most other people were going, as the trade washed unevenly around the available clubs. The Golden Shore might have a lucky week when a disproportionate number of good-looking English girls happened to choose it on their first night. The other clubs would suffer while the short-term holiday-makers continued to favour the club that had looked most promising the previous night. It was hard to break the pattern once established, so the night-spots all competed on arrival nights to tempt the best looking females into their seedy and noisy interiors.

Iannis was excited by the freedom and the easygoing availability of the girls he met in the clubs. It was so much simpler than in London, where he was as likely to be rebuffed as to find an encouraging welcome. His dark skinned good looks were an advantage here, while they were of questionable worth back home. English girls on holiday were much more likely to take a risk with a foreign-looking stranger than they were in Manchester or Leeds. The excitement of someone from a different background added spice to the encounter, and the certainty of being back home the following week meant that the risk of long term complications was minimal.

Iannis met Arif at the bar in his nightclub. Arif was serving some drinks, but mostly keeping an eye on the waiters and constantly scanning the dancers and drinkers. He was wearing the fake Breitling watch that peeped out from the partially rolled sleeve of his genuine Ralph Lauren shirt. He was making significant money from the nightclub for six months every year. The older locals regarded him with some suspicion, and choked on the prices he charged for drinks in his club. No-one over 40 ever ventured inside, nor could they see the sense of paying double the normal price for their bottle of Efes. The younger locals paid the price because it was such a good place for finding their short-term love-affairs.

Iannis sat at the bar casting a professional eye over the operation. He could see how Arif monitored the waiters, just as he himself did in London. He could almost see the brain working as Arif watched the trays of drinks, calculated the prices and watched the till. He saw the slight smile flicker across Arif's face every time a large order of house cocktails was dispatched. Iannis could imagine the staggering profit margin on the unbranded spirits that went into the fruity mix. He also saw Arif's eyes constantly roving round the club, watching the new arrivals, checking for potential trouble, and occasionally lingering over a particularly beautiful visitor. Iannis had watched when some noisy English youths started disrupting the jovial atmosphere. The belligerent exchanges with people who bumped into them, the excessive swearing, and the aggressive body language all indicated a potential problem. It seemed as if it took only a raised eyebrow on Arif's impassive face to bring the club's heavy-duty security men into action. The potential problems were out on the street minus their beer bottles before most people noticed the disturbance. Iannis was impressed.

The two recognised in each other some sort of kindred spirit. They shared an air of quiet, well-groomed, wealthy confidence. They were casually dressed naturally, but expensively. Just as Iannis had noticed Arif's professional eye monitoring every transaction, his own quietly professional observation hadn't gone unnoticed.

"You in the business then?" Arif asked him in a lull in the music.

"Yeah, but not as big as this."

"Where are you?"

"Small place in London. Just here for a week to get away."

"What sort of place you got then?"

"Restaurant and bar, but we have a few other business deals on the go." For some reason Iannis felt a need to project a more dynamic image than he usually allowed himself.

"Business good?"

"Yeah. Keeps us going. Always looking for something new though."

Iannis sensed that there was a potential ally behind the bar. An unformed impulse prompted him to indicate gently that he was interested in business, not too brashly, not too pushily, but enough to open the door a crack.

"Always got to keep moving haven't you. I change this place every year. New lights, new sound, new DJs – gotta keep moving."

"Looks as if you're doing OK."

"Yeah – but there are a few other things that I'm always looking at."

"Same here. No such thing as standing still. You're going backwards if you think you're standing still. That's what I tell my old man. He's too comfortable, too settled. That's when you start going down."

"Better go here. Catch you later. See you on the beach maybe."

"Yeah, buy you a beer if you get down there tomorrow."

"Cheers." And with that Arif reached a fresh beer for Iannis and raised his hand to indicate no money was required. Nothing more was said that night about business or about meeting up, but as Iannis was leaving Arif nodded to him silently. They would meet on the beach no doubt.

Next afternoon Arif indeed arrived on the beach. He didn't trudge down from his cheap hotel like all the holidaymakers. He arrived in his speedboat, with flamboyant style. As he approached the beach, he dropped an anchor astern, and controlled the boat's gentle approach to the shelving sand. At sensible wading depth he tied off the anchor line and stepped confidently from the bow of the boat, bringing a light bow-anchor with him to drop on the sand.

He adjusted his RayBan sunglasses and walked up the sloping beach towards the green-shaded drinks bar that supplied the sunbathers. Iannis had guessed that this was the sensible spot to try to meet up, and had found a sun-lounger close by the bar. He was half-dozing in the shade of the large yellow umbrella when he heard the approach of the powerful speedboat and raised himself on an elbow to watch the arrival. As Arif strolled towards the bar, Iannis nonchalantly raised a hand in the air to acknowledge the arrival.

"Hey man, how's the head today?" greeted Arif cheerfully.

"No problem. Fairly quiet night last night. Saving myself for a last night splash-out tonight."

"Last night? Have to make sure you have a good one."

"Don't worry, I'm going to be in your place in time to meet the girl of my dreams. Hope you have her lined up for me."

"No worries. There should be plenty of chicks there tonight – their last night too so they won't be wasting any time. Anyway, you do any water-ski?"

"Na. Never had the chance. Nice boat though."

"Come on I'll show you how to ski. Dead easy."

The two went easily down the beach, Iannis grabbing his t-shirt and towel as he went. Arif helped him onto the bow of the boat, then retrieved the shore anchor, and hopped on the boat himself. He started the engine but left it ticking over as he pulled the boat gently backwards away from the shore, hauling rhythmically on the stern-anchor line. He stowed the coiled anchor warp with its short length of chain and fisherman's anchor. Then, as the boat bobbed gently on the lapping waves, he settled himself at the wheel and they accelerated ostentatiously away from the beach.

"Wow," shouted Iannis over the noise of the powerful outboard engine. He had planned to act really cool, as if this was nothing new to him, but it actually was a novel experience for someone who had only ever used the safe little day-boats his relatives rented out at their taverna in Thessaloniki. Those watching from the beach saw the graceful curve of the wake trace the path of the boat as it left the bay and turned west towards the headland which hid Gemiler Island and Karacaoren from view. Arif treated Iannis to a fast circuit of the bay and then a slow trickle through the anchorage in Karacaoren, pointing out the Byzantine ruins on the little islands and the secluded rough taverna that served the anchorage.

"Good business here," he confided. "You pay three times what you pay in town for a meal here, and they are full every night."

"How come?" asked Iannis.

"Yachts," came the simple reply. "This bay will be full of yachts tonight, and they have nowhere else to eat. Besides they are used to high prices – they have no idea what you pay in the village for food."

"Ever thought of trying it yourself?"

"Yeah, I will do one year. Enough on my plate with the club in the village, but if I get someone to run it I might do this. Nice life – no crowds, no trouble, just people paying whatever you ask and tipping like crazy. Different sort of people from the ones in the cheap apartments in the village."

They accelerated away from the anchorage and covered the short distance to Gemiler Island in a couple of minutes. Arif slowed again as they passed the end of the island and entered the channel between the island and the mainland shore. As the view opened up, Iannis could see the jumbled remains of houses and churches that seemed to cover all the available land.

"Wow," he exclaimed again.

"This place was a famous old pilgrimage site," explained Arif. "It's covered with ancient stuff. Great sunsets from the top. You should go some day."

They continued the gentle circumnavigation of the island, watching the swimmers, checking the sunbathers on the anchored yachts, and enjoying the experience of being watched by the people they were watching. Iannis was enjoying himself.

They left the eastern end of the island and sped noisily across the open water to another headland on the mainland shore, which hid a series of sheltered bays tucked into the serrated rocky shoreline. Arif slowed again as he approached one of the empty bays, and as they came to a standstill he dropped the bow anchor into the crystal clear water. When he had satisfied himself that they were secure, he killed the engine and flipped open the cold-box that was hidden under the rear seat of the boat.

"Beer?" asked Arif as he lifted a beer and a coke out of the box.

"You not having one?"

"Na. I just drink coke mostly. I like to see others drink but I don't do much myself. That's the difference the religion makes. Not that I do anything else about it, but you sort of grow up in a Muslim atmosphere where alcohol isn't allowed, and it's only the last few years that people are loosening up and drinking as much as the tourists. I haven't got into the habit I guess. Just prefer to have a whisky when I'm relaxing, but I can't be bothered with all the rest."

Iannis took the proffered beer can and popped the seal.

"'Fraid I really like the beer here, so I'll have one."

"Want to have a go at the skiing afterwards?"

"I'll only fall off and make a fool of myself."

"Who's to see you?"

"That's true."

They were not in view of the beach back at Olu Deniz, nor could the anchored yachts see into the secluded bay.

"OK, that's cool. I'll give it a try."

When they finished their drinks, Arif fitted Iannis with a buoyancy jacket, showed him how to fit the water-skis, and gave him the standard instructions about keeping his arms straight, leaning backwards, and letting the boat do the pulling. After a lot of laughter and a few false starts, Arif managed to pull Iannis to his feet on the skis, and he executed a gentle circle round the bay, venturing far enough out to get a good expanse of water before turning back into the sheltered bay. Iannis grinned like a child as he completed another circle, but his arms were aching, his legs were aching, and his stance began to go wrong as they finished the turn. Arif could see him tiring and considerately slowed the boat so that Iannis gently subsided into the water as the speed dropped.

"Well done! You got it."

"That's fantastic. Didn't think I'd get up at first. That's really cool."

They laughed and congratulated one-another before tucking the skis and rope away on the boat and accelerating back out into the wider bay to make their way back to the beach. Arif took a long sweep across the bay and over to the eastern coastline with its great gorges cutting down from the mountains behind. It was a dramatic and forbidding landscape, with tree-covered lower slopes, scree covered heights, and no sign of habitation.

"Used to be great smuggling country," shouted Arif above the noise of the wind and the pounding of the boat over the waves. "Lots of places to hide, and hidden paths up into the mountains. This coast is famous for it."

Iannis nodded as he scanned the coastline and imagined how impossible it would be for the authorities to monitor all the potential landing places. He looked thoughtfully at Arif and wondered again about his new friend.

They approached the beach slowly, taking care to watch out for the swimmers who seemed oblivious to the danger of being too close to a propeller in the water. Arif nosed the boat in to the beach and let Iannis jump off into the shallow water before reversing carefully back the way he had approached. Then with a casual wave of his left hand he once again accelerated away from the watching beach.

Iannis and his two London friends had drifted apart

during the week in Olu Deniz. Attachments to different girls meant that each was more interested in pursuing female company than having a night with 'the lads'. The three met early each evening in the apartment, and without rancour chatted about the different plans for the evening. They expected and didn't mind the fact that they would end up in different places as the night wore on. They started the night as usual with some beer and food in the little pita shop that had become their regular haunt, and wished each other good luck for their last night on the town.

Iannis was the one without a prior arrangement with a girl, but he was relaxed, and looking forward to the excitement of finding someone new as they walked up the buzzing street to Arif's club. They split up at the door, and as the other two went off to find their girlfriends, Iannis circled the floor looking for the unattached girls while trying to look cool and confident.

He gravitated to the bar and ordered another beer. There was a high stool available so he sat there and watched the crowd, still a little thin as it was early. By the time he had ordered his next beer the club was in full swing. The dance-floor was full of t-shirted couples, the tables were crowded, and most of the wall-space was taken up by nonchalant-looking single men, eyeing the crowds hungrily.

Above the noise of the music it was almost impossible to hear what was happening. Two people with heads almost touching had to shout to be heard by one-another. So it was the movement that Iannis saw rather than the crash of the doors bursting open. Like a wave in a tank, the physical push and the recognition of what was happening washed around the club. Those furthest away were dancing or shouting at each other, while those nearer the door had turned to see the intrusion and stopped in their tracks.

A spearhead of about ten armed men had burst through the doors. Most carried what Iannis could recognise as automatic rifles, and wore a uniform that he had seen occasionally round the village. It was the Jandarma, the semi-military police force that was responsible for law and order outside the cities, and particularly for border security and anti-smuggling enforcement. One was making his way forcefully towards the DJ who was poring over his playlist and seemed unaware of the raid. As long as the music blasted out, there was no chance of addressing or controlling the crowd.

Iannis felt a sudden firm touch on his shoulder. Arif was indicating urgently that he should duck down and come behind the bar. He crouched and slipped under the access hatch in the bar counter, and found Arif propelling him low and fast out of a back door into the alley behind the club. As he went he felt a solid, plastic-wrapped package being placed firmly in his right hand.

"Take this. Run." Hissed Arif, before disappearing back through the door into the club.

Iannis listened for a moment before running. He knew that a planned raid by the Jandarma wouldn't ignore the rear exit from the club. But the door he had emerged through wasn't one of the main and obvious back doors. There were two, one at either side leading into the alleys that separated the club from its neighbouring buildings on each side. The door that Iannis had emerged through was a small and inconspicuous one, almost hidden in the detritus and undergrowth in the untidy laneway right behind the club. Instead of running either up or down the lane, which would take him past the ends of the alleys where the emergency exit doors were no doubt already guarded, he vaulted the waist-high fence that separated the lane from the village houses and gardens that ran parallel to the main street. Keeping low and being as quiet as he could, he made his way through what seemed to be vegetable patches and back yards to a point 100 metres along the lane, where he could see the rear of one of the competing night-clubs.

The package in his hand felt solid but slightly malleable. It was about half the size of a supermarket pack of sausages back in London, but was heavier and felt dense. He was just able to stuff it into the pocket of his jeans, where his loose overhanging t-shirt made it unobtrusive.

He could see that the rear door of the club was ajar. There were a couple of men relieving themselves in the laneway, and their voices could be heard along with the escaping noise of the music and chatter of the club. The two finished their business and slipped back inside the club. Iannis squeezed through an old gate in the fence and three paces took him across the lane and through the still unlocked door.

The club was less busy than Arif's, but sufficiently big and crowded that no-one seemed to notice his arrival. He moved a few metres away from the door and leaned against the wall. After a few moments to blend into the crowd he pushed his way to the bar and asked loudly for "another beer".

Standing with his back to the bar, bottle in hand, he watched the bouncers make their routine circuit of the club and wearily secure the emergency exit crash-bar. He had been extremely lucky with the timing of his arrival. He felt his heart still pounding not from exertion but from the drama of the last three minutes. His calculation that, following the raid on Arif's club, the safest place to be was in another club, was one that he couldn't fully explain. However it seemed right when he considered the options, and he knew he didn't want to be wandering along the street on his own, potentially being checked by the Jandarma. He waited and watched as the normality of the place reassured him and slowed his thudding pulse.

After a few minutes he saw a bouncer talking urgently to someone at the door, then hurry over to Arif's equivalent behind the bar. Their heads bent together as an urgent bit of news was passed. To Iannis' surprise, the owner nodded and allowed a slight smile to flicker briefly across his moustached face. Then it was back to business. He seemed relaxed. He didn't seem at all surprised. Iannis guessed that he knew that the Jandarma would not be raiding his club that night.

"Hi gorgeous!" An unexpected voice disturbed Iannis' thoughts in a brief pause in the music. She was smiling cheekily at him, head cocked appraisingly to one side, and waiting expectantly for his response.

"Hi, Janet?" he stabbed hopefully at the name.

"Jane," she responded. "Haven't seen you much for the last few days. Where have you been?"

"Sorry, yes, Jane. I've been around. Where have you been? I've been looking for you," he lied.

"Yeah, yeah. That's what they all say," she parried but with no rancour, and still with the cheery smile on her well-tanned face.

"No really," he went on, partly calculatedly, partly actually pleased to see her and to have the partner. "What are you drinking?"

"Another of those house cocktails since you're asking. Ta."

"Listen, do you want to dance first, then I'll get us both a drink?"

"Yeah. Why not."

So they sidled onto the sticky dance floor, and commandeered a body's-worth of space where they could move and sway to the music. Iannis could feel the tension relax in his shoulders and neck. It had been a dramatic few minutes, and he suddenly felt invincible, having gone from peril to perfectly innocent cover in three easy steps. He stroked Jane's arms and she allowed herself to brush closely against him, their cheeks touched gently together as they smiled with their different reasons for contentment.

Next morning Iannis slumped onto the window seat in the airport bus. It was lunchtime but he hadn't been up in time for anything other than packing. The charter flight was in the early evening, but the tour operator insisted on getting them to the busy airport hours ahead of departure time, so he was grumpily and hungrily complaining about the uncivilised departure from the resort. His packing had been pretty straightforward, stuffing everything into the fake Mulberrry holdall and checking his passport, tickets, money and cards. He puzzled over Arif's package. In the end he placed it beneath the worn underwear in one of the side pockets of his bag. No sign of Arif and no time to go looking for him. Iannis was contemplating the prospect of carrying the package through Dalaman and Gatwick airports. He didn't know for sure what was in the package but he guessed from the feel and weight of it that he had probably the best part of 500g of cocaine in his bag. It wasn't the sort of amount to be caught with, but it was incredibly tempting to take the risk.

He reasoned that he hadn't been checked at any point in his holiday, so no-one would have any reason to pull him aside. He knew from experience that most people walked straight through customs in Gatwick – the officials more intent on minor infringements of duty-free allowances than on drug smuggling. Unless they were tipped off of course – which he knew was why most people were caught. It was generally a well-planned targeting of a mule as part of a long-term surveillance operation rather than a random lucky choice of victim. Since Arif hadn't planned to give him the package and he himself certainly hadn't been part of any plan to smuggle the package, he guessed that the chances of walking through were pretty good – unless they had dogs on duty.

He was still undecided about what to do when the coach arrived at Dalaman airport. He had kept his holdall with him so didn't have to join the scrum of people retrieving their bags from the unloaded piles on either side of the bus. While the others were intent on spotting their luggage, Iannis was looking around and with a weary groan calculating how long the queue was going to take to get through initial security and into the building. Travel really was becoming a nightmare thanks to all the security checking. Perhaps the tour operator was right to allow so much time, but it wasn't a pleasing prospect.

He spotted a motorbike picking its way over the speed-bumps on the airport approach road. It was able to skirt the edges of the bumps so was travelling much faster than the taxis and coaches that arrived in an endless stream. The helmet-less rider swooped round the final bend, disappeared from view briefly, and then noisily sped up the ramp to the upper level where the coaches disgorged their passengers. He wasn't surprised to see the RayBans and the casual panache as Arif slowly rode past the crowds of passengers, scanning them intently.

Iannis stepped out with a raised hand, and the bike pulled into the gap between the emptying coaches.

"Hi man, I thought I'd missed you! I tried to catch you before the bus left but slept in I guess." Arif was his usual cheery self.

"Man! I thought I was dying this morning. I didn't have time to walk up to the village before the bus came. Thought you'd be on the ball!"

They embraced, throwing arms round each other and slapping each other on the back.

"You still got it?" murmured Arif into Iannis' ear.

"Yeah. Don't worry. Right here."

Iannis bent down to his bag and slipped out the package along with a book and his camera. The package was under the book in case the security cameras really did work.

"Give me your e-mail address," demanded Arif noisily. "You're definitely coming back here. You must mail me and keep in touch."

They noisily exchanged e-mail addresses and promises of return visits. They hugged again and gave one another the fond Mediterranean male cheek-kisses. It would have taken a very good security camera to detect the surreptitious transfer of the little package to Arif's jeans.

Chapter 39

Correspondence Summer 2000

To: Iannisk@hotmail.com
Sent: 9 Aug 2000
From: arif13@turknet.tr
Subject: hi
Merhaba Iannis

I hope you are safe home and not missing the sunshine too much. The club is very busy here and business is good.

Thank you for helping me with the unwanted goods when we had visitors. You must come again but next time talk business.

Be careful what you write in e-mails
Arif

To: arif13@turknet.tr
Sent: 12 Aug 2000
From: Iannisk@hotmail.com

Subject: Re: hi

Hi Arif

Good to hear from you. Things here busy too. Lot of tourists around London and things going well.

I'll be back OK, interested to talk business next time. Open to ideas.

Ciao

Iannis

To: Iannisk@hotmail.com
Sent: 20 Aug 2000
From: arif13@turknet.tr
Subject: Re: Re: hi

Merhaba Iannis

Are you going to come back this year? The season here is good right through to end of October. Why don't you come then and we can talk.

Arif

To: arif13@turknet.tr
Sent: 25 Aug 2000
From: Iannisk@hotmail.com
Subject: hi

Hi Arif

I'll check flights in October – should be good. There should be plenty of last minute deals from London, so I'll plan to come second week of Oct.

Ciao

Iannis

To: arif13@turknet.tr
Sent: 25 Sept 2000
From: Iannisk@hotmail.com
Subject: hi
Hi Arif

Booked a deal for Sat 14th October. Flying to Dalaman and staying in same hotel. Flight arrives very late Sat night so I'll see you on Sunday night at the club.

Ciao

Iannis

To: Iannisk@hotmail.com
Sent: 26 Sept 2000
From: arif13@turknet.tr
Subject: Re: hi
Merhaba Iannis

Great to hear you are coming. More time to talk in the day than at night in club. I'll pick you up at the beach bar on Sunday afternoon.

Arif

It was as easy as that. When Iannis looked back years later at the start of the collaboration, it seemed too easy, but he trusted his instinct, and trusted the evidence from their first encounter that he had passed the test that Arif had set him.

.

Chapter 40

The Rodos

Turkish Coast October 2006

Iannis Katharos senior was no sailor. He wondered why he had allowed his son to persuade him to come along on this trip. In the first place he didn't like Turks. He was of the generation that remembered the stories of the so-called "population exchanges" of the 1920s. Greeks of his generation had grown up with the horror stories of Smyrna repeated time without number. He remembered family holidays in the Aegean Islands when he was a child. He heard the men talk in the taverna about their readiness to defend their islands against potential invasion by the Turks. The men told the impressionable young visitor about the guns hidden in the outhouses, and the signalling systems arranged for the inevitable night when the Turks would come. It wasn't a vague uncertain possibility; it was just a question of exactly when they would come. Along with these stories came the confidences about the nature of the enemy. Unlike the honourable and noble Greeks, who had brought civilisation and democracy to the world, the Turks were part of the Barbarian east that had never achieved the civilisation of their European neighbours. Nothing that old Katharos could read or hear would change his deeply held beliefs about the neighbouring nations.

This wasn't just a matter of clinging to half-remembered historical dates and facts. In England people could read or watch programmes about the Norman Invasion without feeling any emotional involvement. It was ancient history that required a real effort to make it relevant to the 21st century. For Katharos, the enmity was visceral. Hearing the stories of the butchery, burning and destruction aroused a fury and a sense of injustice similar to the outrage felt by the western world to the Rwanda slaughter. The driving out of the Orthodox families from virtually the whole Eastern Aegean coastal region left him angry, aroused, and righteously certain that there were crimes that had gone unpunished, and criminals who had inflicted barbarous evil on his fellow Greeks. He was impervious to the arguments from his son who had read more balanced accounts of the events, and who knew that the atrocities were not all one-sided. His son tried to convince him that the politicians of the time on both sides had gone along with the process for their own reasons. Iannis Junior thought of himself as more enlightened, more broadminded and obviously more modern than his father. He was happy to let bygones be bygones, and for him the rights and wrongs had little more impact than the stories in ill-remembered and boring history lessons.

When opportunities to make money came along Iannis Junior had no compunction about collaboration with Turkish partners. He found them pretty much like himself - perhaps just exploring their role in the modern Europe, but confident of their ability to take advantage of the new face of Europe and their geographical jackpot in bridging the East with the West; the Muslim world with the supposedly Christian; and the suddenly fashionable Turkey with its European neighbours who were hungry for something "different".

Iannis Junior had followed his father easily into the family business. The restaurant still operated in one of the bustling side-streets near Marylebone High Street. It provided a sound business basis for all of their other money-making schemes. The family was content to be regarded as the proprietors of a solid if unexciting Greek restaurant, and the financial accounts of the family business fitted with the solid but unexceptional profitability of their kind.

It was an excellent cover for the real money-making activities that they enjoyed. Iannis Junior set foot in the restaurant only to eat and to keep a finger firmly on the finances. He had a long-serving chef who dealt with all the practicalities of the kitchen, and a manager who ran the restaurant with the old-fashioned style that customers came for. The fundamentals were stable even if there was a constant turnover of the poorly paid waiting staff and kitchen porters. The family were content to stay in the background, but the chef and manager knew that Iannis scrutinised every receipt and every invoice, as well as quietly observing what went on in the restaurant, so the usual skimming and dodgy accounting were not even a temptation. It wasn't that they were by nature immune to temptation, just that they knew how closely everything was monitored and how quick their exit would be if anything were found to be amiss. The cautious employment practices of big companies just didn't apply in this world. They knew the rules and stuck to them. But Iannis knew that if he relaxed his scrutiny the story would be very different.

All this meant that Iannis was able to pursue occasional money-making ventures from a solid and respectable base. His father had taught him well. The old man had avoided legal problems by keeping his ambition in check. He saw other dealers grow rich and become increasingly greedy. Simple mathematics didn't work. If it was possible to make £100,000 by importing a small quantity of cocaine, it did not follow that importing ten times the amount would lead to ten times the profit. Drawing attention to oneself was a bad idea whether it was the police or competing criminals whose attention was drawn. The Katharos business was not big enough to worry competing importers, and their unobtrusive and even self-effacing approach kept them out of the mainstream.

Iannis senior had started making some extra money almost by accident. He had come to London after the war when Greece was in turmoil and escape from the civil war was attractive to someone without strong political convictions other than his enmity towards the Turks. He reached London as a teenager in 1948, with minimal resources other than two names and addresses. Ethnic ties and loyalties ensured he found a job, and he patiently built his earnings in London into a solid chunk of savings. His insight into the prevention of fraud in his own restaurant had a foundation in the loose practices that turned out to be so lucrative for him. Watered bottles of spirits, meals that didn't go through the till, modest ripping off of inebriated diners - all had contributed to the accumulating wealth of the immigrant Iannis. His life was a testament to the success of patient and unobserved criminality. He didn't think of it in those terms. He thought of it as a general outwitting of the rest of the world, but all the factors that led him to be able to buy his own restaurant by the age of 40 were based on activities that he preferred to keep secret.

By the 1970s he was making good money from the business and was able to travel back and forth from London to Greece at least once a year. An off-hand comment from a contemporary in Thessaloniki opened his eyes to the money that was to be made from some illicit trade. A small parcel of cannabis resin which easily made its way from Afganistan to Thessaloniki was phenomenally profitable once it reached London. Just as he had applied subtle and carefully moderated criminality to his restaurant business, so he developed his profitable sideline. Careful always to be virtually invisible, and never to be too greedy.

Through the 70s and 80s he prospered. He had married late, and brought his bride from Greece to London. Steadily and unobtrusively Katharos continued to build up his formal and his informal businesses. If other drug smugglers knew of him they didn't take him to be a threat. His contacts were well-tried and trusted. They knew that from time to time Katharos would be able to sell them some "goods", but it was strictly wholesale, and he was never foolish enough to dabble in street-level selling. Had he attempted to elbow into someone else's territory, the quiet and unobtrusive days would have been over. He outlasted all the more ambitious and briefly more successful importers, who allowed their belief in their own invulnerability to lead them sooner or later to their undoing. Some fell foul of their competitors and rivals, others were tracked down by the drug squad, but Iannis quietly lurked in the shadows, known only to the few essential contacts he cultivated, and never sufficiently high profile to come to the attention of the law.

In time his only son was easily assimilated into the business. Iannis Junior showed a fine appreciation of the methodology and style his father had perfected, but gradually became more adventurous. He was more able than his father to dissipate the carefully accumulated wealth, but he did pay attention to the key lesson about staying under the radar of both the authorities and potentially jealous competitors. A quiet life was better than no life. Iannis Junior found it hard at first to resist boasting to friends about the money he could spend, but he was well taught and well warned by his father. As a result, his excesses were discrete and of a very personal nature. The almost puritanical ethos of the old Orthodox religion had mingled with the insecurities of the immigrant to produce a mindset where conspicuous flaunting of wealth could only be followed by disaster. Iannis Junior tried and immediately forswore hard drugs. A brief period of experimentation before the age of twenty clashed with his inherited need for control and self-contained-ness. The idea of being at the mercy of others due to self-inflicted indulgence struck him as stupidly asking for trouble. He had no intention of doing anything to endanger the fundamental nature of his father's success. He just wanted him to be a little more adventurous, a little more modern, a little more profitable.

Old man Katharos was feeling his age. He had insisted on travelling through Greece. They had flown to Athens, and then to Thessaloniki. Although the flights were relatively short, he had found it all tiring. The long night of animated conversation in the family taverna near Thessaloniki left him with what he refused to acknowledge was a hangover. However his thumping head and sluggish brain were a liability as they travelled again on the next day's 55 minute flight from Thessaloniki to Rhodes.

In Rhodes they boarded the Rodos – appropriately named for the location and looking sufficiently luxurious to enable him to overcome the dyspepsia resulting from his overindulgence. The Rodos was owned by an associate of Arif's. He didn't even know the name of the company that appeared as legal owner in the ship's papers. His son had told him that everything was organised according to the wishes of Arif's foreign associates, who were insisting that the usual route for transporting the packages was not to be followed. This last venture was to be especially careful, especially secure. So instead of letting Alex take the risk of transporting the goods through customs and delivering them safely to Hampstead, they were for the first time participating in the actual supply chain. He was not happy with the idea, but the stakes were higher than usual and Arif's associates were not willing to let the package take its chances with the unprofessional Alex as he took his chances through customs in Gatwick. In any case, England was not the final destination this time.

The Rodos looked big to him. Iannis had no experience of estimating the size of these private yachts. A more experienced man would have quickly established that it was a 45ft Cranchi motor yacht. Big enough to accommodate the four key people involved in the trip, but small enough to avoid too much attention from customs and coastguards. There were four guest cabins, with crew quarters hidden somewhere as cramped as they were unobtrusive.

Iannis senior threw himself on the bed in his cabin and cursed himself again. He didn't like all this travelling. He resented being required to change a well-proven formula. The uneasy feeling in his belly might be partly explained by the excesses of his cousins' hospitality, but it might also represent a nagging unease that he was failing to address. Perhaps it was fear of appearing weak to his son. Perhaps he was for the first time stepping outside the league he normally played in. Whatever the reason, he was agitated, tired, and uncharacteristically vulnerable.

The captain of the Rodos was reassuring.

"Do not worry my friend. This is all very routine. Tomorrow I take all the papers and passports to the harbour police, the customs and the immigration, and by midday we will be ready to go. Today it is too late to do any of that, so relax, rest, and enjoy the city here."

Katharos had no choice but to submit to the timetable, and in fact he quite relished the opportunity to wander the streets of the old town. He and Iannis Junior walked through the cobbled history and ate modestly in the least touristy taverna they could find.

Chapter 41
Rodos October 2006

In transit to Fethiye

The Rodos inched its way out of the old Mandraki harbour in Rhodes. The captain had completed the formalities in the Immigration, Customs, and Harbour offices, so they were free to leave Greek waters, and were due to log into a Turkish port within a few days. As they left the harbour, the rolling swells coming across the open sea gave the boat an uncomfortable squirming motion. Old Iannis Katharos did not like it at all. The motor yacht relied on speed through the water to smooth the motion, as it had no heavy keel beneath it, so it was less comfortable than a sailing yacht when it travelled slowly through the water.

As they cleared the north-eastern tip of the island, the captain opened up the throttles and the motion steadied. The boat was still far from comfortable, as it slammed from one wave to the next, but at least it was a definite solid feeling rather than the nausea-inducing wallow at slow speed.

Iannis senior resigned himself to his misery. He tried lying on his bed, but the effort of staying on the bed infuriated him. Each roll of the boat threatened to deposit his heavy body on the thick carpet. The thuds as they hit each wave made rest impossible. He levered himself off the bed and onto the floor of his cabin. He reasoned that if the boat was trying to get him off the bed he might as well save it the trouble. He wedged himself between the bed and the expensive rose-wood dressing table – both bolted firmly in place he discovered. At least there was no threat of falling further, but it was uncomfortable, and distinctly undignified. He didn't want anyone to come in and see him lying in this pathetic position.

He heaved himself to his feet, and carefully made his way out of his cabin and along the narrow passageway to the main saloon. No-one else was around, so he wondered if his son and the two monosyllabic Turkish associates that Arif had brought to them were suffering in their cabins just like him. He looked up the steep steps that led to the elevated bridge, from which the captain controlled the boat. He could see his son's back, and he seemed to be talking to other people, so perhaps they were all up there.

Iannis struggled step by step up to the bridge. He quickly worked out that if he timed his movements to match the boat he wasn't caught mid-pace when it slammed into the next wave. It was important to have both hands and both feet firmly planted each time the hull shuddered with the impact of a wave. He emerged into the crowded space and Iannis Junior made space for him to sit in one of the sturdy seats that were again firmly bolted to the boat's deck.

Once established in the seat, and holding the well-placed grab-rail, the old man was able to see why everyone else was up there. Seeing the horizon and being able to anticipate the waves seemed to have a calming effect on his nausea. Looking to his left he could see right down the north-western coast of Rhodes, with the rocky headlands and olive-covered hills that stretched for miles. Ahead he could see nothing but blue water, but even he could appreciate the beauty of the white-flecked sea and the expanse of hazy blue sky. The sky was clear above them, and at the horizon the merging of blue sky with bluer sea was fudged by the greyish heat-haze that still appeared in October. He breathed easier, and decided that this was a better place for him to survive the rigours of the journey.

"How long will this take?" he enquired of his obviously ecstatic son.

"Only a couple of hours to Fethiye. Isn't it fantastic? This is more like it. You should buy yourself one of these."

Iannis senior wondered again at his son's ability to totally misread his thoughts, preferences and inclinations. He grunted.

Within 10 minutes they were able to discern the shape of the coast of Turkey as the distance from Rhodes to the nearest point on Turkey is little over 10 miles. However their course was not towards the nearest land, but further east. Having gained some shelter from the Turkish coast they ignored the deep indentation in the coast where Marmaris lay waiting, and struck East across the seemingly endless blue towards Kapu Dag and then across the Gulf to the port and welcoming marina of Fethiye.

By mid afternoon the two Katharos men and their two Turkish business partners were sitting in the garden bar at Ece Marina. Old Katharos had endured the long trudge along the unsteady pontoons of the marina, watching warily for the snaking hosepipes and electric wiring that were ready to trip him up and send him headlong into the oily water on either side. He really didn't like it.

But in the bar, he was at last able to extract a rich cigar from the shaped leather case. He lovingly clipped the end before installing it between his fat lips and applied his gold lighter to the waiting tobacco. He savoured the aromatic warmth of the smoke before exhaling generously in a raised stream aimed high above the table. He picked up the brandy glass and drank a first sip of the Turkish liqueur.

"Not bad. Not at all bad. Not Metaxa of course, but not bad."

Iannis Junior smiled knowingly and winked at Arif's friends.

"So you'll survive after all do you think?"

"There is a big difference between surviving and enjoying my son. But this I can enjoy."

"Just look at that," invited Iannis Junior, sweeping one hand in a grand gesture around the view in front of them. The sleek stainless steel flagpoles sported an international display of colour, and framed a scene of white yachts and blue sea, with green encircling hills in the background that provided both shelter and pictorial balance. "What a place! There must be millions of pounds worth of yachts lying here."

The Turkish companions were more relaxed now

they were back on their own territory, and were becoming less monosyllabic. They were keen that these visiting Greeks should realise that Turkey was a modern country, and was not the backward barbarian wilderness that old Iannis clearly anticipated.

"Welcome to Turkey at last," pronounced the senior man. "Let us drink to the success of our enterprise."

A warning glance shivered around the group. They did not want anyone to have the slightest knowledge of their purpose in being there. However the Turk had no intention of going beyond that and was raising his glass inviting the mutual clinking and exclamations of 'Sherife' that came as second nature to all but old Katharos.

"Sherife," he ventured, and cautiously raised his glass to the waiting three. He leaned forward on the chair, and conveyed to the others that they should lean in also so that what he said could be private.

"I trust that everything is organised as carefully as your friend Arif has promised. Today we relax here, and tomorrow we make our way to your rendezvous bay. If we see anything out of place, or any sign that all is not well, the deal is off. Iannis and I will go our separate way back to Rhodes and you will go back to Arif. However if all goes smoothly, we will be rich men by Saturday night, and on our way to Amsterdam. I know you have made the travel arrangements," he nodded to his son, "but I would like to be sure again that everything is in place."

Iannis Junior nodded patiently. He had rehearsed the plan endlessly to his father since he and Arif had conceived the idea for this big, big, coup. It was more lucrative than anything they had done before. In fact it was more profitable than all the previous deals added together. It was going to be the last time they needed to work, and because it was the last time, they didn't need to be small insignificant players. This time people might talk, but they wouldn't know who had pulled it off. They wouldn't be able to pin the deal to Katharos (pere et fils) because of the complexity of the linkage between Greece and Turkey; Turkey and Cairo; Cairo and Sudan; Sudan and the impenetrable DRC; Amsterdam and Lichtenstein; Lichtenstein and London. It was so impenetrably convoluted that only those who conceived it could follow it. There was no way that links could be made between the disparate parts of the chain because it was a new chain, forged purely for this one deal, and never to be used again. That was the beauty of it.

"Don't worry. The flights are booked and confirmed for Sunday." He looked across at the Turks, who were watching the exchange carefully. Any sign of the Greeks backing out and they had their instructions from Arif. They hoped that things were going to go well. "My father is going to have to endure the discomfort of a holiday charter flight to Amsterdam. It is the most inconspicuous way to travel from Turkey to Holland, it is full of late season cut-price holiday-makers. He will hate it, but it is a good way to travel without being noticed. Many people use Schipol as a hub for these flights and the security is not tight. We will conclude the business on Monday, and after that there is nothing to find, no documents, no objects, nothing to stop us taking a more luxurious route back to London. But in fact we will take the train. Again it is inconspicuous, and so many English people are taking Eurostar breaks that the security is slight. In any case there is nothing to fear."

"It is clever. Very low key," agreed the senior Turk. "We also will be low key, but not on the same flight, as you know. We will meet you in Amsterdam on Monday, but not before that and not after that. As you say, it is very secure."

They signalled to the barman to bring another round of drinks, and nodded sagely to one another about the cleverness of the planning for the operation. Old Iannis puffed his cigar but looked reluctant to join in the mood of mutual congratulation.

Chapter 42
The Rodos to Tomb Bay

Oct 2006

The Rodos refuelled in the marina on Friday morning and then gently made its way across the Gulf of Fethiye. Sheltered by the encircling land the sea was smoother and the day more peaceful. They motored across towards Gocek to allow the passengers to enjoy the scenery, but didn't enter the busy marina. Instead they turned South around Gocek Island and pottered down the even more sheltered waters of Skopea Limani.

Tourist gulets occasionally crossed their path, fulfilling late season twelve-island tours. They looked into the bays that attracted the gulets before dropping their lunchtime anchor in a quiet spot round the headland from Kapi Creek. The crew set the table for the four guests and sent the tender round the headland to the taverna at Kapi to bring back some freshly cooked fish and bread. Despite all his preconceptions to the contrary, old Iannis Katharos began to luxuriate in the seductive pleasure of the unspoiled beauty of the place. Now that he was threatened by no further open sea crossings, and he felt secure in the sheltered bay, he was able to appreciate why people spent such time and money on this sybaritic pursuit. He sat back in the canvas director's chair and sipped the cold white Turkish Chankaya wine. He mopped up the remaining oily juices from his plate with the unfamiliar village bread, and sighed contentedly as he contemplated the nearby landscape.

It looked to him as if they could be thousands of miles from civilisation rather than the few short hours they had travelled. A small herd of black goats was nibbling its way along the margins of the bay, while a patient donkey stood tethered in the shade of a wizened tree where the stony beach gave way to the dry grassy vegetation of the gorge behind. He could see an old track leading up through the bushes and scrub until it disappeared behind the rocky hillside at the side of the bay. It brought back boyhood memories of the unspoiled islands he had visited as a child, and he almost winced at the contradictory emotions that were inextricably linked to the old national animosities. Yet here he was in a Turkish bay, undeniably enjoying the food and drink, and contemplating a business venture with his son's Turkish friend that carried a higher reward than any of his previous activities. He didn't dwell on the commensurately greater risks, as he knew they had done everything they could to minimise them. To quibble now would be to question his son's judgement and his trust in Arif.

As the guests lingered and relaxed in the October sun, the crew of the Rodos cleared the debris of lunch before weighing anchor and motoring gently north-west across Skopea Limani to their arranged overnight anchorage in Tomb Bay. The Captain was worried that they would not be allowed to tie up to the wooden jetty where he had promised Arif they would be waiting. He was ready to deploy long stern lines to the shore beyond the jetty if the locals were worried about the weight of his craft damaging the fragile-looking wooden structure.

He needn't have worried. The taverna owner in Tomb Bay was so pleased to see the expensive yacht making for his jetty that he expressed no worries about their mooring. They dropped anchor rather than use the local sunken mooring lines, but made sure not to entangle the taverna's chain and rope that rested on the sea-bed. By mid afternoon they were securely moored to the Tomb Bay jetty.

Katharos senior trod warily across the passerelle to the jetty. He walked carefully along the head of the T-shaped structure to the shaft of the T, and slowly to the landward end. The taverna was an open wooden structure, which seemed to be no more than a framework supporting a roof held together by entwined vines. There were old sailcloth curtains rolled up to roof level on the three landward sides of the structure, while the seaward side was open to the view and to the winds. At the rear of the area was the more permanent structure of the bar, where the owner waited smilingly for the lumbering guest.

"Welcome, welcome my friend," he said warmly as Iannis came within the sheltered area and made his way between the empty tables. "Would you like a beer, or perhaps you would like a shave?"

Iannis raised his eyebrows at this unusual query, and then noticed the sign for the barber's lean-to construction alongside the bar. The barber sat in his own chair reading a paper and nodded his head in relaxed greeting to Iannis.

"I think the answer is yes to both of those," smiled the old man. He made his way slowly and carefully between the tables to the barber's chair, while the barman reached in his fridge for a cold beer. Iannis lowered himself with a grateful sigh into the chair, and relaxed into the old familiar ritual as the barber shook the towel then wrapped it with a flourish round his client's shoulders.

Iannis enjoyed the shave. Turkish barbers were renowned for the pride they took in their work, and Elias was no exception. He lathered Iannis thoroughly, and with an old-fashioned cut-throat – of which Iannis silently approved – he shaved him with gentle touch once, then lathered and shaved him again. The spirit-based rosewater stung his face deliciously, and the soothing cream was massaged carefully into all the freshly shaved skin. To his surprise and delight his head and shoulders were strongly massaged before the barber bowed theatrically and swivelled the chair so that Iannis could stand.

He sat by the bar and sipped his beer. At the jetty there was a brightly painted long local open boat, and across the T of the structure just one other small sailing yacht was moored twenty metres from the grandiose Rodos. The view across the expanse of Skopea Limani and the Gulf of Fethiye was spectacular. Blue sea fringed with green hillsides, and in the distance great grey mountains loomed majestically. A helicopter flew noisily overhead and interrupted the peaceful calm of the afternoon.

"What are they doing?" Iannis asked the taverna owner.

"Rich people going to Gocek to their boats. Fethiye too. They fly to Dalaman and then a short helicopter ride to the marina. Too much money. Too much hurry."

Old Iannis watched the helicopter and then let his eyes drop to the rear of the Rodos where his son was towelling himself after a swim in the bay. He could see how easily the younger man was seduced by the style and the glamour of the yacht. Too much pleasure makes men careless, he thought to himself.

The afternoon slipped gently by as he sat in the shade of the taverna and sipped another well-chilled beer. A few sailing yachts appeared later in the afternoon and circled the bay looking for an anchorage. Each time a yacht appeared the taverna owner roused himself from his newspaper and walked to the end of the jetty, waving an optimistic welcome to the yacht's crew. Only one of the yachts accepted the invitation and reversed slowly back to the taverna's jetty. Iannis watched from a distance as they threw their mooring ropes and made the yacht secure.

"You know these people Tolga?" He asked, as he now knew to call the taverna owner, when he returned to the shady bar.

"Yes, they come every year. Quiet people, no trouble. You will have peaceful night here. Tonight we have lamb shish and we have fresh fish. Fresh this morning. You stay for dinner?"

The old Greek confirmed that they would be

spending some money that night, but was actually not entirely sure what his son and the rest of the crew would be planning. He decided that he would tell them that they were eating ashore. He felt secure in the taverna. He had come to feel well-settled on his ancient wooden chair, and in an unsettlingly inappropriate way was experiencing feelings of coming back to his roots. He dismissed the thought with a wry smile. A Greek feeling at home in Turkey! What was happening? He chuckled quietly to himself as he lifted the cold, condensation-covered glass again. His eye ranged over the nearby rocky hillside, and then over the expanse of blue water stretching to the distant mountainous shore. He sighed. It could easily be Greece. It was undeniably beautiful, but beneath the beauty was the same challenging rocky landscape and potentially treacherous sea from which his compatriots and ancestors had wrested a living. The fishermen on this coast seemed no different from the fishermen he could see from his cousins' taverna in Thessaloniki. The boats were almost identical in shape – having evolved over the generations to cope with the same demands from fishing in the eastern Mediterranean. Was he wrong to have harboured all those hatreds for all of his life? He banished the complex thoughts and worries and tried to settle back to relax in the shade as another helicopter thudded past on its way to Fethiye. He sipped his beer again and watched the machine shrink and finally disappear into the distance.

It was late afternoon when he padded his way gingerly down the jetty to the Rodos. Young Iannis was lying back in the gentle sunshine, while the two Turks were playing cards in the shaded saloon. There was no sign of the skipper, but the deck-hand was making his way laboriously along the near side of the yacht, polishing the bright-work and smoking a cigarette. His unhurried repetitious movements with the rags were reflected in the calm water, and provided the only sign of energy and life in the bay.

The old man stepped on board and lowered himself into the director's chair beside his son.

"Everything all right?" his son enquired sleepily.

"I've just been resting in the taverna. You should have a shave. They are real craftsmen here, just like Athens. Better than anything you get in London. We'll eat there tonight."

"Better tell the crew that we aren't eating on board then. They'll expect to serve dinner for us unless we tell them different."

"I'll leave that to you. You know these people better than I do. But now that you are awake, do you have the information about Alex on the other boat?"

"I'll ring the guys in Kapi and check he's there. I have the list of where he has been all week – they faxed it through earlier – can you believe it they're still using fax here!"

"I want to be sure that everything is set up for tomorrow and we don't have any disruptions to the plan. I worry that someone is watching us and that this is all going to go wrong."

Iannis Junior looked quizzically at his father and chided him gently,

"Look dad, this isn't your usual routine I know, but these guys are professionals. Arif knows what he's doing, and you put the fear of god into Alex so he'll do as he's told. Relax, and this time tomorrow we'll be on our way back to Fethiye – unfortunately. The day after that we'll be in Amsterdam, and by Monday it'll be all over."

"What about those helicopters?"

"Just shuttles from the airport to the big yachts – happens all the time – I checked with the skipper."

"I thought you were getting lazy," chuckled the old man with a smile, "but you were on guard after all."

"I told you, just relax. I'll check the other boat now."

The smug young man went into the saloon, smiling to himself that he had predicted how the old man would check up on the helicopters, pleased that he had been prepared. He went forward to the office-like communications desk where he had left the fax from their contact in Fethiye. It listed each day of the week so far and indicated what harbour or anchorage had been used by Alex that week. With typical efficiency it signed off 'everything in place for Saturday.'

Iannis picked up his mobile phone and dialled the Kapi Creek number. He didn't need to explain who he was. There were a few grunts from him as he received the message and jotted down on the free space on the fax, 'Alex in Kapi, package pickup completed OK Monday, all OK.' He left the paper on the desk by the computer and fax machines – knowing that his father would have a look to see what the message was about, and wanting to show him just how efficient and smooth Arif's operation could be.

Chapter 43

Rodos Raided

Friday 13th October 2006; 22:00 hours

The slate-grey launch, showing regulation red and green navigation lights and a white 'steaming' light, came gliding gently round the headland protecting Tomb Bay. Hugging the coast on the northern side, it felt its way along the shore until it reached the old stone quay which provided an alternative landing place for visitors to the tombs. Nosing gently in to the dock, the navigation lights disappeared as two silent crew stepped ashore and tied lines to the recently installed mooring posts. The peace of the night was scarcely disturbed, and the tourists on their Gulet 200 metres along the bay looked up only briefly from their game of backgammon to note the arrival.

The group leader on board the grey launch gathered the six operational officers around the red-lit navigation table for a last look at the late-afternoon reconnaissance photographs from the Coastguard helicopter. The photographs showed the deep encircling bay, protecting at its innermost point the taverna and T-shaped jetty. The white bulk of the motor-yacht dwarfed the two sailing yachts moored along the T. His finger pointed to the spot on the northern shore of the bay where they had just arrived. It was about 700 metres round the shore from the main jetty.

"Group Alpha, this is the path along the shore that you will take to the jetty. You will go as far as this point and wait until Group Zebra signal you." He pointed to a tree-sheltered indent about one hundred metres before the path reached the taverna. It was safely out of sight of any staff or customers at the taverna.

"Group Zebra, no lights, you will take the dinghy to the bow of the Rodos and insert the spike. Do it quietly and as near to the bow as you can without alerting the crew on board. Then pull back so that you are in the darkness but can get a clear view of the taverna. When you are sure that the target group – all four of them – are on board the Rodos, signal to Group Alpha and wait until you see them on the jetty. Understood?"

He looked round the six faces peering intently at the photograph and listening carefully to his repeat of the instructions already rehearsed.

"What if there are only three, chief?"

"Wait for the fourth. If he doesn't appear in five minutes signal to Alpha that there are three on board. One long flash and three short instead of four. Alpha, you send one man to the taverna to locate the fourth target and the other three continue to the Rodos."

"What if there are only two, or one?" It wasn't a stupid question; it was the voice of experience that knew how often the careful plans were screwed up by a factor they hadn't thought of.

"We can only guess that there will be four eating together in the taverna. It would not be usual for the crew to eat with them, so three crew should be on board. If you cannot identify anyone in the taverna as the targets, we have to assume that they are all on board. Just make sure that you don't mistake people from these two yachts as the target. If they go back to their yachts early that's good. If they are sitting up late in the taverna or in their yachts let's just try to keep them at a distance."

"So what if there are only two we can identify in the taverna?" persisted the young officer.

"It is possible, but unlikely, that the two Greeks and the two locals will separate. Maybe two will eat on board and two in the taverna. I doubt it, because they won't trust one-another, so they'll all want to watch the others. They'll be together wherever they are – and most likely the taverna."

"But if there are only two?"

"Signal 'two' to Group Alpha and continue as planned."

The young officer didn't dare ask about the vague possibility that only one of the targets was in the taverna and the others not visible.

"When you have secured the ship, radio me here, then get ready to take the lot of them to Gocek. Don't give any of them a chance to dump evidence or to interfere in any way. Use the cable-ties to disable them and secure them. As soon as the skipper sees your ID he'll co-operate. The crew have no incentive to cause trouble, so go for the four targets right away. We'll let the specialists search properly back in Gocek, just don't lose anything."

"OK chief, ready to go." The others nodded their readiness to get into action and with a curt dip of the leader's head they were off.

Group Alpha looked like English tourists from a Gulet. They wore an odd collection of safari jackets, boating-style fleece jackets, and trousers that were zipped around knee level for conversion into shorts. On their feet were the sort of stout walking shoes that the English and Germans seemed to favour. They made good time round the rocky path to their holding point and stared intently into the darkness of the bay for a sign from Group Zebra. It was a still night, the voices from the gulet and the rattle of the backgammon dice were clearly audible across the water. One hundred metres beyond them they could hear nothing but the occasional rattle of glasses and an infrequent burst of laughter from the taverna. They had no idea how many people were there, but suspected it was very few. All the better for their purposes if everyone was taking an early night.

Group Zebra were puzzled. When they left the slate-grey patrol boat, they took a route curving out into the middle of the bay and almost to the south coastline, before continuing the clockwise turn so that they approached the jetty from behind the protective bulk of the motor yacht.

They could not see into the taverna, nor could anyone in the taverna see them. They edged quietly to the bow of the Rodos and slipped the anchor spike into place. More like a horse-shoe than a spike, it was a hardened steel bar coated with black rubber. It slipped through a link in the anchor chain, the two heavy ends hanging down either side, while the rubber coating ensured it made no noise. They retreated in the dark dinghy so that they were virtually invisible from the shore.

Now that they had a clear view into the open front of the taverna they were puzzled. They could see that only one table was occupied. Both of the small sailing yachts were showing signs of life. One had lights showing from the cabin below, while in the cockpit of the other yacht two people were talking quietly and occasionally sipping from glasses of amber liquid. At the taverna table was a large hunched man who looked as if he matched the older Greek target. The other figure did not match their remembered photographs of either the younger Greek or the two locals. They waited.

Group Alpha were fretting at their holding point. They waited the five minutes they had been allocated and then waited another one. The group leader muttered his impatience and sent a single flash of his torch into the dark. This exacerbated the uncertainty on the dinghy. There was no sign of the target in the taverna moving, and they had no certainty about the other three. It was exactly the scenario the young officer had stopped himself from raising.

"The other three must be on board. I don't think that target four is talking to another of the target group. Where is the taverna owner? Maybe that's him. That makes sense. The other three have gone back to the boat and left him talking to the taverna guy. Let's signal three to Alpha, so they know to pick up one ashore. The fat guy won't get far."

"OK, one long and three shorts, let's hope this works."

The torch flashed its message from the dark, and Group Alpha at last stretched their legs and moved briskly past the thorny bushes along the rocky path to the taverna. They had understood the message, and one of the group was detailed to check the taverna and the toilet block to apprehend the fourth target. The other three would saunter gently down the jetty looking like crew from the other yachts, trying to raise no alarm until they were within reach of the motor-yacht. The surface of the path became loose stony chips, then pebbles and shingle for the final fifty metres. It was impossible for four men to move quietly on it. They felt like sprinting to maintain the element of surprise, but knew it was counterproductive if they were to maintain their cover as tourists trekking along from the Gulet for a late night drink, or as crew returning late to the sailing yachts. They continued to plod their way noisily along the shore path, cursing the taverna for laying the noisy stone path.

Old Iannis could move surprisingly quickly for someone of his bulk. His alarm registered when he saw the series of flashes from the darkness of the bay. They were too structured and orderly to be random flashes from an innocent yacht's dinghy. He was already on his feet when he heard the first of the crunching footsteps approaching from the northern side of the bay. Tolga heard the footsteps – in the still of the night they sounded like an approaching army. He peered into the darkness, unable to see beyond the lights of his taverna. He was ready to welcome some late customers, probably from the Gulet, so was similarly on his feet and starting to move towards the bar.

As the four figures emerged crunching along the final stretch of shingle to the bar, Tolga called out a welcome, and happily moved a couple of chairs back from a table to indicate that they could sit and have a drink. Although they were dressed like many of his customers, they were moving with more purpose than most. Tolga didn't think it all out right away, but later remembered that they looked different. Prospective customers emerging from that path usually slowed up and paused when they were able to survey the bar and the wooden tables. They usually grouped together and discussed where to sit, before moving hesitantly between the tables. One of the four looked intently at him for a moment then looked inland past him, and strode firmly towards the primitive toilet block. The other three scarcely gave him a glance before walking past him to the start of the jetty, focused entirely on the boats on the outer end. His words of welcome were ignored, and his offer of a drink on the house was obviously irrelevant.

The land-based officer approached the toilet block, mentally rehearsing his approach to each of the two doors. The other three officers were covering the final few paces of shingle before setting foot on the long wooden jetty when a voice rang out and the plan changed.

"Iannis! Fiye! Go! This instant! Go!"

The voice came from the hillside above the jetty, from the impenetrable looking woods on the southern arm of the bay. Old Iannis had not wasted his time in idle chatter during the afternoon. He had learned from Tolga about the old path with its almost invisible entrance just beside the taverna. It climbed up through the dense trees and bushes on the southern curve of the bay before turning inland and up through the steep cleft between the hills. Tolga had told him about the ancient path that he used some nights to return to his uncle's house just over the hilltop behind the bay. With a wink and a wily grin he had hinted that the route had been useful over the years for more than just innocent access to the bay. Old Iannis had looked long and hard at the entrance between the bushes that afternoon.

With an initial rumble and then a blatant roar of exhaust, the engines on the Rodos started. Iannis Junior started casting off the stern lines while shouting imperiously to the skipper,

"Go, go, go!"

The skipper had been roused instantly by the commotion. His habit was to doze in the high central bridge of the boat until everything was shut down for the night. All he had to do was swing his legs off the white leather bench onto the deck and he was instantly in action. He checked that Iannis was casting off from the jetty and hit the button to raise the anchor. The powerful electric windlass turned and the chain started to rattle over the bow-roller. He needed to use the anchor to pull the yacht out from the dock, and then get it raised from the seabed before he could use the engines to motor away. Suddenly there was a solid dull thud and the anchor windlass went silent. They weren't moving. He pressed the 'Up' button again but he heard only a click. Nothing from the motor of the windlass.

Iannis was now screaming at him from the stern of the boat. The first pull of the anchor had tightened the remaining stern line and made the rope impossible to work with. Iannis was not an expert, and he could make no impression on the bar-tight mooring rope and the knot that held them fast.

The skipper knew that the windlass fuse had tripped, and he needed to go below to reset it. He registered the problem that Iannis was having with the stern rope and could see two of the other passengers ineffectually wrestling with it but getting in one-another's way. He planned to reset the tripped fuse and get a knife to cut the rope.

Meanwhile the three customs officers had given up all pretence of being innocent tourists as soon as the voice rang out from the hillside above the jetty. They were quickly but carefully picking their way round the ropes, buckets, and broken planks that made the jetty a continual hazard. They couldn't run for fear of ending up in the water, but they could hear the Rodos' frantic attempts to leave. They didn't panic. They had expected the solid clunk as the hardened steel anchor-chain spike met the bow roller on the boat. They knew that until the crew identified the problem there was no physical possibility of the anchor being raised.

The remaining stern rope was still holding the yacht firm so it was an easy leap for the agile officers from the jetty onto the low bathing platform at the yacht's stern. No weapons were needed. As they flashed their Sahil Guvenlik ID, the two Turks shrugged and resignedly slumped against the polished wood at the side of the yacht. Iannis Junior picked ineffectually at the rock-hard knotted rope, refusing to accept that until the strain was released, it was impossible to free the knot. Alone he ranted at the others and scrabbled at the knot, until he realised the futility of his efforts and stood limply looking at the three officers.

The skipper emerged from the interior of the yacht and silently dropped the knife on the saloon carpet before trying to ensure that the Sahil Guvenlik knew he was simply the hired skipper and not part of whatever it was they were after.

"All secure forward." It was the voice of Group Zebra. The two men had waited in the dinghy for the doomed attempt to raise the anchor, and then expertly hoisted themselves aboard at the bow, using the jammed anchor chain and their quickly deployed boarding ladder. They stood, arms folded, looking menacingly ready for action in the black combat gear that would have been more comfortable attire for the incongruously dressed Group Alpha.

"Tie them up," instructed Group Alpha leader, and the three targets found innocuous-looking black plastic cable-ties biting painfully into the skin of their wrists and ankles. They were bundled onto the luxurious bench seats in the saloon, unable to make any move without causing even more pain where the ties threatened to cut their skin.

The fourth member of Alpha appeared on the jetty.

"How many of them here?" he urgently enquired.

"Three."

"Shit."

"Where is he?"

"Got away. Wasn't in the toilets and I can't find him

in the dark. Must be somewhere up the hillside. Sorry."

Alpha leader didn't respond. He pulled out the handheld VHF from his now ridiculous safari jacket and called the patrol boat to report their partial success and to start the land-based hunt for the fourth target, who was now being referred to as 'the fat Greek'.

The serious search for the fat Greek started early next morning. The coastguards were convinced that no-one could have escaped over the high hills behind the bay. They took all day to search the path from bay to hill-top, and then gradually retraced their steps searching in the vegetation for six metres on either side of the path. Old Iannis hadn't travelled far. The sudden dash up the steep path combined with the anguish of a lifetime's caution shattered on this accursed Turkish shore, proved too much for his aged sclerotic body. Within seconds of shouting his warning to the son whose scheme he should have questioned, he tumbled awkwardly backwards into the dense undergrowth, clutching his chest as a low groan emerged from his clenched mouth. No time for regrets or reflection on why he had allowed fear of antagonising his son to over-ride a mounting feeling of unease. No time to replay the many occasions when he had almost voiced his suspicions, but decided to give his son room for his coup. No time to curse the ease with which he had accepted the explanations of helicopters, of easy passage, and of lack of customs formalities. Just the vague perversely inappropriate feeling that he had been right all along.

Chapter 44

Mugla jail.

Next day.

Alex lay back on the disgusting bed despite his revulsion. He was exhausted, and couldn't bear to sit on the edge any longer. He gave in to the need to lie down, but couldn't stop the whirling worries in his burdened brain. It was mid-morning, and he had heard the clanging activities of the guards as they took other prisoners from their cells and later returned them. He listened carefully for clues to the activities, and waited impatiently for any sign of the guards opening the door to his cell. He had used the zinc bucket in the corner of the cell, and the smell of his urine mingled with the stale legacy of all the previous unwilling inhabitants.

He desperately wanted to ask someone what had been done with Maggie. He worried that his policy of keeping her in the dark about the operation would mis-fire.

She wouldn't be able to answer as cleverly as she otherwise would had he briefed her honestly and fully. It was too late now for second thoughts. The die had been cast in Dublin when the surprisingly effective William had taken charge of events.

He heard different footsteps approaching along the bare corridor. Accompanying the usual heavy clumping of the guards' boots, there was the sharp clicking of a different pair of feet. He could picture the polished formal shoes of an officer. The group halted at his door and the metal peephole rasped open to allow the guard to check the prisoner. Satisfied that Alex was safely on the bed, the guard unlocked and swung open the heavy door.

The guard stood respectfully to one side and saluted the crisply dressed officer who stepped forward into the open doorway. He wore the formal black jacket and trousers of a senior officer in the Navy or Coastguard, Alex couldn't be sure which. The gold rings round the cuffs of the jacket indicated an impressive seniority, and the peaked cap held in regulation style under his left arm bore the gold decoration on its peak of a very senior rank indeed. The impeccably pressed outfit, highly polished shoes and air of careful grooming looked thoroughly out of place in the smelly and undignified surroundings.

"Mr Fox." It was the same semi-questioning statement that had started the exchange on the yacht a life-time ago in Kapi Creek.

"Yes?" responded Alex hesitantly.

"Mr Fox, you are free to go. On behalf of the Sahil Guvenlik I thank you for your part in this operation, and apologise for the inconvenience to you here."

The guards exchanged puzzled looks behind the officer, but knew better than to voice their puzzlement.

"Take Mr Fox to the guard-room, and make sure that he is returned his shoes and other belongings," the officer instructed the still-surprised guards.

"Can you tell me where my wife is please?" Alex could no longer restrain himself.

"When we have completed the formalities here you will be taken to meet her. She is well and is comfortable in Gocek. Do not worry Mr Fox, your nightmare is at an end."

Alex couldn't help himself. Tears welled in his eyes as he struggled to contain the long-controlled emotion. The guards waited uncomfortably, shuffling their feet as Alex wiped the tears from his weary face and shakily stood up to go with them to whatever awaited.

"Maggie!" The one word was all he could say as he threw his arms around her and choked back the threatening tears. Maggie was less successful at controlling herself. She sobbed and kissed him and then held tight as if trying to drive out the horrors with the warm physical reassurance. She more than ever knew she didn't want to be separated from this man. The thousand questions and even the recriminations that had swirled round her brain in the last twelve hours would have to wait. For now she just held on tight and couldn't let go.

Alex had been brought by car from Mugla to the guest quarters in the officers' block at the Gocek Coastguard base. His deferential host had indicated the shower and toiletries available to him, but they could wait.

Alex asked for Maggie, and with a smiling nod of his head the officer disappeared. He returned to usher Maggie into the room, but immediately withdrew and quietly closed the door. He knew they needed some time before being summoned to join the senior ranks for a very late lunch.

"Tell me it really is all OK now - tell me it's over." Maggie desperately begged for the confirmation that the uncertainties and dread of the past night were genuinely the last act in the nightmare.

"It's over. I'm so sorry I've put you through all of this, but I just didn't know how it was going to work out. Believe me they kept me in the dark too. I'm just making sense of it all myself and I really didn't know what was happening last night. There's a guy from the UK Revenue and Customs that we'll meet later. I hope that he can help me get my head around all the missing bits of the story."

"I should be really cross with you that you have been keeping more crucial facts from me - I thought that was all over since Kapi last year."

"I'd understand if you were mad at me, but you'll see later. It was one of the conditions of going ahead with the whole thing that I couldn't talk or even think about what they might set up. It was hammered into me that the slightest unconscious slip could have warned Katharos that things were not on the level, and that slip would probably cost me my life. I had the feeling that my life was the least of their worries!"

"Who was it said 'to understand all is to forgive all'?"

"I don't know but that's exactly right. At least I hope you can still say that later when it all comes out."

"Don't worry, I think I've worked out the overall

picture so it's only the mechanics of it that I need to find out about. In case you had forgotten I'm not totally dense you know."

"Really! Who'd have thought it!"

She hit him quite hard for that, but it shifted the mood from the intensity of the emotional reunion to a light-hearted release of tension. Laughter was waiting to burst out. Smiles and tears were inexplicably interchangeable. The atmosphere had palpably moved on to one of almost school-holiday hilarity and frivolity. The black cloud of the last two years wasn't just lifting, it was being blasted, vaporised and banished with a degree of relief only possible because of the weight of the cloud itself. The upsurge of spirits, and the sudden lightness of heart, were in direct proportion to the previous burden. Alex at last allowed himself to stare his old fears in the face, able to acknowledge them fully now only because they couldn't bring him down. The release from his stinking and oppressive imprisonment into the warmth and cleanliness of the guest quarters, seemed to be a metaphor for the mental and emotional prison he had inhabited since Katharos ensnared him more than two years earlier, and only as he looked back from the sunny relief of his release could he acknowledge the full horror of his previous state. He shuddered at the memory and shook his head as if to rid himself of the last vestige of that stinking blanket of blackmail and deceit that had threatened to overcome him.

Chapter 45

LUNCH

Tony Ambrose sat in the 'honoured guest' seat, to the left of the senior officer commanding Regional Special Services along the south-west coast of Turkey. It was a rare occasion of quietly smug satisfaction at a job that had worked out better than they had dared hope.

Unseen by the privileged lunch party in the officers' mess was a group of four bemused English holidaymakers in a little hotel dining room in Gocek. Just as they were about to sit down to lunch an official car had drawn up at the hotel entrance. The group was summoned to the foyer to hear a formal greeting delivered by a young lieutenant chosen for his facility with languages. In perfect English he conveyed the greetings of the regional commander of joint naval and coastguard operations, and hoped they would accept the commander's gift of two bottles of the officers' mess special reserve champagne. He asked them to please make use of the champagne to raise a toast over lunch to the commander's special guests, Captain and Mrs Fox, who were engaged with meeting some very important officials over a formal lunch at the Coastguard base.

"I told you so," whispered Patricia to the bemused party. "I knew things weren't as they seemed. Oh I'm so glad I left that note for Maggie. I do hope they know we didn't think they were in the wrong."

Meanwhile back in the officers' mess, the putting-together of all the pieces of the puzzle was progressing apace. Tony Ambrose was able to give some explanation but he also wanted some from Alex.

"What I can't understand is how you got the whole show started in the first place. How on earth did you manage to convince someone senior enough to listen to the story without throwing the book at you right at the outset?"

Alex laughed.

"Well believe it or not, that is down to the most unlikely group of people I have ever met, who I would never have guessed could help me find a way out of the mess I was in."

"I think you'd better explain," said a puzzled Ambrose.

"Not Lavinia?" guessed the shrewd Maggie.

"Well actually Lavinia and her book group. If you met them on the street you'd think they were the most ineffectual group of upper-class twits that you could possibly imagine. But yes, it is Lavinia's book group that deserve the thanks for getting this started. And believe me they're going to get a big thank you from me as soon as I can get there."

Alex had the attention of the whole table. It was

outside the experience of the naval and coastguard officers, never mind Her Majesty's Revenue and Customs, to imagine how a book group could start a process that led to one of the most significant seizures in a smuggling operation for years.

"I think it might be to do with the fact that it was Dublin," started Alex. "There is something about the Irish mentality that makes things possible. It was a very strange experience to be quizzed by that group and to find that they could take on board the most outlandish story as if it was the most natural thing in the world, and then go on to assume that they could help find a way out of it."

Alex took them back to the night when Lavinia had found him amateurishly extracting the negative from her dark-room. He described the scene later in Delaney's restaurant when they questioned and probed him. They didn't disapprove, and they seemed to be able to identify with the way life could work out. 'Once one thing goes wrong, everything starts to go wrong ' wasn't a far-fetched idea to them.

He described how Lavinia subtly created the atmosphere of shared problem-solving, and he had found that almost effortlessly the mood shifted from blame to communal solution-seeking. Perhaps because they were used to reading a great variety of fiction and exploring far-fetched plots, they didn't find his story to be shameful or unbelievable. Like reading a complex book, they all focused on understanding the issues and the characters, not on reacting with blame or judgement.

He related how William, exuding empathy for someone whose business had gone wrong, had helped him explain the sequence of events that took him from safe and humdrum management consultancy to involvement with frightening criminality. He remembered how it felt to be able to explain and share that feeling of falling uncontrollably down a helter-skelter of increasing complexity and irretrievable implication in criminality. And they nodded, sympathised, and helped him explain it all.

Sinead, who he thought wouldn't say boo to a goose, had paper and pencil on the table between the wine glasses, and had deftly drawn diagrams showing the key players and their relationships - highlighting the steps along the way and annotating the diagrams and names with notes about dates and involvements. Steve had treated the whole story as if it happened every day - it was just another example of the ways of the world, no more remarkable than the way restaurants charged excessive mark-ups on the wine they drank that night. The atmosphere of 'So what?' had enabled Alex to calmly sort out in his own mind more clearly than ever before just how he had been manipulated.

He still couldn't quite get over the way in which the book group didn't just take on board the story, but the way in which they assumed they could help him find a way out of it. The blind optimistic faith in being able to sort things out was not an Anglo-Saxon characteristic. Something of the Celtic suspension of disbelief was necessary to avoid being defeated by the enormity of the problem, and to sustain the belief that it was solvable.

Add to that the assumption that it was possible to make contacts at the highest level, and the totally un-English process started to make sense. Once they had set out on Sinead's pages the outline of the story and the seriousness of the league they were involved with, they made the easy leap to the conclusion that only someone at the highest level could make the right people listen and create an escape route for Alex.

He hadn't quite believed it when James asked to borrow a mobile phone so that he could ring a friend in the Irish prime-minister's office in order to get the name of the right person to talk to. Here was a guy who was unemployed, couldn't afford his own mobile phone, but could call up people in the corridors of power and chat to them as if they were old friends. Alex had quickly realised that this was just what they were. James had old friends from school days, and from his bank job, who had fingers on all the buttons they needed.

The rest fell into place with remarkable ease. William made sure that Alex received the guarantee of immunity before implicating himself with HMRC, and accompanied him when a three-way meeting was quickly arranged between Alex and the UK and Irish officials. Hours rather than days seemed to be needed to get the right people together.

Once the Customs people had checked out the story, and made the connections with the longstanding but unprovable suspicions they harboured about Katharos, the operational officers began to get excited about the prospect they had on their hands.

"One thing I don't understand," Alex addressed Tony Ambrose, "is why such a relatively minor player prompted such a high level of response. Katharos had been an illegal for years, but by all accounts he was a minor player in the great scheme of things."

"Ah," said Ambrose. "This is where the other key to the mystery lies."

"Go on then," Maggie was impatient now to know it all.

"It really goes back to human nature really," Ambrose was enjoying himself. "Picture the two young men in the story. You have Iannis Junior, all his life playing second fiddle to his father, and desperately needing to impress both his father and his Turkish friend Arif. Then you have Arif, who was making a good enough living, but was really competing with Iannis to be the big guy. Arif was desperate to break out from the small-time smuggling and crime that he was involved in. So you have two dangerous factors in the same scenario – each amplifying the other's bravado and willingness to take risks, and neither willing to admit fear or caution. Then their need to prove themselves meant that they weren't as discreet as they should have been.

"There had been rumours on the international scene of a really big operation that was going to involve Turkey and London. Informants on the ground had been feeding in snippits for almost a year about the hints that these two young players were incautiously dropping when they wanted to impress people – usually girls they never suspected were informers."

"Good old human nature!" agreed Alex. "But we were still talking about small packages that I transferred – so why so much attention?"

"You really don't know what you were dealing with this time do you?" Ambrose looked sympathetically at him. "Probably just as well."

The Turkish officers were as satisfied looking as Tony Ambrose. The whole bi-national group of officers looked like proud parents about to spring a birthday surprise on an excited child. The look of unsupressibly smug delight was injecting an air of carnival gaiety that needed all the formality of the surroundings and the uniforms to keep in check.

"The way these things work you can't infallibly join all the dots at the outset. It takes an experienced pair of eyes to sift the rubbish from the worthwhile bits of intelligence, and then something of an imaginative leap to see how it all might fit together. We end up with a long series of 'if's, and most of the time they don't come to anything, but this time they really did."

"So for goodness' sake tell us!" erupted Alex.

"Sorry. Of course. We knew that Iannis Junior was crowing about a big operation that was a once-in-a-lifetime. We knew about his link with Arif, who was making similar hints in Olu Deniz. Quite separately there was an operation ongoing for years trying to crack down on the trade from the Congo. You've heard of "blood diamonds?"

Alex and Maggie nodded silently.

"Well, there had been a few quite successful operations run through South Africa and Zambia that had disrupted some long-standing supply routes. The section in Interpol that co-ordinates intelligence about diamond smuggling reported that new routes were being sought after the successful disruption of routes through Angola, Zambia, and Sierra Leone. You might remember the fuss about UN vehicles being implicated in the smuggling?"

Alex and Maggie shook their heads.

"That's by-the-by. The key point is that everyone was on the lookout for indications of a new route, and there were obvious suspicions that a route up through Sudan to the Eastern Mediterranean should be guarded against. There were enough snippits of information to make a viable scenario, and the Arif to Iannis link completed the possible picture. You happened to provide a hugely tempting key to the operation to all the right people at just the right time. It was fantastically lucky that you made the right contacts and that the right people joined the dots as they did. We couldn't believe our luck, and didn't want you to know just how much was riding on your operation."

"I'm rather glad I didn't," breathed Alex. "But what value are you talking about?"

"Oh the value of that specific shipment isn't the main issue. It was substantial no doubt, but the key thing was predicting and disrupting a new route. It enabled us to trace back at least a few steps down the chain, and while the big players are still sitting safely in DRC, they will have been shocked at the loss of a route, and hopefully driven to try other methods that we'll also be able to identify and block. It also means that a substantial amount of money is not available for the purchase of yet more weapons for the DRC warlords."

"I really would like to know how much I've been carrying in my anchor locker," begged Alex.

"I'm afraid you'll just have to guess that until my masters decide what if anything they are going to say in a press release. Sometimes these things are the material for boasting and publicising, other times they are kept very quiet. It's up to the politicos to decide what's to happen this time. The key thing is that the funds for buying more weapons have been denied to the bad guys, and we have continued to make clear that we are on their case. They have to work harder to find routes for their disgusting merchandise and that takes time."

"Oh Tony, that's not fair," groaned Maggie. "I've got to know what we've just carried."

"And I'm not allowed to tell you," parried Tony. But relenting when he saw Maggie's face he said, "Work it out for yourself. Alex can guess the weight of the package, probably 4 or 5 kilos, and it is public knowledge that uncut diamonds of basic quality fetch at least $2000 per carat on the market. These are likely to have been high quality uncut, so the value might be many, many times that. A carat, before you ask, is about 0.2 of a gram."

Maggie's eyes focused on a distant point on the ceiling as she worked out how many 0.2 grams were in a gram, and how many grams in 5 kilos.

"Gosh." Was all she managed to say.

Chapter 46
Dublin: November 2006

The book group

Lavinia sat watching the faces of the others in the book group as they struggled to keep a coherent critical discussion flowing. Her own distraction was probably affecting all the others and legitimising the uncharacteristic lack of focus and energy that was dragging the process down.

"I'm not at all convinced by the denouement," ventured Steve, passing judgement on the final resolution of the latest LeCarré novel.

"Oh I don't know," mused William. "I rather like it when the loose ends aren't all tied up and the good guy doesn't necessarily come out well at the end."

"I hate that," declared Sinead, surprising herself with the vehemence of her assertion.

"Perhaps it depends on one's view of life," suggested

James bravely.

"Go on James," prompted Lavinia, tuning in to the conversation again.

"Well it seems to me that some of us are better than others at organising things and putting life into a structured system." He smiled privately at Sinead as he said it. "People who are good at that probably also like books to be orderly, and don't like loose ends left hanging about. Others of us are less structured and more able to live with a bit of a mess in life, so we are more accepting of a book that reflects that imperfect and messy state. A neat and tidy ending would seem a bit unrealistic to us."

They continued to debate the extent to which their personal characteristics determined their reaction to Salvo's uncertain fate at the end of the book. They disliked the easy categorisation but had to agree that there was at least an element of truth in it. The good-natured challenging and analysis left them in a reflective and introspective mood as Lavinia poured the teas and coffees that wrapped up the evening.

William was watching Lavinia with a distant, wary, longing. He wondered if his caution at actually declaring and resolving his feelings was based on the need to avoid exposing himself to fresh hurt and disappointment. Was it more comfortable to live with his enjoyably proprietorial fantasy about Lavinia, rather than to risk translating it into an imperfect reality? He suspected that the answer was 'yes', it was much more comfortable and less threatening, for now at least. But what, he wondered, would happen to that comfortable state if Lavinia found a lover? Was it better to live with that unresolved risk than to take a chance with reality? His inaction seemed to be the mute answer, unsatisfactory though it would be to a different personality.

James and Sinead exchanged eye-contact meaningfully. James had come to value the drive for order and resolution that Sinead brought to their relationship. His own nature allowed him to wallow in unresolved and unsatisfactory possibilities without ever precipitating the simple actions necessary to achieve clarity and definite answers. His ability to avoid issues had been thoroughly demonstrated in his working and private lives, leading to disaster and frustration in each. He was unspeakably grateful for the sublime counter-balance to his ineffectual nature that Sinead injected into their joint existence.

Sinead for her part loved James for the very characteristics that he found weak and even despicable in himself. She had spent her entire life experiencing the inner existence of an ordered person: one who could analyse, categorise, and organise the details into solid, dependable ways of looking at the world. There wasn't much room left for the dreamy uncertainties that seemed to be so enjoyable to others. The book group had answered that quest for the different side of life in more ways than she had expected. The enjoyment of fiction, and a consciousness of the rich variety of approaches to conveying stories, provided a positive emotional bonus for her. It was quite different from the logical, analytical dissection of literature that she had previously experienced. She had gradually come to value the way in which fictional accounts could usefully deepen her own insights and understanding in the real world – a world where the complexity of human emotion and motivation led to a messiness and apparent irrationality that usually disturbed her. The stories in themselves weren't the answers, but the thought processes that they prompted helped create analogies and insights that had their parallels in her experience of the world. It was complex, but more satisfactory than her old 'cut and dried' viewpoint.

But it was James, or perhaps Sinead's acceptance of her feelings for James, that had been the real revelation. How strange that the simple steps she had taken to do something about her dissatisfaction with her ordered and predictable life as one of 'the girls' could have led to such a reward. There was an amplification of possibilities, a terrifying and exhilarating multiplication of avenues that led not only to potential pain and anguish, but equally to possibilities of pleasure, excitement and comfort in the confusing cocktail of a relationship. Where was it going to lead? She put off resolving that issue. Her structured mind came to her rescue with the highly rational escape route that required the completion of her accountancy studies before addressing the long-term issues with James.

Steve was used to uncertainties and unresolved wishes. He watched the others and envied the relative straightforwardness of their issues. He experienced an amused impatience with James and Sinead. He longed to shout at them, "Get on with it for goodness sake!" But he didn't. He watched the way William's eyes followed Lavinia, and saw the flickering twitches of smiles as William allowed himself his undeclared fantasies. Just like his reaction to the book, William preferred the world of pleasing dreams and possibilities to the harsh concrete of the declared affection and the spurned advance.

But what of Steve himself? He was learning to more

truly value each day and the enjoyment it brought. His illness had at one time given him a short life-expectancy. At that point he had managed to climb beyond the despair and depression that rode on the back of the feelings of unfairness and persecution. He had achieved a philosophical stasis where the mundane was very truly just that. Conversely the pleasures of friendships, and the disproportionate elation at little daily successes, achieved a colour and value that injected an unexpected quota of humour and joy into his life. The horizon had gradually gained distance, so now he was adjusting to the complexity of seeing a longer life again, and puzzling with the questions of how it was going to be filled. His hard-won philosophical foundation gave him a wry, un-fussed relaxation about the future. After coping with the lack of a future, he was hardly going to let its reinstatement prove negative. So he watched himself with something of the air of a benevolently amused spectator. His lightness could be misinterpreted by others as superficiality, but in reality it was a perspective that had emerged out of the worst of times and the deepest of despair.

Lavinia was puzzled. She loved the little group she had fostered – loved them collectively and individually. It was one of the liveliest symbols of her re-invented self. But she was experiencing a disturbing dissatisfaction in an unfocused and annoying way. She couldn't find the reason for it, and she was unsuccessfully trying to pin it, like a cardboard donkey-tail at a children's party, on each inappropriate theme that inhabited her mind.

She knew really that it wasn't the group. They could be annoying, but they were also stimulating, helpful, challenging and amusing. Each of them brought a necessary facet to the group, and she didn't want to change the mix at all. She had re-established an active relationship with Hermione, and they met more frequently than they had for years. Her photography was working well – more pleasing prints and more opportunities to submit them for competition and exhibition. She was even selling some.

The photographs took her mind back to the strip of negatives; the heart-sinking moment when she found Alex in the dark-room; and the exhilaration of the dinner in Delaney's. Her little group had unassumingly blossomed into the most creative, dynamic and effective team that she could have imagined. She pictured it as something equivalent to the parental joy at seeing one's children take off and excel in the world. It was probably the high spot of her life to have seen poor Alex taken in hand by her unlikely squad, and changed from a confused and defeated mess into a hopeful and positive agent in the affair. Perhaps that was it. Perhaps after the highs that they experienced in extracting the story from Alex, and then so unexpectedly finding a way out of the maze for him, the excitement could only be followed by an emotional low. It was probably the natural counter-swing in emotions after the incredible positives they felt when the contacts they made reacted helpfully, and Alex emerged with a way out of his hell.

The celebratory party last week had been exuberant, delightful, and deservedly self-congratulatory. Alex and Maggie had been so hugely grateful to them. He really meant it when he said they had saved his life, it wasn't just the usual hyperbole. But why was she left feeling deflated? Why were even the memories of the warmth of that evening somewhat bitter-sweet? She dismissed as usual any possibility of feelings of romantic attraction. At first it was just the learned reaction that she had demonstrated countless times in her successfully solitary life. Almost immediately it was also the rational rejection of the possibility of a relationship, as Alex had even brought Maggie to the party – what greater evidence did she need?

Lavinia sighed; William dreamed; James squeezed Sinead's hand; and Steve quietly smiled.

ABOUT THE AUTHOR

Jack Dylan is a reclusive Irish writer. A career in business and psychology provided raw material for a library of books. The Turkish Trap (previously published as Dolphins in the Bay) is the first and will be followed quickly by more in the same style. Dylan plans a volume of short stories and a collection of poetry. Both will be available in Amazon books.

Follow Jack Dylan on Facebook:
https://www.facebook.com/JackDylanAuthor
and on Jack's website:
www.jackdylan.co.uk

Printed by Amazon Italia Logistica S.r.l.
Torrazza Piemonte (TO), Italy

16883193R00194